Praise for Teresa Noelle Roberts's
Knowing the Ropes

"I cannot wait to see if there is more written by Teresa Noelle Roberts. [...] I highly recommend this book and author to those readers who like a little kink in their romance."

~ *Night Owl Reviews*

"In *Knowing the Ropes* Teresa Noelle Roberts paints a beautiful picture of a woman who is not afraid to take that step towards fulfilling her most intimate needs and darkest desires with a man who can show her the pleasure of pain. [...] A brilliant story that will captivate you from beginning to end."

~ *Guilty Pleasures Book Reviews*

"The kink and sex between Selene and Nick was scrumptious and had me turning virtual page after page."

~ *Fallen Angel Reviews*

Look for these titles by
Teresa Noelle Roberts

Now Available:

Duals and Donovans: The Different
Lions' Pride
Foxes' Den
Fox's Folly
Cougar's Courage

Knowing the Ropes

Teresa Noelle Roberts

SAMHAIN
PUBLISHING

Samhain Publishing, Ltd.
11821 Mason Montgomery Road, 4B
Cincinnati, OH 45249
www.samhainpublishing.com

Knowing the Ropes
Copyright © 2014 by Teresa Noelle Roberts
Print ISBN: 978-1-61921-677-8
Digital ISBN: 978-1-61921-451-4

Editing by Linda Ingmanson
Cover by Angela Waters

First Samhain Publishing, Ltd. electronic publication: February 2013
First Samhain Publishing, Ltd. print publication: February 2014

Dedication

To my dear friend and writing support, Dayle Dermatis (aka Andrea Dale, Dayle Ivy, and the other half of Sophie Mouette, among other pseudonyms), for helping me "whip" the long-ago first draft of this novel into something much stronger. Thank you, sweetie!

To my editor, Linda Ingmanson, for working with me to smooth out the rough edges.

And to Jeff. Always yours.

Chapter One

Selene Daniels hesitated outside Declan's Grille, heart pounding, stomach roiling and nipples practically pushing through her soft red cotton bra, and tried to imagine what awaited her within.

The Boston Kinksters United munch was on the other side of that door. And once she stepped through it, who knew what might happen? At the very least, she'd start arming herself with information she'd need in her future career. There was a definite line between consensual kink and abuse, and it was important for someone who worked with domestic abuse survivors to understand where that line was.

More to the point, it was important for Selene to know where that line was, for herself. Knowing what she did about relationships gone horribly, violently wrong, both from her volunteer work and from what she'd seen in her friend Molly's family, she sometimes thought she was crazy to crave pain mixed with her pleasure, to want so desperately to give up some of the control other women were fighting to regain.

Yet she did want all that. She'd fought wanting it for her entire adult life, but damn it, she was almost thirty and already making big changes in her life—quitting her steady IT job at the University of Rochester and moving to Boston to pursue an education doing something that might make less money but felt like her calling. Why not make another big change and pursue her other, kinkier dreams?

They'd had a speaker in one of her grad-school classes, a woman from Boston Kinksters United who'd talked about the differences between consensual BDSM and abuse, and special considerations when counseling kinky people. After Alison spoke to the class, Selene had e-mailed her, asking to get together for a coffee and ask a few more questions.

Alison wore a discreet slave's collar, a simple silver necklace that locked in place, and she'd probably done all kinds of edgy, wildly erotic things that Selene wouldn't dare try, but she was a smart, self-assured forty-something who didn't seem like she'd take shit from anyone unless it amused her to do so. Talking to Alison had given her the courage to come to this munch.

And this munch might change Selene's life.

Then she chuckled at herself.

She'd felt this nervous, this excited, this sure that she was on the cusp of something marvelous and romantic and life-altering when she went to her first junior high dance. Twelve years later, that night was still the stuff of jokes with her best friend Molly.

At least this event wouldn't involve crepe-paper flowers and spiked Kool-Aid punch and all the boys clustered on one side of the room pretending not to stare at the girls, and vice versa. Probably no water-balloon fight, either, although, given the heat wave oppressing Boston, it might not be a bad idea.

And chances were she'd never share this adventure with Molly, even if it turned out to be a comedy gold mine. Molly wouldn't get her obsession with ropes and floggers and spanking, her need to yield, at least for a few hours, to a man's sexual whim and will.

Not after what Molly had seen growing up. Selene knew instinctively there was a world of difference between an abusive asshole like Molly's father and the woman who hadn't figured out yet how to get away from him and two people whose fantasies aligned to create kinky sparks—but since she couldn't really articulate the difference to herself yet, she'd be damned if she could to Molly.

That was why she was here, to get a little insight into her fantasies. Not so she could explain them to Molly, of course, but so she could explain them to herself.

Maybe then she could figure out why her past relationships had a lot more fizzle than sizzle and move on to a relationship with plenty of sizzle. Hell, she'd take the sizzle without an actual relationship, at least for a while.

The butterflies inside Selene's panties offered the opinion that even if this one meeting didn't change her life, it could lead to some seriously hot dates.

It was just a meeting, she assured herself. That was all. A chance to educate herself and maybe make some new friends. Anything else that came from it was gravy.

At least if you thought of gravy as coming in flavors like "Scary Yet Sexy" or "Risky But Worth Doing".

Taking a deep breath, she opened the door and walked in.

Her knees didn't buckle. So far, so good.

When the hostess asked if she could help her, though, all Selene could do was make a fish face, not sure if she should outright ask for Boston Kinksters United or if there was a discreet code phrase she was forgetting.

The hostess smiled at her obvious attack of nerves. "Oh, you'll be wanting the function room upstairs," she said with a trace of a brogue. She lowered her voice. "Don't worry. They're nice people."

Selene thanked her and scooted up the stairs, taking a deep breath before entering the function room.

Gingerly she opened the door and walked into...

A disappointingly ordinary restaurant function room, with a table set against the far wall, sporting crudités, cheese and crackers, a couple of chafing dishes, and pitchers of water and what looked to be iced tea.

Almost as much of a letdown as a dingy gym decorated with paper flowers.

The old-fashioned, dark-paneled room decorated with photographs of the Irish countryside was a more attractive space than the gym of Seneca Lake Consolidated Junior-Senior High, but even though she'd known this was a social gathering, not the sort of dungeon party she'd experienced only via erotic fiction, she'd imagined something a bit more exotic. This could have been an office party for a small company.

About thirty people sat at tables, eating and chatting, or milled around with drinks in their hands. Most were as ordinary as any random collection of people she'd find in any Boston restaurant.

Just to add to the air of business-function normality, there was a check-in table where a pleasant-looking, burly, bald man with a name tag that read "Joe-Bear" gave a cursory glance at her driver's license and directed her to make a tag for herself. She thought briefly about making up some ridiculous pseudonym but went with Selene instead.

Then she stood at the edge of the room. Alison would be here, she knew, but she couldn't spot her new friend anywhere.

She looked down and realized she was fidgeting, rubbing her hands together.

Time to get a drink and some snacks so she'd have something to do with her hands besides wring them. Maybe she'd have the guts to strike up a conversation with someone once she got there.

As she filled her glass, someone tapped her on the arm and said, "Hi, Selene."

Once she finished jumping out of her skin, Selene managed to say, "Thank God you're here."

Alison smiled. "I invited you. It would be pretty rude to desert you. Sorry I couldn't meet you beforehand, but the timing just didn't work out. Want to meet a few people?"

Selene nodded, wondering if her face was red and why the ice cubes in her drink were clinking so much against the side of the glass.

Damn vibrating ice cubes. Must be someone's idea of a joke.

With drinks in hand, Alison took her around the room and introduced her to more people than she could keep track of: all genders, and as far as Selene could guess from chatting briefly, a cross section of straight, gay and bi, doms, subs and switches. Most of them seemed pleasant, and a couple of the men, while not on a Daniel Craig level of panty-melting hotness, were intelligent and easy enough on the eyes and might be worth getting to know better for purely base motives.

But no one seemed inclined to grab her—or anyone else, for that matter—by the hair and have his deliciously wicked way with her. Not that she expected such things in a restaurant, really...but a girl could dream, and often did, of outrageous, sexy things, and some small part of her had hoped to walk into a den of very fun iniquity, even if Alison had made it clear this wasn't that kind of party.

The sheer normality was both a relief and a disappointment. Selene wasn't sure exactly what she was ready to get herself into—but dammit, parts of her wanted to find out.

Parts of her, face it, were aching and dripping to find out, even if her brain wasn't as ready to spring into oversexed, possibly risky action as those less-than-sensible parts were.

Luckily, it didn't seem like she'd have to make any decisions on the subject today. Her fantasy life had been in overdrive ever since she'd decided to come to the meet-and-greet—okay, ever since Alison spoke to her summer-semester class and Selene realized that there were seemingly sane people, right here in Boston, living out the fantasies she'd written off as too scary to live out—but so far all the fantasizing had been just as pointless as the previous worrying. She'd gotten a few good orgasms out of the fantasizing, so it hadn't been *totally* pointless, but this was no depraved orgy.

Maybe the depraved orgy happened later?

Would that be good or bad?

They were talking with another woman, a cute, tomboyish Latina with a pierced nose and a T-shirt that sported two cartoon girls kissing, when Alison screwed up her face and said, "Selene, Betsy, let's get something at the bar!" The way she said it made it clear it wasn't the bar she was thinking about but getting away from the man who was bearing down on them.

"Great idea," the other woman agreed, "and I don't drink."

The guy wasn't bad-looking, sort of a rumpled Michael Douglas circa *Romancing the Stone*. But clearly there was more—or less—to him than met the eye; Alison grabbed Selene's left arm, Betsy took her right, and they deliberately marched her toward the stairs.

The man accosted them before they got there. "Ladies, who is your lovely friend?"

Betsy with the pierced nose and Alison looked at each other. "My date," Betsy growled, putting her arm around Selene possessively. "Sorry, Craig."

His name tag read Master Craig.

Sheesh. Selene didn't know much about real-life BDSM, only what she'd read (and since a lot of that was fiction, she took it with several pounds of salt), but it seemed pretentious if not downright tacky to expect random people you weren't involved with to call you Master.

"What a shame. My dear," he said, addressing Selene, "when you're ready to stop playing at submission with another woman and submit to a real master, let me know." It was unfortunately clear that he wasn't joking.

She pulled away with a theatrical, obvious shudder and filled her voice with ice. "Excuse me, I think you're in the wrong place. The caveman party's next door. Go join the other throwbacks."

He sputtered and seemed to search for an appropriately cutting response. Then, abruptly, he glanced over Alison's head toward the door, turned on his heel and stalked away.

"That," Alison said once he was out of earshot, "was Craig. I used him as the model for at least two of the bad-dom types in my Intro to the Scene workshop."

And then Alison turned around and beamed.

Curious, Selene followed the other woman's gaze.

A solid, olive-skinned man had just come in. Like Alison, he looked to be in his mid- to late-forties, with some gray salting his dark hair. Not precisely gorgeous, Selene thought, but if you could bottle the aura of alpha-in-a-good-way male that hovered around him, you'd make a fortune selling it to other, less confident guys. He waved at Joe-Bear as he came through the door but didn't stop for a name tag, heading straight for Alison instead.

Alison stood taller as he approached, and her fair, freckled skin flushed a little.

If she had a neon sign that flashed "Woman in Love" over her head, it would have been more subtle.

Selene grinned. "I take it that's your master?"

Alison's smile grew broader. "Yes, that's Garth. I'll introduce you in a bit, okay? He had to run some errands this morning, and now I need to catch up with him."

Catch up with him wasn't the phrase Selene would have used for the kiss that followed, or for the way they snuggled together afterward as if they'd been apart for days rather than a few hours.

Betsy sighed and whispered to Selene, "God, I envy her."

"No offense, but I wouldn't have pegged Garth as your type."

The other woman laughed. "He's not. Wrong plumbing and too much of a top. But if I could find some nice, queer, switchy girl who looked at me the way he looks at her, I'd be one happy woman."

"Ah, that new-love smell!" Selene had to make a joke. Otherwise the intensity between the couple, and the intensity of her own reaction, a gut-clenching mixture of envy, arousal, and fear, would make her too uncomfortable.

"Hardly. They've been together forever. Ten years at least."

Selene looked at the couple. Garth wasn't grinning the way Alison was—his wasn't a face made for grinning—but the way he stood with arms around her and the expression on his face spoke of possessiveness, pride, protectiveness and deep affection. Alison, who on her own had looked like the capable managerial type Selene suspected she was during business hours, seemed softer, younger and much happier. All her abundant energy was focused entirely on Garth.

It was almost too intimate to watch.

Alison might be a slave, but her master was clearly just as dotty about her as she was about him, and their love had endured over many years.

Now, that was a surprise.

Selene could picture these two as a cute old couple like her mom's parents, still holding hands and smooching and being adorable together—only in Garth and Alison's case, also still being kinky, if less energetically than in their younger days.

Sweet, hot and yet somehow disturbing. With all that intensity, how could Alison keep from getting swallowed up whole?

Maybe she had been swallowed up and was too happy to care. But that was okay if it was consensual, right?

Hoping to dispel the tension roiling inside her by doing something, anything, Selene took a drink but got nothing but a few melting ice cubes.

She started back toward the buffet table, then turned, still walking, and said to Betsy, "Back in a few. I'm going for more...

Oh God, I'm sorry."

The last bit was muttered into a broad chest.

Chapter Two

A large, firm hand patted her reassuringly on the shoulder.

An affable male voice said, "No problem. Saves us the trouble of having to come up with some lame reason to introduce ourselves. I'm Nick McCutcheon."

Selene looked up.

Her breath caught.

She'd managed to bump into someone absolutely gorgeous. Where had he been hiding? He must have sneaked in while she was talking with someone far less interesting.

Tall. Broad-shouldered. Amazingly blue eyes. Mahogany-colored hair in a neat ponytail. Good cheekbones. Confident, assured posture. A charming smile. And he must have shared Garth's bottle of Eau de Alpha Male.

Oh yeah.

Nick might not match her fantasy Sexy Pirate, Ruthless Billionaire or Demon Lover in every particular—face it, jeans and a retro Hawaiian shirt just weren't as devastating as knee-high boots, a bare chest and a cutlass, a custom-made tux or whatever scrap of leather Demon Lovers wore—but he came damn close.

And he had an air of good humor about him that she hadn't considered for her fantasy lovers but would be something she'd definitely want in a real-life one. Even a dom couldn't be all imposing and serious and stern 24/7, or he'd be impossible to deal with.

She was pressed up against him, feeling the heat of his

body. Smelling him—green, herbal cologne overlying a spicy, masculine scent that she thought was just him.

Her body tingled. She wanted to cling to him, pull him closer, kiss him.

Do a hell of a lot more than kiss him. The only problem would be deciding which delicious fantasy to beg him to fulfill first.

Jesus. Talk about moving too fast.

She forced herself to step away. "Selene Daniels. And again, I'm really sorry, but at least my glass was empty or you'd be wearing iced tea."

"Let's get you that refill, then." He walked with her over to the buffet.

No, he walked her to the buffet as if he were escorting her into a formal dinner. The proprietary air might have been weird from someone else but worked on him.

"Is this your first time here?" Nick asked.

"That obvious?"

"More that you don't look familiar, although I haven't been around much in the past few months, so for all I know you've become a regular since I was gone."

She felt herself blushing. Damn her fair skin anyway. "No, first time here. First time at anything like this. I'm even new in Boston. Moved here at the start of summer term; I'm at Lesley for social work."

Blushing *and* running on at the mouth—way to sound adolescent! She was usually much calmer than this, even talking to a sexy man, but Nick's presence, his sheer sexuality and aura of dominance, turned her into a nervously babbling teenager.

Nick's body language changed subtly, making him look bigger somehow, more commanding. "You're lovely," he said, almost as if it had taken him by surprise. "You'd look even lovelier in a cage next to my bed. I'm looking for a new sex slave. I think you ought to start begging for the opportunity to please me." His voice purred with silky menace, quite unlike his earlier slightly flirtatious but basically friendly tone.

Selene backed a step away, bristling and sputtering. Gorgeous guy or not, kinky event or not, this remark was way out of line. He made Creepy Craig sound normal by comparison.

Even if the idea of being his little sex slave, locked in a cage until needed, was something she'd go home and dream about while she and her Magic Wand spent some quality time together. Definitely a hot fantasy—but you just didn't say something like that to someone less than five minutes after meeting them.

He had a twinkle in his eye, though, a slight smile playing on his lips. Maybe he wasn't serious.

She hoped he wasn't serious, because she didn't want to have to do something vile to him with a plastic fork. She didn't think the plastic would be up to the task.

Craig had been almost as outrageous, and he had been serious.

She didn't want to believe Nick was serious. But if it was a joke and she stabbed him with a fork, it would be hard to recover.

Only one thing to do, then. Treat it as the joke it had to be—loudly enough that, if she was wrong, she'd make a fool of him.

She gave in to her impulse to crack up, and crack up loudly. "I see you like teasing the newbies," she exclaimed between whoops of laughter. "That's number five from Alison's Doms to Duck list, right? Or was it six?"

The twinkle in his eye got brighter, and he broke into a goofy yet charming grin that reminded her of the kind of likeable geek boys she'd dated in college, the kind who'd sometimes forget plans because they were caught up in a computer game but could always get her to forgive them by making her laugh.

"Give the lady a Kewpie doll! She got it in one! And she passed the common-sense test."

"Test?" She couldn't decide whether she should be annoyed or amused and settled for a little bit of both. She probably ought to be more annoyed than she was, but between the smile, his general brain-melting sexiness and the fact that it was kind of funny, the annoyance couldn't work up a good head of steam. "What would constitute failing?"

"Trying to take me up on it." Then his face changed, got a little more serious. "I'm glad you laughed. I was trying to be clever and realized just too late that it might not have been the smartest thing to do. If it hadn't come off as a joke, you'd have been justified in throwing your drink at me or remembering you had to walk your nonexistent dog and leaving. It was out of line."

"No problem." Any irritation with the "test" dissipated in the wake of the apology. "I can't imagine anyone taking it seriously for more than a second or two."

"You'd be amazed. I'd bet that kid would buy it and probably kneel and start begging. Notice I didn't try it on her." He pointed toward a little Goth waif with tousled dyed black hair wearing a minute black T-shirt that read "Take Me", a microscopic black leather skirt and a collar that looked like it came from PetSmart. Her nametag read "slave kat", the lower case apparently deliberate. If someone hadn't been checking ID at the door, Selene would have guessed she was still in high school.

"I cheated this time, though. I saw you talking with Alison when I came in, and she looked like she was actually enjoying the conversation. That's a good sign."

He smiled again, a smile that went better with the silken-menace voice he'd used earlier. "I wasn't kidding about the lovely part. The rest was a joke—a bad one—but I got this teenage urge to bring the conversation around to sex, even in a silly way, as soon as I saw you."

Oh really?

Selene's ears—and nipples—perked up.

Even though he'd been joking when he'd made his voice go all silky and menacing, she'd bet he'd do it when it mattered.

At the thought, her mouth went dry.

Her pussy was another story.

Oh boy, was it ever. She was flooded just talking to him.

She knew she shouldn't go home and act out her most dangerous, decadent fantasies with someone she'd just met—but that didn't mean she couldn't think about it in loving, explicit detail.

The voices of her mother and thousands of female ancestors warned her that it was far too soon to tell if he were Mr. Right.

She told them to shut up. Looking at someone as a potential kinky Mr. Right was a great way to get in way over her head. At this point, she needed a friend with benefits, a playmate, someone trustworthy who'd help her explore some of her fantasies and see if they worked.

Could Nick be that man?

It was probably premature to consider it seriously, but her body was definitely of the opinion that the answer was yes, yes, yes.

He could apologize when he stepped over the line. That put him ahead of half her ex-boyfriends right there.

Nick's eyes were following Selene's red sundress and mane of light brown hair as she headed toward the restroom when he noticed a potential problem. Craig Whittaker was hitting on the little lost barely-of-age lamb.

That wouldn't be a problem if the girl had been reacting with the feminist rage Craig could call forth in the mildest of women, but she seemed to be hanging on his words, wide-eyed and excited. Craig had an arm around her and was grinning like a hyena that had just met a particularly dumb gazelle.

Time to intervene.

Nick put on his best I'm-in-charge face and headed across the room toward Craig and his victim, moving casually but with purpose. He pretended he was walking past the pair but instead stopped abruptly and faked a double-take. "Craig," he said, sounding much friendlier than he felt. "Good to see you, man! Heard about your daughter getting into Dartmouth Medical School. Your wife must be thrilled."

The "lost lamb" pulled away from Craig, frowning. "You have a daughter older than me? And a *wife*?" she said, her voice squeaky with disgust. "Does she know you're here hitting on someone younger than your kid?"

Craig was undeterred. "You need a man with experience, Kat, someone to guide you and shape you. A true slave needs..."

"You are so full of it. Tell that to your wife, asshole!"

Craig drew himself up taller. "You, little girl, are not a slave. You're not even a submissive. A real submissive would know her place."

And he walked away.

Young Kat's eyes widened. "I'm sorry," she said, sounding as crushed as if she'd just buried her mother. "I'm sorry, sir. I don't know anything yet. I don't know my place, like Master Craig said, and I..."

Then, to Nick's dismay, she dropped to her knees and burst into tears.

This, inevitably, was the moment when Selene came back.

Of all the ways he could think of to impress a woman,

having a weeping teenager groveling at his feet was pretty low on the list, unless by "impress" you meant "impress her with what an asshole you are". She probably thought he'd tried that joke on the kid and the kid had taken him seriously.

That was obviously what was going through her mind when she stormed over, saying, "Nick, what did you do to her?"

"Nothing," the girl sobbed. "He was just there. He's being nice to me, more than I deserve. I screwed up bad. I yelled at a master. I can't believe I did that! Aren't I supposed to kneel to...someone?"

Selene rolled her eyes at Nick over the girl's head. She looked concerned, but he could tell that she was also fighting not to chuckle.

That made him feel less guilty about his own urge to laugh at poor melodramatic small-k kat and how quickly things got ridiculous. Then again, Craig was good at making things get ridiculous.

Nick quickly gestured at Craig's back. "Someone didn't take no well and started ranting at her about 'true slave behavior'."

"But that's true, isn't it?" Kat said in a small voice. "I said no, and a real slave never says no. At least that's what the masters I've talked to online told me."

"Oh, puh-lease! You shouldn't believe everything you hear online, girlfriend," Selene said. Then she mouthed, *Go get Alison.*

Good call. The newbies, especially the youngest and most hapless, were her special charges.

By the time he came back with Alison, Selene had one arm around the crying girl, saying, "Obviously a case of brains melting in the heat. You forgot tact. He forgot he was married. His brain melt was worse than yours. And there's nothing wrong with saying no. Doms aren't gods, you know. We just like to pretend they are—as long as it's fun."

Two things entered Nick's head simultaneously.

One was that he liked Selene's attitude. She was kind but not squishy about it, and he bet she didn't take shit from anyone. She might take orders, if it entertained her, but not shit.

And she got it. She might be new to the scene, but she got that it was about people shaping fantasies, not fantasies shaping people.

That was more than Natalie ever understood. She really thought it was all about living out *The Story of O*, and never mind that half the stuff in *The Story of O* wasn't even physically possible, let alone a good idea.

Part of him immediately felt guilty for the negative thought about Natalie. Yeah, she was a little bit crazy, but for a while, crazy had been hot, and he'd encouraged her.

The rest of him decided that he wasn't leaving without Selene's phone number and e-mail—or ideally, with Selene herself.

As Alison whisked Kat away, probably to the women's room, Selene grabbed his arm. "So," she asked conspiratorially, "what really happened?"

"Pretty much what you heard. The guy's been part of Kinksters for a while. He came in with this 'I am a true Master and superior to anything female' thing, but people come into this with all kinds of crazy ideas; we figured he'd learn. Then he gets pulled in as a contractor on my software project, and I find out he's married."

"I suppose it would be too much to hope that it's an open marriage?"

"Not likely if he hasn't mentioned a wife to anyone here, let alone brought her to meet the gang. So when I saw him hitting on Kat, I thought I should drop the wife-bomb. The rest, you saw, although you missed the amazing way he turned being wrong back on her."

He spouted off Craig's most appalling, taken-straight-from-cheap-porn lines in what he hoped was a good imitation of Craig's arrogant, slightly nasal voice.

Selene sputtered with laughter. "My God—him! This has to be the same idiot who hit on me earlier, the one who used lines that would make a Neanderthal blush. That poor kid! I'd been envying her courage. At her age, I wouldn't have had had the nerve to come to something like this. But maybe it's just as well. I missed out on some good clean dirty fun, but at least I had a chance to grow some common sense before I got started."

Common sense. What a concept. Yes, he could definitely get to like this woman. The big brown eyes, cute smile and killer curves didn't hurt, but the attitude really appealed to him.

Chapter Three

The meet-and-greet ended at five o'clock. Alison and Garth came over to say good-bye to Selene and Nick. While Garth and Nick chatted, Selene touched Alison's arm and asked, "Confab in the lady's room?"

Alison let Selene pull her just a few steps away. It occurred to Selene that Alison probably didn't want to interrupt Garth to say where she was going, so she was staying in sight. Then Alison leaned in and whispered conspiratorially, "If it's about Nick, he's a great guy. He's one of Garth's best friends, and he's pretty much the opposite of a dom to duck. I'm going to do the responsible-friend thing and say you should just talk and smooch tonight, but if you wind up playing, I know he'll play safe."

Selene hugged her and whispered back, "Thank you! I'll try to behave—but no promises!"

And so kinksters spilled out onto the muggy streets of Boston singly and in twos, threes and larger groupings. Selene found herself with Nick, drifting toward an early dinner somewhere. He had a place in mind but hadn't actually told her where, and she found she liked the feeling that she'd put herself into his hands in this small way.

The more she talked with Nick, the more his cool blue gaze and warm smile distracted her, and the more she felt his body language sync up with hers. No, not exactly in sync but one step ahead, anticipating her next movement and influencing it, as if starting to mold her already. She watched his big hands, imagining them alternately caressing and slapping her breasts, her thighs, her ass.

She looked down at his feet when she imagined her fevered thoughts were too obvious in her eyes, then imagined herself kneeling there, naked, trembling, wet.

Actually, she didn't need to imagine the wet and trembling part. Her panties already felt suspiciously damp and her knees were shaky.

They walked more or less in silence. Between traffic noise, noise from the perennial construction along Atlantic Avenue and the melting heat, talking seemed far too much like work. Even the breeze off Boston Harbor was sticky.

By the time they crossed a bridge over Fort Point Channel, she was wishing she'd worn flats, even if they wouldn't have looked right with the outfit. She prayed that the restaurant would be an informal place where she could slip her shoes off under the table.

Once she saw the restaurant, her feet breathed a sigh of relief.

The Barking Crab was a tribute to the beachside clam shack. Rough picnic tables covered with butcher paper—they even provided crayons for doodling. A mix of fried and steamed seafood, with a few more sophisticated but still basic selections. And outdoor seating on the harbor, so she could kick off the damn heels and relax. "It's a tourist trap," Nick said, "but it's fun."

Soon they were drinking cold beers—he'd recommended the fascinatingly named Smuttynose, from a brewery in New Hampshire—and awaiting plates of fried scallops, fried calamari and steamed mussels. Selene hadn't eaten a great deal that day and the frosty, hoppy beer was making her feel pleasantly euphoric.

Or maybe that was Nick.

She stretched out her bare foot, brushed it against his calf. Hard muscle under soft denim. Nice.

Yeah, Nick might just have something to do with the euphoria.

He took the hand that wasn't holding her beer.

No, he didn't exactly take her hand. He covered her hand with his and closed his fingers around her wrist. Then he looked into her eyes.

A slow, sensual smile opened on his face as he said, "That's better. Isn't it?"

It wasn't really a question, but he was giving her an out if she wanted it.

She didn't. That firm grip on her wrist hinted at so many things she'd dreamed of. "Oh yes," she breathed. "Better." She dropped her voice a notch. "And wetter."

It may have been purely coincidence that the woman sitting behind her giggled at that second, but Selene was sure she'd overhead.

Heat flared in Selene's cheeks and, to her surprise, between her legs. She squirmed in her seat, less from actual embarrassment than to enjoy the pressure the movement put on her swollen lips.

Under the cover of the first round of food arriving, Nick leaned forward. "So, you enjoy a little bit of public embarrassment? I'll file that away for later."

"You're so confident that there'll be a later?"

"What do you think?" He ran one fingernail down the tender inside of her forearm.

His nails weren't sharp, but she still shivered.

"What about the common-sense test?" she asked. Her voice sounded a little desperate to her own ears, grasping at verbal straws. "Don't I fail it retroactively if I go home with you tonight?"

"If you come home with me and let me lock you in a cage, then yes. But to do that, I'd need a cage, and where will I find one in downtown Boston on a Saturday night?" He laughed. "I'm regretting that test. It's making us both think we have to be sensible, and right now I'd rather be impulsive."

"Would it help if I said I wasn't thinking of much of anything except you?" Had that really come out of her mouth? "Okay, you and food. I'm starving." She grabbed a ring of fried calamari and popped it into her mouth, hoping the squid would keep her from saying anything too stupid. Calamari had the texture of bubble gum, in her experience, and it was rude to talk with your mouth full.

Damn it if this place didn't manage to make calamari tender. Delicious too, with a nice, crunchy coating and a bit of spice.

Much tastier than what she'd been expecting but not nearly as effective for keeping her safely quiet.

"Try it with a bit of the banana pepper," Nick suggested, picking up a calamari ring and a piece of yellow-green pepper. She thought for a second he was demonstrating the proper technique.

He wasn't.

He reached across the table and held the food before her lips. "Try it," he urged.

Her mouth opened of its own accord.

He brushed his finger across the pout of her lower lip, making her shiver.

She opened her mouth slowly, took a tentative nibble to test the pepper's heat, then parted her lips wider and engulfed the food and Nick's fingers.

Unfortunately, there was only so much room around the morsel for tongue and fingers to work their wiles upon each other. She did her best, though, sucking and nibbling on his fingers while he moved them against her tongue, tantalizing something besides her taste buds, which were already busily dealing with piquant pepper and warm, spiced calamari. She found she was leaning forward to take him, wanting to feel more, liking the sensation that he was filling her mouth.

She wanted him filling her mouth with his cock, wanted him to move in her mouth as he was now—no, harder, more forcefully, claiming that piece of her as his.

She arched her throat, tried to convey the fantasy through what she did to his fingers, and discovered that the calamari and pepper were interfering.

She coughed.

It didn't stop the lovely, depraved images running through her head. Frankly, it fit with them, because the blowjob she was imagining was the kind where you might find yourself almost choking on cock but not wanting to stop. The kind where you'd actually revel in the bit of discomfort because your lover was getting off so much on thrusting hard into your throat.

On the other hand, cock couldn't actually end up in your windpipe, but a stray piece of food could, and nothing spoiled a flirtation like a Heimlich maneuver and a visit to the ER.

Regretfully, she pulled away and actually applied herself to chewing and swallowing.

The pepper-and-squid combination was delicious, all right, but not as delicious as his fingers.

She thought of his cock deep in her throat, imagined how he might taste as he poured into her, felt herself flushing.

She forced herself to giggle. "Something more delicate might have worked better," she said, making her voice stay even. "Maybe a taste of one of the dipping sauces next time."

Something about the way Nick smiled in response let her know that he knew exactly what she'd been thinking, because he'd been thinking it too. Not just oral sex, because that was what you always thought about when you teased someone like that, but a very specific kind of oral sex, the kind that was claiming, almost brutal. "I don't know. Are delicate morsels what you prefer?"

"Delicacy has its place. But so does less delicate, and that was perfect. Just considering other possibilities that might be...perfect in different ways."

"Oh," he said, smiling luxuriously, "we have time to try all sorts of morsels. This is just the appetizer."

How in the world, she thought, shifting in her seat for the pleasure of feeling her slick lips rub together, was she ever going to get through the rest of dinner without begging him to take her on the table?

When they dragged themselves out of the Barking Crab and started heading toward South Station, Selene's country-bred common sense informed her she was going to get on the Red Line back to Cambridge.

Her body had other ideas. She knew it was too soon to go home with Nick. But for once in her life, she was going to play the game her way, not by the rules.

"Time to get you home," Nick whispered. "Otherwise I'm going to rip your clothes off right here, and it's too nice a night to get arrested."

For a second, she thought about saying no, that things were moving too fast, and that sexual heat or not, it was too soon to know if they were suited in any other way.

But did it matter if they weren't? It could be great if tonight turned out to be more than hot sex, but hot sex had been sadly lacking in her life lately, and they wanted each other so badly she could smell their desire over the estuary-exhaust-fume-and-hot-pavement stench of the summer night.

She meant to say yes, but instead, she found herself stretching to meet Nick's lips without speaking a word, wrapping her arms around him as he drew her close. Their lips met, and any vestiges of inhibition Selene had went up in flame. Hell, she was surprised their clothes didn't go up in flame as well. Nick's big hands gripped her ass, grinding her against him. He was hard, jutting against her belly but not quite able to tease her clit through their clothes. His cock was close, though, so close and so hot. She could almost feel him moving inside her, his cock mirroring the pulse of his tongue in her mouth, mirroring the blood throbbing in her clit.

Without breaking from the kiss, he nudged her legs open with his thigh. She took the hint immediately, straddling him. His hands moved her hips back and forth, a subtle but inescapable rhythm. He twitched his leg against her.

For an instant, Selene remembered they were on a busy street in the heart of Boston and told herself to hold back.

Then it dawned on her that they were, indeed, on a busy street in Boston, where she knew almost no one. In the short time she'd lived here, she'd passed by plenty of couples making out, not to mention couples arguing, people smoking things that definitely weren't legal, and one guy having a boxing match with an imaginary opponent. Only the boxer had registered in any detail, and if she'd been in a hurry or talking on her phone, she might not have noticed him except as one more obstacle to avoid on the street.

She was in public—surrounded by people—and yet in some ways completely private. People might see, but chances were they wouldn't care, and if she and Nick did succeed in shocking a stranger or two, those strangers needed to get out more often.

The dichotomy of being exposed yet anonymous sent a frisson of desire through her already needy body, heightening her sensitivity, her arousal, her awareness of Nick's kiss, his possessive, sure hands, his cock pressing against her, his thigh between her legs. She couldn't hold back any longer. She swayed her hips, grinding herself against him, her wet sex soaking through her panties and skirt and onto his jeans. Blood thrummed in her ears. Nick's kiss became even more insistent, claiming her.

Despite the heat, Selene started shivering.

Nick's lips traced their way to her ear. "Come for me," he whispered. "Get yourself off, here on the street."

Selene hadn't thought she was in any danger of actually coming so publically—but the deep burr of his voice in her ear pushed her over. Burying her face against Nick's chest to stifle a scream, she shuddered and clenched as she fell into the fire and exploded.

He held her close as she trembled. When he softly kissed the top of her head, that simple gesture came close to setting her off again. When she stopped shaking and looked up at him, he mouthed, *Good girl.* She clenched, setting off an orgasmette, a mini-detonation that echoed the huge one.

"I think," she said in a voice that had taken on a weird Marilyn Monroe quality, half breathless, aroused woman and half lost little girl, "it's time to get someplace more private. Like you said, too nice a night to be arrested." She paused for effect, then added, "Too nice a night to be handcuffed by anyone but you."

"I prefer rope," he said, putting his arm around her waist. "Come on. My car's at Post Office Square."

Chapter Four

In the darkness of the parking garage, Selene took a deep breath and asked something she probably should have asked earlier. "This is a play date, right—not a date-date? I'm still learning the ropes, and you seem like a guy who knows your ropes—and whips and all that other stuff—but I don't know what else I want. My last relationship ended pretty badly and..."

"You too? That sucks, but at least we're on the same page about keeping it light and fun and seeing where it goes from there. BDSM can fuck with your head and heart if you let it. Sometimes a play partner you like and trust is the safest way to go."

It was exactly what Selene needed to hear. After the fiasco with Will—she'd almost married him, for heaven's sake, just because everyone seemed to expect it and he'd wanted it so badly—she needed to keep things light and sexy-friendly. So why did her heart sink a little to learn Nick was in the same place in his life?

She could have brooded on that for a while, but luckily, Nick came out with the perfect distraction. "Now that we've got that settled, take your panties off."

Selene stopped in her tracks. "Did you say...?"

"Take your panties off." He pulled her closer, whispered in her ear in that throaty, intense voice she was starting to recognize as his dom voice. "I know we haven't talked about limits, so this is a request rather than an order. But I'd like it if you did." He guided her hand to his cock, straining against his jeans. "Feel how much I like just thinking about it, and imagine how much I'll like it if you do."

Utter icy terror coursed through Selene's veins. She couldn't just take her underwear off in a public place, could she? People just didn't do that.

Then again, people didn't usually caress other people's cocks in public, even stealthily in a dark corner, but she was making no move to snatch her hand away. Nick's grip on her wrist felt right, and his denim-shrouded cock under her captive hand felt even more right. At the moment, they were alone, but someone could come across them at any time—and rather than scaring her, Selene had to admit, the idea jacked her already fierce arousal even higher.

And hell, the panties were so saturated at this point that they weren't even comfortable. "I'll need my hand back," she whispered, giving Nick one last stroke as he let her go.

Slithering the panties to her ankles was easy enough, no worse than slipping out of a bikini bottom under a towel so she could do a quick change. Getting them from around her ankles without tipping over in her high heels, though—that was a bit of a challenge.

Especially when a loud group of teens barged, laughing and shoving each other, into their part of the garage. Selene froze, knowing the panties were visible if any of the kids bothered to look, but knowing they'd be far more likely to look if she bent over.

When the kids passed, she braced herself on Nick's shoulder and stepped out of the panties.

At least that was what she meant to do, only they caught around her left ankle. Holding on to Nick, she kicked out with a little more force than she intended. The panties flew off her foot and skittered under someone else's car. She chuckled nervously, but when Nick echoed her, it turned to a real, honest laugh.

For a second, she thought about trying to retrieve them,

then thought better of it. No point in ruining her dress or Nick's shirt for a five-dollar pair of panties.

And it wasn't like she was going to need them again tonight.

Selene hadn't given a lot of thought to what kind of car Nick might drive, but she hadn't been expecting a bright red Prius. The surprise must have registered on her face.

"You were expecting a muscle car? Or maybe a Ferrari?" He chuckled and added, "When I win the lottery, I'd love a vintage Mustang and a big pickup for the country place I don't have yet, but for the life I live, this is perfect. Sometimes it really is all about the gas mileage."

She laughed. "I can respect that, though I still can't get over that gas is cheaper here than in New York. Not that it helps much, since nothing else is and the extent of my driving these days is moving the car from one side of the street to the other for street-cleaning, since driving in town terrifies me."

"You get used to it, but it's still sucktastic, just a sucktastic you've learned to cope with."

She reached for the passenger door of the Prius, but Nick beat her to it, opening it for her so she could slip in. She kicked off her heels again almost immediately, sighing with relief.

Nick got in, closed his door and whispered, "Hike up your skirt."

A little thrill went through her. She raised herself slightly in the seat and flipped her skirt up behind her. The pragmatic gray upholstery was coarse against her ass, not living up to the cool, smooth leather she'd always imagined, but it certainly made her aware of her bare skin and Nick's scrutiny.

"I see you read *The Story of O.*" Nick's voice was rich with amusement.

Selene felt herself blushing. "It made an impression, even if every single character was crazy as a red-assed bee."

"As long as you know that, everything will be fine. But I should I have been more specific, because we've all read *The Story of O*, and while the bare ass on the seat is lovely, it wasn't what I had in mind."

He reached across her body to grab her seat belt. The sudden proximity, the scent of his body, overwhelmed Selene's senses. She moaned and embraced him, needing more contact, needing him in a way she'd never needed.

For a tantalizing second, Nick let her hold him, her face pressed against his side. Then he slipped out of her arms and settled back into his own seat. The seat belt clicked into place. "I love strapping down a willing woman," he teased, only she had the feeling that while he was teasing, he was in no way joking. "Now tuck your skirt up under the belt. I want you bare."

If she hadn't been wet already, those words, in that tone, would have done it. She flooded at the command in his voice, or maybe at the way she didn't even think about disobeying. In the low car, she'd be exposed to truckers, maybe even to people in tall SUVs... They probably wouldn't see much in the dark, realistically, but the important part was that she *felt* exposed. Vulnerable. Open.

"I'm going to stain your seat," she said as she tucked up the soft folds of her skirt. The fabric felt silkier and more sensual than she'd ever noticed before, caressing her hands, caressing her bare thighs as she drew it up.

His smile seared her skin. "Worth it. Now open your legs."

She did, trembling with anticipation of a touch, a further order.

"Beautiful. God, you look so sexy right now." He ran one finger over her slick pussy lips. She arched up, straining for more, but she didn't get it.

Even that light touch had coated his finger with her juices. He made a great show of sucking and licking them off, his eyes closed as if he was focusing on the flavor, basking in the moment. Selene felt it herself, low in her belly, a tightening and fluttering that combined lust and anticipation and a hint of anxiety about the adventure she'd plunged into when she'd only intended to test the water. If just getting into the car had left her this wet and trembling and Nick—she glanced over to check—straining in his jeans, what was the ride going to bring?

As it turned out, Nick kept his hands on the wheel for most of the trip to his place in Jamaica Plain, occasionally touching her thigh but nothing more intimate, none of the caresses her swollen clit and dripping pussy so desperately craved. Whenever they stopped, he turned to look at her, open longing in his eyes, but he didn't do anything more.

Mostly they talked. Some sexy banter to tease them both further, but also the everyday things you might discuss with any new friend: jobs and childhood homes and dreams, and in Nick's case, the awkwardness of working on the same programming project with Craig. "Luckily Craig's odd and abrasive even by code-monkey standards, so no one wonders why I avoid him. Everyone does."

Selene laughed at that—wound up as she was, probably more than the remark merited. Muscles clenched as she did, and the giggle turned into a gasp. For a few minutes, the conversation had distracted her from her arousal, from her half-naked state. The movement brought it all back to her, and suddenly her heart raced and her blood pounded in her ears. She worked her fingers helplessly in the material bunched up around her hips so she didn't put them between her legs. Just the lightest flick of her finger now would bring her off, grant her at least a little release from the painfully delicious pressure building inside her. But she instinctively knew that wasn't a good idea. He'd tell her if he wanted her to play with herself, she was sure of it. The self-denial, and Nick's denial, his pretending he didn't notice her state though the look in his eyes said otherwise, was perversely pleasurable, reminding her that at the moment, Selene was under Nick's command.

Because she chose to be there.

It felt just as amazing as she'd always imagined.

For a second, she flashed to Nick's serious eyes as he'd said how BDSM could fuck with your heart. It was starting to make more sense. But she wasn't going to let that happen.

Chapter Five

Nick's condo was the second story of a refurbished Victorian home in a pleasantly funky section of Jamaica Plain. As they entered, Selene breathed a sigh of relief at the blessedly cool, air-conditioned air, then looked around the living room.

Although she wouldn't have admitted it for the world, she was mildly disappointed that it was just an ordinary condo, and a single-guy condo at that, not bad but basic. The couch was deep burgundy leather, expensive-looking and almost new; the easy chair across from it was well-loved and upholstered in a rather battered deep green fabric that didn't clash but certainly didn't match. A desk in one corner held a computer. Most of the rest of the décor was chosen for function rather than form and looked like it came from someplace along the lines of Ikea: chrome shelving for storing books and media, a plain coffee table, simple lamps, a throw rug. Two doors led out of the room, one an open archway that went to the kitchen, the other leading to a hallway that, she guessed, led to the bedroom and bathroom. All perfectly decent, but not the den of iniquity that, on some level, she'd been hoping to find.

The only den-of-iniquity touches, and those were mild, were three framed photographs, artistic black-and-white female nudes. The model's face was hidden. She wasn't in bondage, although she wore a leather collar and cuffs, and in only one was she kneeling—actually curled on her knees in the yoga pose called the child's pose, her long fair hair spread in front of her—but something about her body language spoke of submission and pride in submission. They were all the same model, an elegantly slender, graceful-looking woman with tattoos and rings in her nipples.

"I want to be like her someday," Selene said, hardly realizing she said it out loud.

Nick shook his head. "No, you don't. I know the model, and trust me, you don't want to be like her."

"How about that flexible and that thin?" It was only after she said it that Selene, distracted by the sheer sensuality of the images, picked up on his cool, serious tone. Clearly there was a backstory she didn't know—probably didn't need to know, though she couldn't help but be curious.

To her relief, Nick laughed. "That flexible, I can understand. But I like your body just the way it is. And," he added, his voice taking on some of that hot, menacing quality that had attracted her from the start, "I'm looking forward to seeing more of it."

Mesmerized, Selene reached around and started to unzip her dress. He reached behind her, caught her wrists. "Oh, I'm glad you're as eager as I am, but we need to talk a little more— with our clothes on. Things we should have talked about before, really, but dammit, woman, you make it hard to think." Another devouring kiss, and then he steered her toward the couch.

"Pull up your skirt before you sit," he added, almost as an afterthought. "Being naked would distract us both too much— but a little distraction will keep you honest."

And then he proceeded to ask her a series of no-holds-barred questions that made her squirm on the leather couch in a combination of embarrassment and lust.

After they'd gone over her experiences (fairly varied in the vanilla area, but limited in the kink department to light, playful spankings and a few experiments with silk-scarf bondage) and the things that were absolutely off-limits (she asked about his absolutely nots as well and was relieved to hear they agreed on the things they'd never, ever want to do), the subject turned to her fantasies.

"What draws you to BDSM?" he asked.

"I'm not sure I can put it into words. There's so much… It's always been part of my fantasies, ever since I was little and made my brother's GI Joe do unspecified evil things to my Barbie."

That cracked him up, but once he stopped laughing, he encouraged her to go on.

"Part of it is the idea of giving up control. The couple of times I've been tied up were heavenly, even though the guy who did it to me was probably a bigger sub than I am. He was just doing it so I'd tie him up and have my wicked way with him the next night. I'd love to be restrained more severely." And how. She was getting wetter simply talking about it, imagining Nick spread-eagling her on the bed or putting her into some of the exotic rope-bondage positions she'd drooled over while surfing the Net. "And I'd like to take that further, to give up mental control once in a while, to put myself into good hands and say, 'You're in charge now.' To please you if that's what you want, or to take what you give me, your choice."

"How far are you willing to go with letting someone else make the decisions for you? How about…erotic dares, maybe? Like would you want to be told to have sex with someone else?"

"Maybe. Depending on the circumstances. Especially if it's a woman. I've had my bi fantasies, and I've kissed women before. The idea turns me on, but it never seemed like the right time go further than kissing. So being 'ordered' to do it…might be hot, as long as it was something she'd do anyway." She grinned and felt herself flushing.

"Consent's definitely key, even if we're all pretending we're forcing you. How about erotic pain—my flogger or cane or paddle against your skin, alternating with caresses? Because I know I'd love to redden your ass before I bent you over and fucked you."

The words touched her core like skilled fingers. She squirmed, the leather couch tantalizing on her ass, but she couldn't form words to answer.

"I take it that's a yes?"

Her voice seemed to be taking a vacation somewhere, but she made herself speak. "Oh God, yes." With all her darker fantasies within reach, Selene began to tremble. "But what if I can't actually take it? What if I chicken out?"

Nick had been standing over her, looking stern and fierce and glorious, but suddenly he was sitting next to her, putting his arm around her shoulder, drawing her close. "If that happens, we stop and try something else. It's that simple."

Snippets of erotica and posts from FetLife danced dangerously in Selene's head. "Not to sound like a clueless newbie, but I am one. Is that really okay? Aren't you supposed to be in charge?"

"For as long as it's fun for both of us." He kissed the top of her head, a gentle, tender gesture that nevertheless burned into her skin, into her spirit. "No matter what assclowns on the Internet say, it's all right to use your safe word. This is all new to you, and I may try something that doesn't feel good or freaks you out. If I do, I want to know—and I want to know whether you want me to stop or just slow down and let you get used to the sensation."

Tension fled her body, tension she hadn't been aware she was holding. "Red versus yellow. I'm new, but I've read a lot." She leaned against Nick, aware of the skin beneath their clothing, aware of his heat, his strength and of a kind of tough gentleness she had never imagined in a fantasy dom but was glad she'd found in a real-life playmate. "And I'd like to try some of what I've read about, please."

"Like what? What do you want to try first, Selene?"

Her mouth went dry as her pussy got impossibly wetter. "You said you liked rope," she said, "and I'm curious about that." She looked up and made herself meet his eyes. They looked bluer than she remembered, impossibly blue, almost navy. She could get lost in them. "And some light pain. I've been spanked, but never by someone who was really into it, and then whatever you think would be a good next step for a very curious beginner."

"You and I are going to have so much fun," he said, grinning. Nick kissed her again, a deep, devouring kiss. Then he stood and pulled her to her feet.

His eyes were still merry when he looked at her, but when he said, "Undress," it was in a voice like dark chocolate and whisky and sex, a voice that that stroked Selene's core. His posture changed. His eyes became molten, heat within their blue depths. Even if she'd wanted to disobey out of a sense of mischief—and she was a bit surprised she didn't want to—she didn't think she could have.

Selene had thought he'd looked commanding before at times, a dominant in action. Now she realized she'd just gotten a taste. This man she was just meeting contained the funny code-monkey she'd been getting to know, but he seemed to be more somehow. Bigger. More intense. Scarier in some ways, but at the same time, safe. She could put herself into his hands.

She undressed in record time, letting her dress crumple to the floor, tossing her bra carelessly aside. "Shoes?" she asked, surprised by how hard it was to speak.

"Lose 'em. Heels are overrated. I want to be the only thing that hurts you or gets you off-balance tonight."

Relieved and smiling a little at his good sense, she kicked the shoes away.

She wasn't sure what she expected next, but it wasn't for Nick to examine her so intently. He circled her twice, then settled back in front of her, staring unblinkingly like a cat studying its prey. *The next thing will be that little butt wiggle before he pounces,* she thought. A cartoon image of Nick as a cat popped into her head, and she fought back nervous laughter.

She lost the battle.

Suddenly, Nick, springing like the cat she'd envisioned, was on her. His big hand grasped her jaw and throat, gently but with unmistakable authority. No pressure, no physical danger, but a definite sense of menace, of claiming. "Something funny?" he growled. The dark gravel in his voice worked with the hand on her throat, freezing her in place. She shook her head, barely able to move even that much. She couldn't think, could barely breathe from sheer sexual tension, but oh God, she might just come. He wouldn't hurt her, but it was like a roller coaster or a monster movie where you got scared at something that wasn't actually dangerous and enjoyed the hell out of the adrenaline rush.

"Very good. Stay right there. Don't move." Nick stepped away, leaving her bereft as soon as he opened a side door and disappeared from view. He returned quickly, set something she couldn't see just beyond the open archway and returned, holding two hanks of rope. "Hold your hands out in front of you."

When he wrapped the rope around her left wrist, Selene's heart started beating so fast she thought she might crack a rib. It was natural-colored and looked like a thicker version of the twine her grandmother used to trellis peas, but it felt surprisingly soft against her skin. She closed her eyes, wanting to focus on the sensations of Nick touching her, of the rope moving against her skin. He made a snug band around her wrist, then repeated it on the other side. When she opened her eyes, Nick stood before her, holding the ropes that connected to her wrists. He tugged on the ropes. "Follow me."

He led her to the wide, open doorway that led into the kitchen. It was perhaps a dozen steps, but with the ropes holding her, with Nick leading her, it felt both instant and endless.

There were rings set in the wooden doorframe, spray-painted to match the dark green trim. One set was at roughly shoulder height, another single one above her head. Selene gulped. So much for her first impressions. This was definitely a den of iniquity—just a subtle one.

Using the rope ends, Nick secured her wrists to the rings at her sides. There was a bit of play in the ropes; she'd be able to shift around, change position a little. Still, she wasn't going far, and knowing that was a delicious feeling. "Next time we'll try something more elaborate," he whispered, "but I wanted you to experience the feel of hemp rope. Feel the safety of bondage when I flog you for the first time."

She shuddered violently at the word *flog*. It evoked vicious images of the British navy circa *Master and Commander*, a title that seemed much sexier when she was bound in a doorframe waiting to see what evil things Nick might do. But he was right about the safety of bondage. She felt...embraced, as if Nick's hands and not pieces of rope were holding her in place. Delightful.

Nick leaned in and whispered in her ear, his voice a sinful caress, "Are you ready?"

All she could do was nod.

"Stick out your ass." Wordlessly, breathing shallowly in little gasps, she obeyed. Nick ran his hand over the curve of her butt. "Beautiful. You have the perfect ass for spanking, round and heart-shaped and just the right combination of firm and soft. The kind of ass that makes a man like me think evil thoughts." He demonstrated by grabbing one of her cheeks hard. It should have been uncomfortable, would have been under other circumstances, but instead it made her gasp and clench. "Very nice." He lightly smacked the area he'd just grabbed, then struck the other cheek. Back and forth a few times, light and only mildly stingy, but making her feel warm, swollen, pink. Selene moaned and thrust her butt out more, hoping he'd take the hint and pick up the pace. "Oh, you're a natural at this. But spread your legs more. I want to see the juices dripping down your thighs."

As she obeyed, Selene's face flamed, abashed that he'd see

she was already soaked, her thighs already slick. Then she had a revelation. She was embarrassed because she thought she should be and because she'd had the bad luck to date a couple of guys who were intimidated by how sexual she could be. But Nick wasn't intimidated. Nick craved her desire, wanted to see its evidence on her skin.

That knowledge aroused her even more.

Realizing this didn't make her face feel less heated, but it was more a flush than a blush now, pure sexual excitement.

"Ready?" Nick asked again, but before she could answer, his hand struck hard.

Selene squealed and jumped in place. It hurt. That was her first reaction. It stung and burned, and instinct told her to pull away. But he stroked the skin he'd just smacked, and the throbbing discomfort shifted to a throbbing pleasure. "More, please," she said before she could help herself—not that she wanted to help herself.

"Of course. But don't you dare come until I tell you to."

Come? Selene wanted to chuckle. Spanking might be a huge turn-on, but there was no way she could come without more direct stimulation. She was safe, although she had to admit the order not to come was exciting in itself.

That thought fled after a few more blows, a few more caresses, and instead she found herself wondering how she was going to manage to hold off coming until she got permission. She tried to count at first, but somewhere around twenty, her brain turned off its ability to do anything that rational and linear. Her ass felt huge, hot and swollen—but not as hot and swollen as her cunt. She throbbed all over, between the sweet, decadent ache in her pussy and the tender ache in her abused butt. Her head swam. She didn't want to beg. She really didn't. It was such a cliché, and she'd sound stupid, and...

And if she didn't get permission to come, she was going to do it anyway. The combination of pleasure and pain was driving her mad. "Please," she whispered, her voice doing that Marilyn Monroe thing again. "Please, may I come?"

Nick spanked her again in response, a quick flurry of blows she couldn't quite process. "Aren't you forgetting something?" he said, a hint of super-villain evil laughter in his voice.

Selene made a desperate guess. He'd never said anything about calling him *Master* or *sir,* but demanding—obliquely—at this point was a great way to fuck with her already foggy head. "Please, may I come, *sir?*" she gasped out and was rewarded with a hearty, "Come now," and another good smack.

The orgasm seized her and wouldn't let go. She bucked and thrashed and howled wordlessly. A flood of moisture escaped her pussy. She strained against the ropes as she arched back, all her muscles tightening and then releasing abruptly so she sagged, using the ropes to hold her up. Her pussy still convulsed, but more gently. Nick embraced her from behind, murmuring soothing nonsense like someone might say to a crying child. "Hush, I've got you. You're all right. I've got you."

"More than all right. Wow." He felt so good against her, so hot and hard and yet so safe. His cock, rampant inside his jeans, pressed against her tender butt, but right now she was more interested in his strength, in the protection of his arms.

At least at first. Then her brain started coming back on line just enough to remind her the night was still young, she was still horny, and Nick was still fully dressed. She pushed back against him, grinding her ass against his crotch. The denim of his jeans felt harsh and coarse, as if she could feel every individual thread at ten times their actual size against her delightfully abused flesh, a weird and wonderful sensation, but not as wonderful as the way Nick reacted. One of the hands that had been around her waist travelled up to her breasts, pinching first one nipple, then the other, exactly hard enough.

The other strayed between her legs to circle her sensitized clit. Within seconds, Selene felt stars dancing on her skin and groaned something that she meant to be *please,* though it didn't sound much like English.

"Come, Selene," Nick growled in her ear. "Come for me."

She flew apart again in a burst of light, a different sensation than coming as he spanked her, but just as heart-poundingly, cunt-clenchingly good. Not as devastating, though—she could stand afterward without relying on the rope, and could even formulate an answer when Nick asked her, "Are you up for a flogging? Or would you rather move straight to the part of the evening when we fuck like crazed weasels?"

Two things occurred to her. One was that he sounded smugly certain she wanted to fuck him, and normally she'd be tempted to make him work for it no matter how interested she might be—but since she'd realized she wanted to fuck him about three-point-two seconds after meeting him, she couldn't be bothered to pretend offense. The other was that he was asking a trick question. Luckily, it was a trick question with an answer fairly obvious to her lust-saturated brain. "Both, please. First the flogging and then the fucking." She hesitated, then added, "Unless, of course, you have another idea."

"I like the way you think. Now spread your legs a little more." She complied, wondering if he was moving straight to the fucking after all. Instead, he crouched down and half crawled between her legs to grab something that had been tucked just out of her sight on the other side of the doorframe: a flogger with dark green falls and a leather-wrapped handle.

She shivered in delight.

Once he stood again, he reached around Selene's body, dragging the falls across her breasts. They were suede, deliciously soft as they passed over her nipples, but she suspected they were heavy enough to make an impression when he wanted to. Not *Master and Commander* at all, though. This wasn't the kind of whip that would draw blood but the kind that would draw her in a sensual spell. It already was, moving so lightly and lovingly across her skin.

Now Nick moved to her back, letting the strands of suede tease from her shoulder blades to her ass, and lower, onto her thighs. Just feather-light caresses at first, nothing more. Then he started to strike lightly, again starting at her shoulders and working down. The suede danced on her skin, kissing it. On her shoulders, it felt like a massage. On her hot butt and the tender inside of her thighs, it stung in a beautiful way. When she was sighing and pushing back for more, Nick stepped up the pace, hitting faster and harder. Now he was focusing on her ass and thighs, and there was a definite sting to the dance, the falls snapping against her in a way that made her yelp but also made her rise up on her toes in delight. So good. She could get lost in this rhythm, ride the sensual sting forever. Nick had stepped up the pace again, but it was gradual enough that her pleasure caught up. A couple of times, a good whack caught the spot where her ass and thighs met or curled around to her inner thighs, and she yelped. But the constant rhythm of the suede, though stingy and thuddy, was also soothing. Selene was aroused, keenly aware of Nick behind her, of the flogger on her skin, of her hard, crinkled nipples, aching, empty cunt and throbbing clit. At the same time, she felt no great urgency to do anything about the arousal. Maybe it was because she'd already come a few times, but there was something meditative about the way Nick was beating her, about the steady assault on her senses. She was having an in-body out-of-body experience, and she loved it.

She might have been happy to stay in that blissed-out place for the rest of the night if Nick hadn't said, "Come now"—while he let the lashes flick up over her pussy. It was light, light as the first caresses had been, but that contact and the command in his voice were enough to shatter her, send her flying into pieces, then abruptly back down to earth. She sagged in her bonds, limp and happy. Nick's arms wrapped around her from behind, supporting her.

"Once you've caught your breath," he whispered, "I think

it's time for the crazed weasel fucking."

Selene couldn't manage to talk coherently yet, but she couldn't agree more.

Chapter Six

They might have run into the bedroom or they might have floated. In any case, she wasn't paying much attention to the trip, just to Nick's firm hand on her tender ass, guiding her.

She had only seconds to look around the bedroom—a big bed with a heavy dark-wood frame, low-slung dresser, more erotic photography on the walls. Then Nick started to undress, and all she could do was stare, not even able to muster the brain cells to help him.

Nice chest and surprisingly muscular shoulders. Not much hair on his chest, and his skin was very fair, fairer than her own, but it made him look like he was carved from marble. Long, lean legs, defined enough that she could see the cut in his hip muscles, a little dimple she'd love to lick. Maybe it wasn't a perfect body, but damned if she could see any faults in it.

Then again, after what he'd just done to her, he could transform himself into Jabba the Hutt, and for a few minutes he'd still look pretty good to her lust-dazed eyes.

She managed to unfreeze herself long enough to draw down his bikini briefs.

All that and a fat cock too? Damn, she was a lucky girl!

Instinct and desire made her drop to her knees, open her mouth expectantly. He shook his head. "Tempting, but not now. I want to fuck you while your ass is still warm from my hand. Get up and bend over the bed. Stick your bottom out for me."

She posed herself as directed.

The sound of a tearing condom wrapper, a few agonized seconds of waiting, and Nick's hands gripped her hips and his cock pushed into her.

No preliminary teasing, because she was so wet there was no point in waiting. One push and he was in to the hilt, his balls against her tender ass, his fingers digging into her, and all she could do was gasp, "Fuck, yes!"

"Come on my cock," he said. "Come all you want." And that was the last articulate thing either of them said for a while.

He wasn't gentle, not at all. Wild and rough and fierce, not lingering for her pleasure, but chuckling under his breath every time she gasped or moaned. He pounded into her, and she drove back onto him, trying to make it even harder, trying to take him so deep inside her that when he came, she'd taste it. He slapped at her ass and thighs, and each slap drove her a little further toward madness. With each thrust, her breasts bobbed, rubbing her nipples on the chenille bedspread, stimulating her further.

And then he turned his attention from her ass to her breast, slapping at those.

The orgasm, she swore, didn't start in her cunt, but on the deliciously abused surfaces of her breasts and butt, and its waves rippled inward until she was contracting around Nick and making the kind of crazy noises she'd always thought were sure signs of faking it.

Nick swore and bucked into her as he came. The hand still braced on her hip clenched, and that little extra pleasure/pain pushed her into another orgasm. Then his weight sagged on her, and they both collapsed onto the bed.

Nick woke up feeling a bit smug, a bit possessive, and a bit infatuated.

And whatever his brain might have to say about feeling that

way—"stupid" and "crazy" featured prominently—the rest of him was too busy paying attention to the throbbing of his cock to listen for long. Never mind that they'd woken up in the middle of the night and fucked again, that time more slowly, with Selene exploring his body as thoroughly as he'd explored hers the night before.

Did it damn well too, eagerly and adventurously. And she knew how to let him lie back and enjoy while she rode him but in a way that still left him feeling in charge. Very hot. And definitely worth repeating.

He felt a bit like a kid, all wrapped up in his shiny new playmate, without the slightest bit of perspective. But perspective was highly overrated, Nick reasoned, compared to enjoying the moment—the bright morning, Selene's silken body against him, still pliant with sleep but starting to stir, the scent of last night's sex rising off her and stimulating him toward the next round, and no place in particular to be except...

He sat up and swore at the clock, which assured him it was nearly noon.

Selene went from dozing to wide awake in an instant. "What's wrong?"

"Minor annoyance," he soothed. "I'm supposed to go to Garth and Alison's today. They're having a barbecue to show off their new pool. Which wouldn't be a problem if I hadn't told them I'd be there early to help them set up, and it's not early anymore."

He ran one hand over Selene's curvaceous side, wanting nothing more than to bury himself in her body. Curling up for a little more sleep with her came a close second. But he'd made a promise. Dammit. He threw himself from the bed, saying, "So, since we can't spend all day in bed, want to come to a pool party instead? It's going to be hot again—and not just because of you."

She grinned. "Sure, though I'm kind of lacking a bathing

suit. Or clean clothes, for that matter. Anything I can do to help us get out the door?"

"Feed the cats upstairs?" He handed her a key. "Kate and Stephanie are away this weekend, and I said I'd look after them. Their place is laid out differently from this one; you'll walk right into the kitchen, and the cat food should be right out on the counter. Don't let the little furry con-men get to you too much; Kate and Stephanie spoil 'em wicked, and I was up there for a while yesterday."

After that warning, Selene wasn't too surprised to be mugged by a fat, elderly orange tabby and a half-grown Siamese, both crying and wrapping themselves around her ankles, trying to convince her they hadn't been fed or petted in weeks. It was tempting to stay and give them all the attention they craved, but she figured if she did, she might hold Nick up—and if she'd planned to do that, there'd be more interesting ways to do it.

When she came back downstairs, the shower was running.

Selene tried to stop herself, telling herself firmly that Nick was on a schedule, that he would have asked her to join him in the shower if he'd figured he had time, that it probably against some submissive's code to take that much initiative.

Then she decided, *what the hell.* She had to take a shower anyway, and if he didn't want to take the time to fool around, it wouldn't take much longer for her to rinse off with company.

She shucked her dress, left it in a silky red heap on the kitchen floor and stalked into the bathroom.

Nick definitely had his priorities in line. Towel warmer. Plushy, big towels. Slate tiles on the shower walls. Dual showerheads, the kind that delivered a wide, soft spray like tropical rain, strong but gentle on her skin as she slipped in. It was just about the perfect temperature for this already warm morning and for bodies sticky with sex and sweat.

Nick didn't turn around when she joined him, but something in his body language shifted. Selene translated it as "pretending not to notice".

Fine. Two could play that game.

She grabbed the soap—it was a hefty bar, slightly irregular in shape and smelling like lemongrass—worked up a lather and started to wash his back.

He managed to maintain his pretense of silence for about fifteen seconds longer, until she ran her soap-slick hands down his spine to cup his butt.

Only then did he turn his head and say, "It took you long enough. Now keep going." He sounded unspeakably smug and entitled, but tongue-in-cheek about it.

She wasn't sure whether the appropriate response was to say, *Yes, sir*, like a good little sub or to respond teasingly, as his tone dared her to do.

Interesting question. As far as she could figure out, if she was cheeky, she'd get spanked for being naughty. If she was "good", she'd get spanked as a reward for being good. Talk about your win-win situation!

So she said, "Yes, sir," in a slightly mocking voice, with a sarcastic little knee-dip and head bob like a Victorian maidservant trying to cover the fact she thought her employer was an idiot. Then she stuck out her tongue at him. She kept on washing his butt as she did. Why move her hands away from those glorious globes one second before she had to?

"Oh, you are so asking for it!" Nick wheeled around, raised his hand as if to give her a good smack on the ass. "But I liked the sir. Keep using it for the rest of the day."

Selene dropped the soap, letting it fall into the water without even trying to recover it. She could feel every muscle, every nerve, every square inch of skin, yearning toward Nick's hand, craving the sharp sting and the fire that followed in its wake. Without even really meaning to, she turned around and cocked her ass out, presenting a better target.

He lowered his hand to his side without touching her. "Which is why you're not getting it right now. You want it too badly. Don't you, girl?"

With the last sentence, his voice shifted to that deep and ominous timbre that make her clit tingle.

"Answer me, Selene," he insisted. "Were you hoping for another spanking?"

It took her a second or so to find her tongue, which seemed to have cleaved to the roof of a mouth as dry as her pussy was drenched.

She hung her head, studying the off-white enamel surface of the tub as if it were studded with emeralds, watching the soapy water swirl its way down the drain as if it were an oracle. "Yes, sir," she finally admitted.

Why was her voice so small? It wasn't anything to be ashamed of. Nick knew what she liked. That was why she was here. And he couldn't be under any illusions she wasn't...well, she preferred the more elegant "wanton" over "horny", but they both described the way she felt around Nick. He seemed to like her that way, like that she wanted him and what he had to give her.

But she couldn't speak up.

"I couldn't hear you." He raised her chin, and that gentle, proprietary touch made her tremble.

This didn't help her ability to talk.

"Well, if you can't answer me," he said, affecting nonchalance, "I guess I'll have to find someone who can talk to take to Garth and Alison's today. Pity," he added with a hilariously languid gesture that looked like it belonged in a costume drama on a debauched aristocrat played by someone along the lines of Ralph Fiennes, "they were looking forward to getting to know you better. But a woman who can't talk is no fun at a party. Unless she's gagged, of course, and it's not that kind of a party."

The hand that had imitated Ralph Fiennes reached for her nipple, pinched hard and deliciously. "Last chance, Selene. Were you trying to make me spank you?"

He twisted as he pinched, sending a shock of sensation, painful and exquisite, through her. Her "yes" was less an answer to his persistent questioning than an affirmation, a proclamation, a cry of delight. But it was audible, all right.

And saying it broke the dam. After that, she was able to look into Nick's amazing blue eyes and admit, "Yes, sir, I was hoping for a spanking."

"Greedy, aren't you?"

Was that a trick question?

She decided that it probably was, and that it didn't matter.

"Yes I am...sir." She took a deep breath. "I feel like a kid in a candy store. A weird, twisted kid in a strange candy store, but you get the idea."

Nick grinned, the kind of grin most commonly described as either "shit-eating" or "cat that got the cream", depending on who was talking. "The candy store's not going to close on you. But sometimes you need to eat something besides candy."

He tweaked her nipples affectionately, then moved his hands to her shoulders. "I'll redden your lovely ass another time. But I've been thinking ever since dinner last night about using your mouth—and since you're such a self-confessed greedy, impatient little thing, it'll do you good to wait awhile."

He pressed on Selene's shoulders, but she was already sinking to her knees, trying to do it gracefully, like she could imagine the fragile blonde in the pictures in his living room doing. It didn't quite work, but she didn't wobble too badly.

Nick didn't seem to care. At least, Nick's cock wasn't voicing any complaints, and the rest of him seemed inclined to go along with it.

Selene tried to remember if she'd ever sucked cock in the shower before. She must have. Her sex life might have been fairly non-kinky until last night, but not lacking in adventures of other sorts. But she couldn't remember when, where, with whom.

Not now. It was as if, at this moment, she was newborn, brought into being by Nick, for his pleasure—and hers. Definitely for hers.

The water fell on them like warm rain. Drops temptingly beaded on Nick's cock.

She licked them off, feeling the heat of him through the cooling water.

A teasing lick around the head, circling him like a lollipop, savoring the pleasure.

She'd been thinking about doing something like this long before they'd gotten to the Barking Crab, and the calamari incident had made certain she'd keep thinking about it.

She wrapped one hand around the base of his cock, cupped the other around his balls. She opened her mouth wider, stretched it around the satisfying thickness—not too much, just enough to feel right in her mouth—and began to work him over, slowly and deliberately taking in his length.

Hands clenched in her damp hair, he pushed her head forward onto his shaft, then yanked her back again.

The fantasy from the restaurant.

He *had* been thinking what she'd been thinking. She'd known it.

"I said I wanted to use your mouth," he said. "When I want it leisurely and sweet, I'll lie down and get comfortable." He punctuated his words with thrusts, pushing himself into her mouth. His hands controlled the movement of her head, and his grip on her hair hurt, but in the good sense of hurt, the sense she was learning that she craved even more than she'd imagined, and she felt helpless, but that was the way it should be right now. It was as if he'd put a collar on her with his words and his touch and the callous way he was using her mouth.

No, not callous, because it was exactly what she needed, exactly one of her fantasies, and it seemed clear to her that Nick not only knew that but was turned on precisely because of it, because her fantasy and his collided so precisely.

Nick's cock became Selene's world: all she could taste, all she could feel, all she could hear, even the little noises it made as it moved in and out of her wet mouth. The warm water pouring over them layered a soft sensuality over the harder, raw sexuality of the moment and locked them into a private tropical paradise.

Vision didn't matter; she closed her eyes. The strain in her thighs didn't matter; in fact, it felt strangely good, a little sacrifice she was making for her dom. He pounded into her mouth, and it should have been uncomfortable—okay, it was uncomfortable, but it was also remarkably good. She could feel the answer building between her own legs, lava hot, slick, needy. Yet she didn't start playing with herself, as she'd often done in the past while giving her boyfriend du jour a quick blowjob. She was getting a lot of pleasure from his sleek length, the musky hints of precome, the calculated brutality of his thrusts.

Was it possible to come without being touched, to explode from a fantasy fulfilled so perfectly?

Her legs started to shake.

"My balls," Nick gasped, and she understood. She stroked, a gentle caress with a hint of fingernail. Repeated it. Found the spot between his balls and ass where many men liked a bit of attention and applied pressure there.

Nick thrust faster, using her mouth like a pussy. Selene could barely breathe around the force of it, but she could tell she wouldn't need to for much longer.

She shimmied her hand, vibrating on the sweet spot as she

took a particularly deep thrust, one that hit the back of her throat enough that she should have gagged but somehow didn't.

"Oh sweet Jes..." His words broke off into a roar that echoed around the confines of the bathroom, and her mouth flooded with Nick's come.

Selene convulsed as pleasure passed through her, a quick, shimmering shock that was a shadow of Nick's loud explosion, a shadow of the staggering orgasms she'd had the night before.

But unmistakably an orgasm—hands-free—from the sheer amazing rightness of the experience.

Weak, she sat back in the tub, letting the water and the joy wash over her.

"Wow," Nick said quietly, and "Wow," she echoed.

And then, once they'd both started breathing again, Nick drew her to her feet and washed *her* back.

Chapter Seven

She hadn't known what to expect from Garth and Alison's house. Something about Garth suggested that he ought to be living in a British manor house to match the lord-of-all-he-surveyed air, but she knew that was about as likely as Nick's condo really having turned out to be the debauched pleasure palace of her most fevered imagination. Back in central New York, she wouldn't have blinked at the pleasant early twentieth-century house set in a wooded lot. It was charming—lavender lining the front walk, a big side porch looking out over the side lawn, and modest wooden columns by the front door that suggested that the original builder was going for the upwardly mobile market with pretensions of elegance—but not spectacular.

She'd done a bit of house-hunting, though, before realizing that with the proceeds of selling her house in Rochester, she would be lucky to find a tiny condo in an outlying town that wasn't even on a commuter rail line. This close to Boston, a house this nice on such a large lot might as well be a lordly manor as far as she was concerned. Either they'd gotten it years ago as a fixer-upper, or they were...not exactly rich but more than comfortable.

The driveway and the street were already crowded with cars, everything from oversized, overpriced SUVs to hybrids to classic soccer-mom minivans to a few beaters held together with bubblegum, duct tape and the power of prayer. Many of them sported the same small sticker: black-and-blue stripes with a red heart.

Selene suppressed a giggle at that and wondered if she would have figured it out if she hadn't been clued in.

The backyard was hidden, the view from the street blocked by a tall wooden privacy fence—made sense with a pool, she supposed—and as they approached the house, Selene could hear a buzz of voices from behind the fence. There was a gate in the fence, but instead, Nick guided her to the porch steps. Several strangers and Betsy from yesterday were ensconced in chairs on the porch, drinks in hand, chatting. Betsy was drinking what looked like iced tea; the others had beers or mimosas.

"Hey, Nick, Selene," Betsy said calmly. "Herself's out back, imitating a very small force of nature and somehow making food magically appear from the air. You know the Alison magic—you think, just *think* that chocolate chip cookies might be nice, and suddenly they're there, and don't ask how she baked them in this heat, but apparently she did. Himself is around somewhere."

"Grill," one of her companions, a boyish Asian woman with her short hair slicked back like a dapper Jazz Age gentleman, said, gesturing in the appropriate direction. "Since the man who said he'd help with grill duty was running late." The woman winked at Nick as she said it, but Nick looked a little guilty.

The expression, Selene decided, didn't suit him at all. She much preferred the gorgeous, confident alpha-male face. And that made her feel bad for making him late, although certainly he hadn't been fighting back when she joined him in the shower.

They headed into the backyard, following Betsy's gesture.

Nice new pool.

Slightly straggly plantings clearly stuck in to disguise the aftermath of construction, including a couple of potted ficus trees that looked like they'd been appropriated from someone's office for the weekend.

A deck so shiny and new that she guessed it had been put in with the pool.

Various people milling about and a few splashing in the pool. Not a huge crowd, maybe twenty people.

Garth was manning a stainless-steel grill that would give Selene's dad a heart attack from barbeque lust.

Alison was just stepping out the back door with a pitcher of what looked like margaritas in one hand. She wore a long, floaty turquoise silk-gauze skirt, a little matching halter, bronze sandals with moderate heels, a copper bracelet set with turquoise on her left arm. It looked gorgeous with her coloring but more formal than what most of the other guests were wearing. She seemed to find it as comfortable as shorts and sneakers.

It made Selene feel a little better about her dress and utterly inappropriate high-heeled sandals, although she still planned to kick them off as soon as possible so she wouldn't sink into the lawn.

Alison put the pitcher of drinks down on a long table set up by the pool and met them halfway.

"It's my fault we're even later that Nick thought we'd be," Selene told Alison breathlessly. "I begged him to stop at TJ Maxx on the way in; I have no idea where my bathing suit is right now and I..." She stopped talking at Alison's knowing smirk and just held up the TJ Maxx bag to prove that part of the story, at least, was true. "I've never picked out a bikini so fast in my *life*. Didn't even try it on. I hope it fits."

Nice outfit, Alison mouthed before adding out loud, "No problem. I knew you guys weren't dead in a ditch."

Garth joined them, slipping his arm around Alison's waist. "Morning, Nick. Oh, sorry, afternoon." He didn't smirk at the two of them the way Alison did, just maintained the same calm half smile, but his dark eyes were knowing, and there was a world of kindly teasing in his voice. Oh yeah, he knew what they'd been up to last night and why they were late today. Thankfully, he seemed to approve.

"I don't believe we got officially introduced yesterday, but Alison told me a bit about you. Garth Saxon." He extended his hand.

For a split second, Selene panicked. Was she supposed to do something...something subby instead of just shaking his hand? Genuflect or kneel like that silly undergraduate yesterday or something?

Deep breath. *Pool party. It's a pool party. Not a play party.* Nick had already made that clear.

Just to be on the safe side, she glanced at Nick, who gave a slight, encouraging nod. She followed his cue and took Garth's hand, large, slightly calloused and definitely strong. What her father would call a good handshake, firm but not bone-jarring. "Selene Daniels. I really appreciate you and Alison letting me tag along on such short notice."

"My pleasure." His dark-eyed gaze traveled up and down her body, and she was suddenly sure Garth knew she wasn't wearing underpants. The lack of a bra was obvious. She was no Pamela Anderson, but her breasts, being real, were affected by gravity.

The dark eyes flicked over to Nick, then met hers. A slow, lazy grin grew out of his half smile, very Cheshire cat. Oh yeah, Alison was a lucky woman. Garth wasn't as handsome as Nick, but she was willing to bet he was an E-ticket. That look alone was enough to make her shiver, enough to flood her brain with vague but intriguing images of the ways he could reduce a woman to a puddle of happy goo if he put his mind to it.

And then he released her hand as if nothing had happened, and looked so unperturbed that she questioned whether it actually *had* happened. Maybe she'd imagined that heated, assessing look because she was intrigued by him—his relationship with Alison, his air of natural authority so strong that even Nick deferred to him a little.

That must be it. Garth wouldn't have actually been flirting her when he was all cuddled up to Alison like that, would he? Not when he obviously adored and lusted after his wife. He had too much class for that.

The sun glinted off Alison's locking choker.

Not just wife. Slave.

Garth and Alison played by different rules, rules she couldn't begin to understand yet.

And maybe if she was lucky, she'd get to find out what they were.

She was here with Nick, and while they hadn't made any commitments beyond having fun and exploring her fantasies, it seemed tacky to be speculating about his friend. His very married (whatever else the relationship was) friend.

But she couldn't help it.

Not, she realized quickly, because she was seriously interested, but because that moment underscored that she'd stumbled into an erotic fairyland, a world where anything might happen.

If she'd been wearing panties, they'd be damp. Maybe she'd better get used to going without them around this crowd; otherwise, she'd have to carry spares in her purse.

Nick put his hand on her butt, a little, friendly gesture that the party guests milling around them wouldn't notice.

Then he pressed in discreetly, letting her feel again how tender her ass was.

Yup, underwear was definitely optional when she was around Nick. Although it might come in handy sopping up some of the moisture welling between her legs so it didn't run down her thighs.

"Nick, I could still use a hand setting up the sun shade," Garth said. "Alison tried, but it's not a job for short people." He gave his tiny partner a kiss on the top of her auburn head. "Mind if I borrow you?"

"No problem. Just a second." Nick moved so he was looking Selene in the eyes, then put his hands on her hips and pulled her into a kiss.

A kiss that short-circuited Selene's brain, curled her toes and reinforced the notion that, as long as she was seeing Nick, she might as well give up on panties and save on laundry. A kiss that involved nipping at her tongue, sending thrills of lust through her body.

A kiss that wasn't nearly long enough.

Then he whispered in her ear, "You're in a virtual collar while we're here, Selene. Call me sir, obey me, all that stuff. You're mine today, do you understand?"

She nodded mutely, too confused—or maybe the proper word was excited—to speak. Did that mean he would...

As if reading her mind, he added, "Trust me, I'll find ways to take advantage of this. This isn't a play party, but Garth is an accommodating host."

Selene felt her cheeks flaming, felt her sex melting. "Yes, sir," she mouthed. "Thank you."

She forced herself to look up and drown in his intense blue gaze. Those eyes seemed to see deep inside her, see parts of her that she herself had been afraid to look at, let alone reveal to anyone else. How could he know her so well after so little time?

He didn't really know *her*, she reminded herself rather sternly. He'd figured out some of her fantasies, including some she hadn't known she had, like this, used his experience and his cleverness to ask the right questions and make the right guesses. It didn't mean he had some secret insights into her heart and soul. It just meant he was smart and damn good in bed.

And what was not to like about that?

It was impressive that he'd figured out her hot buttons

better than long-term lovers had—definitely a good recommendation for sticking around and seeing what crazy and utterly erotic idea he came up with next.

"If you and Nick are going to be busy, Master, I'll give Selene the ten-cent tour," Alison said. The "Master" was said completely naturally, at the same tone and volume as everything else, cuing Selene in that, while this wasn't a play party, most of the guests were not precisely shockable. "And you can change into your suit if you'd like."

Nick nodded his approval.

Twitchy with arousal and fighting the feeling she'd fallen down a rabbit hole and turned into Alice-in-Leatherland, and expecting at any moment to see a white rabbit—in this crowd, would that be a furry, or maybe a pretty woman in a little teddy, fishnets and bunny ears and tail?—Selene let Alison take her arm and guide her into the house.

The kitchen was open and bright, with white appliances, a breakfast nook on one end and a green countertop that looked like malachite but wasn't. Joe-Bear from yesterday was reducing carrots to carrot sticks, stopping long enough to ask Alison if she wanted more celery done.

"Your guy's here. Go enjoy the party," she said, ruffling where his hair would have been if he'd had any as she passed. "Thanks for helping out."

The kitchen led into a formal dining room with cream chair rails and forest-green upper walls. They didn't linger but moved on quickly through a living room decorated in jewel tones, with William Morris touches applied with a light hand. A wide-screen TV dominated one wall, which should have looked incongruous but somehow didn't. Alison pointed out the office—desks and computers and two walls hidden with floor-to-ceiling bookcases—then whisked her to the stairs.

"We have a changing area—a glorified shed, really—by the pool, but with so many people here, almost everyone'll be changing in the spare bedrooms."

Up the stairs and into the first bedroom. It was small and painted a lovely shade of sky blue. The white wrought-iron bed sported an old-fashioned white chenille bedspread and blue-and-white-striped pillows, like you'd expect to see in a summer house on Cape Cod. The mermaid art on the walls was all topless, and some of them were smooching each other, making it a slightly funky summer home, but every other detail was there, right down to a scattering of shells on the dresser. Tote bags and clothes were tossed here and there. They must belong to the people already in the pool.

Joining them sounded like a great idea. The house was lovely, but it didn't have central AC, and while the downstairs had been bearable, this little bedroom was warm and sticky.

"Well," Selene said, "I guess it's time to see if this thing actually fits. If not, I'll jump into the pool in my dress and take my chances with chlorine." She took the suit, a black-and-white zebra-print bikini, out of the bag and started snapping off the myriad tags.

When the door closed, she figured Alison had stepped out to give her a little privacy, but when she glanced up from her struggle with a particularly recalcitrant tag that was holding the two pieces of the suit together like Siamese twins, the redhead was still there.

"Give me that," Alison said. Selene complied, expecting her to produce scissors from a dresser drawer or something like that.

Instead, she dropped the bathing suit unceremoniously onto the floor, put her arms around Selene and kissed her.

Not a friendly peck, not one of those hostess-Hollywood-Eurotrash air kisses on the cheeks.

A wrap-your-arms-around-someone, pull-them-close, let-them-feel-the-soft-heat-of-your-lips-until-they-yield-to-you kiss.

Perhaps at some other time, some time when she was sane,

in control of herself, not half melted from Nick's caresses in the car, Nick's whispered promises and threats, Garth's flirting, the whole atmosphere of the party—completely mundane on the surface, yet buzzing with an unconventional sexual current—Selene might not have yielded so quickly, so utterly, to the kiss.

But she did.

Opened her lips to the soft but insistent pressure, nibbled on those delightful lips delicately flavored with Alison's dark lipstick and an undernote of vanilla-and-honey lip balm, enjoyed the small, skilled, firm fingers tangled in her hair, opened her mouth to a sweet, cinnamon-tasting kitten tongue darting in to tease all the surfaces of the inside of her mouth. Reveled in the sheer delightful novelty of a petite, curvaceous body in her arms instead of a big male one, breasts against her breasts, a sweet floral-and-spice scent filling her nostrils.

Selene had kissed girls before. It had never been anything more than pleasant, but she'd always wondered if it had been the chemistry with those particular girls that caused the lack of spark or maybe the fact both she and the girls she'd kissed had been spectacularly less than sober. Kissing Alison—a sober, grown woman who knew what she wanted—seemed to be a different story. Far more than pleasant. She wasn't about to change teams on a permanent basis, but she could definitely see the appeal of playing for both teams.

She ran her hands down Alison's back, savoring the animal softness of silk, the fine lines of her body. Cupped her hands over the curves of Alison's ass—they were compact enough to fit nicely into her hands—pulled her in closer so their pelvises rubbed together.

Alison did the same, grasping firmly at the still-tender curves of Selene's ass.

She gasped into the other woman's mouth at the surge of sensation, the warmth radiating out from her slightly bruised skin and pulsing in her nipples, her cunt.

Selene had been damp to start with. Now she was flooding.

She gasped into Alison's mouth as the pain/pleasure flooded her. She ground her mound against Alison's.

She was pretty sure Alison was also a panty-free zone, based on what both her hands and her mound were feeling.

And her clit—her clit that felt as huge and swollen as a cock—kept brushing over what felt like jewelry.

Alison was pierced.

That surprised her.

A lot of people had body jewelry these days. But Selene associated it mostly with artists and the tattooed chick who dished out the falafel at her favorite food truck, not someone as sophisticated as Alison. Not someone who fell, without a doubt, into the category of grown-up.

But she could feel the firm press of metal, both there and possibly at Alison's nipples.

Hottest. Feeling. Ever.

Her hand moved, without her volition, slipped down Alison's thigh and around toward the front. She took the edge of Alison's skirt and bunched it up, not caring that someone might come in at any moment, just consumed with the need to see Alison's ornamented lips. To touch them.

To see if she could make another woman come.

A tiny but surprisingly strong hand grabbed her wrist.

Alison chuckled deep in her throat. "Oh, sweetheart, Nick's going to have so much fun with you—and you with him. But slow down!" Alison's voice sounded husky, aroused, amused and more than a little regretful. "This is just a kiss to welcome you to the family. That's all for now."

"To the family?"

"Nick's like Garth's little brother. We see a lot of him, and I have a feeling we're going to be seeing a lot of you too. You'll take good care of him for us, won't you?"

Chapter Eight

Selene blinked, stunned by the sudden change of tone from sex goddess to concerned friend. "Uh, I'll try. But we're not... I mean you know we just..." She shook her head, saw from Alison's expression that the older woman had her number. "Okay, Nick's sexy as hell and we're having so much fun it's probably illegal, but we just met, and neither of us is looking for anything serious. This is all so new to me—I don't want to get in over my head, and Nick was pretty clear he wants to keep it casual. Friends who play."

Alison's smile was knowing as she said, "So he says. But take good care of him anyway. Friends take care of each other. Right?" She patted Selene's arm, as casually as if they hadn't been kissing like crazed things a moment before. "See you outside, sweetie. Gotta keep the party lubricated. In margaritas, that is."

The bikini fit, although it showed a little more of Selene's butt than made her entirely happy. She craned her neck to check the mirror. It was a nice view—maybe Nick's appreciation of her round ass was rubbing off on her, because she didn't remember it looking that good, and it wasn't like she'd been working out.

And thank goodness, she couldn't see any evidence of the night's activities on display for all the world to see. She was tender, but there were no bruises except for a few faint marks hidden beneath the zebra-print bottom. Not that anyone in this crowd would be shocked—envious, maybe, but not shocked— but she wasn't sure she was ready to share the evidence of the night's adventures with all the guests.

Which didn't explain the surge of lust she'd felt at the thought of going out to the pool sporting obvious marks of kinky play or erase her small whimper of disappointment when she realized there were no black-and-blue handprints, no flogger marks, nothing anyone would notice.

So much for being concerned her fantasies wouldn't work in reality. If anything, they worked too well. No wonder people like Craig-the-asshole and that girl he'd tried to pick up took the game too seriously. It was brain-scramblingly seductive. Far too easy to mistake role-play for reality when you were this high on hormones, or to mistake lust for love.

That brought her up short.

She wasn't likely to think of herself as a mindless doormat, and she suspected that if she showed signs of it, Nick would stop her. If Alison didn't do it first. Selene was still reeling over how non-doormat-like the first self-proclaimed slave she'd met was. But the other...that was a danger.

Face it, she was already head over heels in lust with Nick, hooked on his hot body and even hotter imagination. And it would be way too easy to slip from there.

She needed to take care, to make sure she didn't convince herself she was falling for Nick when what she was simply enjoying the fantabulous sex. That, she figured, was what Alison meant by taking care of Nick: guarding both their hearts so nothing stupid and painful happened.

Even if it wasn't what Alison meant—people as in love as Alison and Garth tended to want their friends just as happily paired off—it was what Selene would do.

She took one last look in the mirror and went to join the party.

The day had passed swiftly...and, to Selene's profound

disappointment, surprisingly normally. Sure, Nick kept pulling her aside and caressing her, and a couple of times had her fetch drinks for him or perform some other small service. Sure, Alison kept grinning wickedly and flirtatiously at her.

Alison in a bikini was an erotic force of nature. She had a surprisingly tight, lovely little body. And who'd have guessed about the tattoo starting somewhere below her teeny turquoise bottom and working up onto her gently curved belly? A chained rose. A lot of the other guests also sported suggestive tattoos or piercings, but Alison wore it better than say, Joe-Bear and his boyfriend. They were obviously hot for each other's stocky, hairy, tattooed bodies, but the view didn't do much for Selene.

But then a couple showed up with kids in tow, and the older couple from next door dropped by, as did some of Garth's and Alison's coworkers, and while the edgy undercurrent remained, nothing happened.

Not until much, much later. Not until after dusk, when most of the guests were gone and mosquitoes and black flies drove the remaining ones inside.

Finally, it was down to Garth and Alison and Selene and Nick. Alison was settled at Garth's feet, not kneeling, Selene had noted, but leaning back comfortably against her master in a way that seemed as sweet and loving as it was dominant/submissive. Selene was curled up next to Nick on the love seat. It was funny that it seemed so natural. Just because they'd had wild monkey sex, even wild kinky monkey sex, didn't necessarily mean they'd be one hundred percent comfortable with each other, but already, they seemed to prefer to be in easy touching distance if not actually touching.

It all felt very cozy and relaxed and pleasant.

And then the bomb dropped.

"So," Nick said, "I hear you were kissing Alison."

Selene felt her eyes widening, her cheeks burning. She nodded, suddenly unable to speak.

She wasn't sure why she was so embarrassed. Kissing another woman wasn't something she did every day, but other people did it on a regular basis. Maybe it was Nick's tone, both richly amused and scolding. Maybe it was that both Garth and Alison were in the room.

Or maybe it was that the heat of embarrassment blurred with another kind of heat that flared from her lips to her nipples down to her groin as she remembered that kiss.

"Not very generous of you two not to share, was it?" Garth looked rather sternly at Alison as he said that. "You know the rules."

Was Alison going to be punished for what they'd done? Imagining dark and terrifying possibilities based on erotic novels and kinky websites, Selene sprang to her defense. "It was just a little smooch. You didn't miss anything."

Only when the words escaped her mouth did she admit to herself that some of the dark possibilities rushing through her head sounded more intriguing than alarming, and that if there were any *interesting* punishments being handed out, she wanted her share.

Nick and Garth exchanged significant looks. She remembered how Alison had said they were like brothers, but *brother* wasn't the right word. Best friends, two sides of a coin and definitely coconspirators, but the situation that was rapidly unfolding just wasn't a brotherly one.

"We'd like to be the judge of whether we missed anything or not," Garth said.

Nick nodded. "So we want a recap."

Time for that deer-in-the-headlights feeling again. She should be getting used to it by now, but apparently it wasn't one of those things she got used to easily. "But..." Wasn't it a little tacky to perform like that, like two women kissing was something that only happened for men to enjoy? Ms. Manners probably didn't cover it, but she'd bet Betsy or some of the women she'd volunteered with at the Rochester domestic violence hotline might have a pretty strong opinion.

Alison hopped up off the floor and closed in for the kill—or rather the kiss—without hesitation.

Selene froze.

"Selene," Nick said in that deep, menacing voice. "Virtual collar. Remember what we talked about?"

She tried to think through her panic. Was this something to protest, to safe-word?

Her brain was sorting through it all, weighing modesty and embarrassment and political correctness and where this fairly innocuous order might lead, and whether she really enjoyed this kind of being told what to do in the first place.

Her body had its own views, which were much less complicated and much less concerned with social niceties, political correctness or even common sense.

Her body informed her, with a surge of lust, that she wanted to kiss Alison again. In fact, her body thought doing more than kissing Alison sounded pretty exciting. Those ghosted rings were terribly sexy, and that complex tattoo had drawn Selene's eye and her heated imagination more than once during the party. Did it extend all the way down to her mound, like it appeared to? She'd certainly wondered before—she'd be willing to bet most women, no matter how straight, had—how another woman would taste, how her soft skin would feel under her hands. This might be her chance to find out.

And her body informed her even more strongly that she wanted to kiss Alison because Nick wanted her to. It was a damn fine idea on its own merits but made irresistible by Nick's wish, Nick's desire.

She rose, met Alison halfway.

Alison smelled vaguely of chlorine and sunscreen, and her kiss tasted of Pinot Grigio, which she'd been sipping instead of margaritas or beer, and she twined around Selene like an affectionate cat.

The men watched quietly, but Selene was acutely conscious of Nick's fierce blue gaze and Garth's dark one. What had felt natural when she and Alison were alone together now felt awkward, like a performance—and the part of Selene that had reveled in being made to come in front of South Station found it all the hotter for that, hot enough that her nipples ached almost immediately. Blood pooled in her pelvis, making her feel drowsy and grounded and very sexy. Alison's skin blazed under her hands and Alison's hands ran over her back and ass and upper thighs, leaving trails of pleasure in their wake, and she made little wild noises into Alison's mouth.

"Would you like my slave to make you come?" Garth asked politely, as if he were offering her another drink or perhaps some ice cream.

Chapter Nine

"I...uh..." Selene's body ached to say yes—her juices were dripping down her thighs, her breasts strained to be touched, and every vague fantasy or idle thought she'd ever had about being with a woman *or* being put on display was pulsating through her cunt—but her brain locked down, unable to let her say yes or no.

"I'd really like to, sweetie," Alison said, looking up at her with soft eyes. "Master is very fussy about which girls I'm allowed to play with, and I came home from our coffee date talking about how hot you were."

"Let's be honest," Garth interjected. "We've spent a few happy evenings imagining you and her together, and that was before I even saw you."

If Selene hadn't already been blushing, that would have made her cheeks flame, the idea that she'd been a matter of bedroom banter between this sexually dynamic couple.

That made her even hotter.

But still she couldn't speak.

Nick got up, slipped his arms around her from behind so she was sandwiched between his tall, hard body and Alison's tiny, soft one. "You're allowed to say no, Selene. But I want you to do it. Want you to let Alison use you for my pleasure and Garth's." One big hand cupped her sex through her dress. She moaned, arched, felt Alison's breasts press against hers as she ground her ass against Nick's impossibly hard cock. "And yours too. I can feel how wet you are," he whispered. "You soaked right through your dress as soon as I touched you. Will you do this for us, Selene? For all of us?"

To feel Alison's hands and tongue on her while Nick and Garth watched...

"God, yes," she finally admitted, pure lust getting the better of anything else.

"Undress her," Garth commanded Alison.

As if in a dream, Selene let Alison unzip her dress and let it fall to pool at her feet. As if in a dream, she helped Alison out of her clothes.

Alison was beautiful, Selene's stunned brain registered.

Selene had already guessed Alison had a genital piercing— but not that she had a neat triad of rings, two in her labia and one in her clit hood, or that her nipples were pierced as well.

The rose-and-chain tattoo extended down to her bare pubic mound, with chains going down her outer lips. Selene didn't want to imagine how much that must have hurt, but the effect was lovely.

Then Alison knelt with practiced grace in front of Selene.

Nick ran his hands up Selene's body to cup her breasts, then stepped back and sat next to Garth.

Selene felt like she should look at the redhead in front of her, but her eyes followed Nick. She met his blue gaze, smiled nervously. "Good girl," she heard him say, and the words burned in her veins like a drug. "After Alison's had you, I'm going to use your mouth." Selene clenched.

Alison slid one arm around her hips, pulling her closer.

Warm breath teased her aching clit.

Alison's fingers brushed against her opening. "You're drenched," she said, and Selene felt the words reverberate through her pussy.

"Please," she whimpered, all nervousness drowning in waves of desire.

Alison's hot mouth closed on her clit at the same time first one, then two, fingers penetrated her.

Alison's tongue was soft and sweet, but she let Selene feel the gentle pressure of her teeth as well, notching her arousal up yet another level.

Nick stroked his cock through his clothes and smiled at her in a way that caressed her almost as much as Alison was. She couldn't look at Garth, didn't dare to see if he too was touching himself.

Instead, she looked down at Alison—at the sweep of her red hair, at her small, neat breasts, the rings in them not visible from this angle, the line of her pale, freckled back. At her delicate beauty.

At the beautiful woman pouring wave after wave of pleasure through her with lips and tongue and fingers.

Delicious.

The redhead pulled her fingers out, reinserted them at a different angle, beckoned at Selene's G-spot as she licked and suckled her clit.

Selene's nails dug into Alison's shoulders as she came, clenching around the fingers inside her, grinding against the sweet tongue. She felt her knees buckling, took a deep breath, tried to steady herself.

Alison flicked her tongue, and Selene realized there was no hope. None at all. One orgasm segued into another, or maybe it was one giant one, and there was no way she'd be able to stand much longer.

Strong arms surrounded her from behind, held her up for Alison's final ministrations. Kept holding her, stroking her, murmuring how beautiful and hot she was, as Alison stood, gave her a final kiss and retreated.

"But," Selene said weakly, "shouldn't I... I mean I'd like..." Alison had made her come so wonderfully. Wouldn't she get to return the pleasure?

"Some other time," Garth said, understanding her

incoherent mutterings. "Right now, I'm going to be greedy and drag Alison away. Master's prerogative."

The other couple wasn't out of the room before Nick had Selene bent over a sturdy-looking table. "Was going to use your mouth, but I couldn't let Alison's fingers have all the fun here," he said, his voice harsh and choked with lust as he ran his fingers over her dripping pussy, making her gasp and buck.

Garth's and Alison's footsteps stopped. She didn't dare look, but she knew they were frozen in the doorway, watching.

Nick didn't take the time to undress all the way, just unzipped, pulled a condom from his pocket. It was a matter of seconds before he was pounding into her, filling her completely, riding her hard. With each thrust, her breasts bobbed, and she was so hot and sensitive that the movement of air over her nipples felt like the touch of a hand. As Nick's body crashed into hers, she felt the lingering tenderness in her bottom, sending more thrills through her.

Hard but patient, not a quick, brutal fuck but an extended, brutal one, and she was loving it.

She wasn't sure she could come again, but she didn't mind. She was on a wonderful plateau, riding the sensations, savoring his fat cock slamming into her, and it was all good.

Then Nick slapped at her breast, and as the bright red shock of good pain layered with all the other sensations, she realized she was wrong. She could come again.

Deep convulsions tried to suck Nick's cock so deep inside her it would never come out.

Nick froze, buried to the hilt in her, then roared something that might have been words. Although she knew it made no sense with the condom on, Selene swore she could feel his come burning into her.

When her head cleared enough for curiosity, she glanced toward the door.

Garth and Alison hadn't made it out of the room. He'd

picked up his tiny slave and was fucking her against the wall, her legs and arms wrapped around him, his hands under her ass, moving her up and down.

Nick collapsed onto the couch, then patted his lap to indicate Selene should sit there. "Might as well enjoy the rest of the show."

Chapter Ten

The next weekend, the heat continued unabated. It peaked on Sunday, prompting another barbecue/pool party at Garth and Alison's. This one was smaller, just their closest friends from Kinksters United.

"So, you ever hear anything from Nat?" Betsy asked Nick as she plopped some marinated tofu onto the grill at a safe distance from the burgers.

Nick liked Betsy, but he suddenly wanted to dive into the pool fully clothed, drink and grill tongs in hand. "Not really," he said, knowing that there was more to the question than idle curiosity. Always was with Betsy. He flipped a few burgers, hoping to dissuade the line of conversation. He was in a great mood after a wonderful, sex-drenched Saturday night with Selene. Why spoil it by thinking about his ex? Right now the most serious thing he wanted to ponder was whether his linen shirt was actually fusing to his skin thanks to sweat.

"I was afraid of that."

He shrugged. "She dumped me. 'Asked to be released', but yeah, dumped me. We don't have a lot to talk about anymore." Especially now. A few months ago—hell, a few weeks ago—he'd have been thrilled to hear from her, especially if she was showing signs of wanting to come back. He'd have known it was a stupid idea, but he'd have still been flattered, and face it, hard as a rock at the thought of her slender, pliant body kneeling in front of him again or wrapped around him in bed. But Selene had changed that. She might be Ms. Right-Now, but Ms. Right-Now had done a number on any remaining illusions that Natalie was anything close to Ms. Right.

Oh, Natalie was two hundred pounds of pure sex in a one-hundred-pound body. He still got turned on remembering some of their better times. But Selene had reminded him of something very important: sane chicks were just as fun and a lot less stressful.

"She's disappeared off the face of the earth," Betsy said. "Last I heard, she'd met some new dom on the Internet and was going to North Nowhere New Hampshire to move in with him. Which scared me to start with because it seemed awfully fast, and you know Natalie's not the type to make sure the guy's not on America's Most Wanted. And now her blog's deleted, her e-mail bounces, her cell phone's been turned off, and maybe that's just because she's practically in Canada and had to change services, but as far as I know, she hasn't given anyone a new number or e-mail. Not me, not Janna and Steve, not Debbie, not Alison and Garth. No one. Hell, I even swallowed the urge to barf and asked Craig yesterday. He's tried to track her down and couldn't. It's like she stopped existing."

Craig might be the world's biggest asshole, but he knew his way around the Internet, including, rumor had it, some creepy stalker's tricks that could find people who didn't have a listed phone number. If he couldn't find her, it wasn't a good sign.

Nick tried and failed to shut out the ugly images that started flashing through his mind: Natalie in trouble. Natalie trapped in the home of some psychotic redneck. Natalie locked in a cage for real, not as part of a sex game, starved and abused.

Natalie's body stashed in the New Hampshire wilderness somewhere, never to be found.

"You know Natalie gets one hundred percent focused on whoever she's with," he said, trying to convince himself. "When she first started seeing me, I had to remind her it was okay to get together with her friends, even to take the time from me to call you guys. If she's found the dom of her dreams..."

"You mean the psycho control freak of her dreams?"

Despite his worry, Nick laughed. "From me, that would have sounded bitter. From you, it's just the truth. I could see her letting someone encourage her to cut all her old ties and start fresh. It's weird, but not necessarily bad," he added, not believing it. For someone whose old friends were drug-addled losers or otherwise poisonous, sure, but Natalie's friends were mostly good people, people a lot more sensible than she sometimes was.

"Oh yeah, it's bad. Maybe she wouldn't think to call me. It's a classic girl thing to get so into a new relationship you lose touch with people. Queer or straight, kinky or vanilla, we all do it sometimes until our friends are like, 'Are you dead?' But Debbie says she's missed two scheduled photo shoots."

At that news, Nick could only say, "Oh shit."

Natalie was a flake but not about professional responsibilities. Once she committed to something, whether her day job, her work as a fetish model or a volunteer activity, she took it seriously—too eager to please, he thought, to let anyone down. If she'd blown off her commitments to Debbie, something was very wrong.

"I'll call her mom," he promised, "see what I can find out. She'd have told her mom where she was moving, even if she didn't tell anyone else." Natalie's mom had probably been more upset by the breakup than either Natalie or Nick had been. Apparently, he'd been the first boyfriend who didn't set off all of Mrs. Sherman's mom-alarms.

"Thanks." Betsy blinked, and he realized she was fighting back tears in a very un-Betsy-like way. "I'm sure I'm overreacting, but one of my friends from high school dropped out of sight like Natalie has. We all thought she'd run off to New York with her new boyfriend." He had a sickening knowledge of what was coming before she said it. "They found her body out by Quabbin Reservoir six months later."

Wordlessly, he offered Betsy his margarita.

And Betsy, who didn't normally drink anything more potent than iced coffee, took a big slug.

Selene climbed out of the pool and headed, dripping, over toward the grill or, more to the point, toward Nick. "Please tell me summer in Boston isn't always like this!" she moaned melodramatically, throwing herself onto a redwood deck chair with a squish of her waterlogged bikini.

"If it's any consolation, it's probably ten degrees hotter farther inland."

"That's not much of a consolation, seeing that we're not there. You ready to take a break from grilling and swim?"

"Actually, I think I'm ready to take a break and find someplace quiet inside for a few minutes. I need some downtime."

"Heat getting to you? Or something on your mind?" His expression was too serious for a party. Grim, almost.

"Just thinking on some stuff I heard today. Nothing to do with you."

"Can you be more unclear, or would that be painful?"

Nick forced a laugh and discovered he didn't really need to force it once he started. "It's kind of complicated, and I'd like to bounce stuff off you. Want to go inside?"

They ended up in the small game room off the living room. Nick closed the door, sat down on a well-loved couch. Selene, still damp around the edges, opted for the floor.

"Okay," Nick said. "Short version: Betsy thinks a mutual friend is in trouble. Half of me thinks Betsy's overreacting, and the other half is convinced she's right and wants to ride off to the rescue even though I don't know where I'd go or what I'd rescue her from."

"What kind of trouble?"

He hesitated, not wanting to say, as if saying it would make it real. "She met this guy, a dom, on the Internet..."

"So it could be anything from a broken heart to a broken neck? Or maybe nothing?"

Nick nodded. "Pretty much. Only, I know her, and she'd be more likely to end up in the broken-neck category. Natalie thought..." He corrected himself quickly, not liking the implications. "Thinks limits are for wanna-bes, and wants to give herself totally to someone, and her ideal dom was a hardcore sadist who would treat her like a toy—a thing."

"In other words, she's an idiot."

"Not an idiot. Half broken—she lost her dad really young, and I think some of her weirder ideas go back to that—and half dedicated to this lofty ideal of submission. Like a nun or something, only...a sex nun, if that makes any sense. If she met someone who was worthy of that devotion and knew what to do with it, it would be sweet and romantic in a bent sort of way, like what Garth and Alison have, only even kinkier, but the broken part means she's just as likely to meet a nutcase and think it's okay."

He thought he'd sounded detached enough, cool enough, but evidently not. "An ex of yours?" Selene asked. When he reluctantly nodded, she said rather than asked, "The pretty blonde in all those pictures in your house."

He nodded in confirmation.

For some reason, his instinct was to say, *I don't love her*, but he bit it back.

For one thing, he wasn't sure it was true. He was pretty sure he wasn't in love with Natalie anymore, but he still felt something, or he wouldn't be as concerned as he was.

For another, he figured saying that when the question hadn't come up was the best way to make a woman assume he *was* still in love with Natalie.

Selene put her arms around him, slipped into his lap. "I

can see why you're worried something bad happened to her. Hell, she's a thin, gorgeous blonde stranger you used to date, and I'm still worried something bad happened to her."

"That," Nick said, "isn't exactly reassuring."

But the feeling of Selene's body against his, clad only in a tiny bikini, was.

Or maybe distracting was a better word.

It didn't seem fair to Natalie—even if she was fine, just in the thoughtless stage of infatuation—to be so aware of Selene's round, creamy breasts almost popping out of the minimal little black-and-white top, the curve of her hip and heart shape of her ass so nicely accented by the bottom. Something about an almost-naked woman got to him every time, and never mind that in this case he'd seen Selene naked, had gotten to explore the now-hidden mysteries of breasts and pussy pretty thoroughly.

He wanted to explore all over again, just in case he'd missed anything.

"Are you trying to distract me?"

Selene pulled away, looking torn between guilt and mischief. "To distract myself, actually. Otherwise, I'm going to keep wondering about your friend..."

"Natalie." Saying the name made the situation feel that much more real.

"About Natalie. About how easy it is to be dumb even if you're smart. I went to those Internet sites sometimes. I kept meeting guys who were obviously more clueless than I was, or who didn't know where the shift key was, or who couldn't type because they had one hand down their pants, so I gave up pretty quickly. But if I'd met someone who talked a good game? I like to think I'm not stupid, but I can be impulsive. Think about how we met. Not exactly reasoned and thought out."

She stopped, then turned to look up at him, eyes like a doe's—that big, that nervous. "I'm babbling," she said. "Please give me something else to do with my mouth."

She tilted her head, obviously hoping for a kiss, but acknowledging that it had to come on his whim, not hers.

And Nick gave her one.

Oh, he gave her one. A rough kiss, harsh and demanding, hands pulling at Selene's hair.

Because he was drowning out images of Natalie, of all the bad things that could happen to...well, to any unlucky woman, but especially one whose major masturbatory fantasy was losing her identity, becoming a mere thing for a man's pleasure.

And Selene moaned deep in her throat, wrapped around him, opened to him as if she were using him to drown out ugliness too—maybe worry for a woman she didn't know, maybe belated nerves for some close call. Maybe fear that she too had jumped too quickly and she'd better enjoy herself while she could, in case she needed to make a rapid escape.

He worked loose the knots holding her top in place as he kissed her, sighing as the slip of damp stretch fabric slithered to the floor and her breasts pressed against him, skin on skin.

He cradled them between his hands, toying at the nipples as he mounded them closer together. His mouth still covered her, drowning out any noises she might be making, but he swore he could taste her aroused, contented sighs.

When Selene had made the remark about giving her something else to do with her mouth, he'd imagined Selene on her knees, his hands knotted in her hair, claiming and guiding her, her lips wrapped around him. And God yes, the image made his cock ache with need. Such a sweet mouth on that girl, such a sweet, greedy, fuckable mouth. Or maybe his cock nestled between those lovely breasts. No, not nestled— sandwiched, enjoying warm oil and the delicious friction of Selene's flesh, one of those acts that felt purely selfish, just taking his pleasure, an act of dominance that involved no pain, no force, just orgasm for him and teasing enjoyment but no coming for his partner.

But now, as his tongue danced in her mouth, another thought was taking over.

Power through pleasure.

Chapter Eleven

Who said the sub always had to be the one on her knees—or that she wasn't getting a kind of power out of being there? Giving pleasure could be a way of claiming someone, and he intended to claim Selene. Still kissing her, Nick steered Selene to the couch, then broke off the kiss so he could order her to sit down.

Lips swollen from kissing, damp hair in Medusa-like tendrils and tangles, Selene shook her head slightly, less a negation than a clearing, before saying, "Uh, wet bathing suit, sir?" her voice small but not exactly humble—more kiss-dazed.

"Well, take it off."

A lazy grin wakened and spread across her face as she solved the problem. The bathing suit bottom made a satisfying plop as it hit the floor.

He gave her a gentle shove, and she sat back on the couch. "Spread your legs," he said, trying to sound authoritative but to his own ears sounding more eager. Greedy, even.

Was that a bad thing? No, he decided as he gazed at her pink folds, lightly slicked with moisture. Her dark curls were matted from her swim, and it made her look wetter yet, as if she'd just been licked into oblivion.

Like she soon would be.

"Wider," he commanded, and without waiting for her to comply, he knelt down between her splayed legs.

"What are you..."

"Hush." With one hand, he pulled back her outer lips,

bringing the inner lips into greater prominence, making her clit stand out, ready for attention.

"Wait a minute, is this some kind of dom trick? I lie back and enjoy and then get punished for being greedy or selfish or something?" She sounded skeptical but not particularly alarmed at the prospect of punishment.

Good, she'd figured out that at this point "punishment" was just a code word for "an excuse to play harder".

A sharp slap on the inner thigh left a pretty red handprint on white skin, made her wince one second and smile dizzily the next. "That's for trying too hard to be clever," he said, grinning as he did to make it clear he wasn't annoyed, just seizing an excuse. "I wish I'd thought of that, actually, but now you'd be on to the trick."

"But...shouldn't I..."

Nick resisted the urge to snort with laughter, because it wasn't fair to Selene. She'd figure out for herself, with a little more experience with him, why it was funny. "Selene," he said, forcing his voice into what he thought of as DomSpeak. "We've agreed that today you're to do what I tell you. I'm telling you to relax and enjoy yourself, because right now I feel like tasting you. I like making you scream, Selene. Will you scream for me if I lick you?"

Eyes wide with anticipation now that it had finally sunk in this wasn't a test or a trick, just good old-fashioned oral sex, she smiled and nodded.

He positioned himself, gave a slow, sensuous tonguing from the juicy opening of her cunt up to her eager clit, savoring the combination of her sweetly smoky juices and overtones of chlorine. Usually, pool water wasn't on his list of favorite flavors, but blended with essence of Selene, it was damn tasty. "There," he said, "not so hard to handle, is it?"

Then he set to work to carry out his threat-or-promise.

Licking delicately at her pouting lips.

Sucking at the juices that flowed from her cunt, wishing he could just stick a straw in, drink them down. She tasted that good to him, that rich and hot and musky.

Nibbling.

Suckling at her protruding clit and inner lips, drawing them into his mouth, working them with lips and tongue until he could sense more juices had flowed, then going back to eagerly lap those up.

Such a hot, sweet, drenched cunt. So tight, and yet so accommodating, opening to his fingers, yet hugging them, squeezing them convulsively as Selene got closer and closer to the edge.

His cock ached to be in there. But dammit, his clever sticking-condoms-in-the-pocket-of-his-jeans trick worked only if he and the jeans were in the same room—and he'd changed into shorts long ago, accidentally leaving the precious condom in the changing room.

And when Selene couldn't hold back anymore, when she was writhing and mewling, pushing her mound against his probing, exploring mouth, begging for release, he pushed into her wet cunt with two fingers as he swirled and spiraled around her swollen clit.

"Now," he breathed, talking around her sex, vibrating her clit with his breath. Whether that did it or the command or whether his timing was that good, Selene arched up, shrieked, clenched at his fingers so hard it seemed to clench his dick at the same instant.

Shattered.

But he wasn't done yet. Not by a long shot, not when that quivering cunt tasted so good, not when seeing her lose control like that under his tongue and fingers made him feel like a god.

Selene's eager little body seemed to crave every bit of pleasure he wanted to give it, came again and again and still seemed greedy for more.

God, he loved that in a woman. Natalie...well, Nat was wonderfully sexual, but in a different way. More rough-edged. She craved the harsh stuff, pain and roughness, and couldn't relax into anything gentler. It had been a great excuse to try some new wild things—but damn, sometimes he'd missed the basics, like the sheer pleasure of making a woman come on his tongue until she didn't know what day it was.

The dull ache in Nick's cock and balls was getting more distracting, but he was determined to keep going until Selene begged for mercy for her oversensitive clit. Didn't she ever tire? Not that he wanted her to—it was just impressive to find someone so responsive, so orgasmic.

So hot and wet and delicious.

Finally, she raised her hand, pounded it on the cushion, muttered, "Enough." When that didn't work, she jerked on his ponytail, trying to raise his head.

Mischievously, he pretended not to notice, giving a few more broad licks, pumping a few more times with his fingers.

"Hey," she protested breathily. "My turn to play!"

He looked up at last.

She pulled him up to her, licked her juices off his chin. Then she wriggled out from under him, encouraged him out of his shorts and onto the couch.

She looked so beautiful—so natural and right—kneeling between his legs, her eyes still soft and hazy from coming, her mouth slack and red with desire, her chest and tits mottled and flushed from coming so much.

Nick tried to tell her as much, but Selene's lips descended onto his cock, and he lost the power of human speech.

The room smelled of sex and chlorine, smelled of Selene. His skin was saturated with Selene. He was saturated in her, wrapped up in her, and he loved it.

Her eyes closed in concentration. Her face was red, scrunched up, distorted by his cock, and that just made it more beautiful from his point of view.

One hand, slicked with her own hot juices, around the base of his shaft, the other playing with his balls. Her mouth clung and suckled, her tongue swirled, and he wanted to hold on to the moment, to enjoy the sensation a little longer. Then, oh God, she used one finger to gently circle his anus, not entering, just teasing that sensitive opening.

That undid him. Opening his mouth in a silent roar, gripping her shoulders convulsively, he poured himself into her waiting mouth, into her throat, thinking, *Mine, mine, mine!* but unable to make even that much of an attempt at English.

With his last energy, he pulled her up onto the sofa next to him.

Selene roused first, stretched, whispered, "I'm starving."

He realized he was too. All that time at the grill—had he even gotten around to grabbing a burger for himself?

If he had, he'd burned it off.

"Shhh." He pressed a finger to his lips. "I think Alison would commit hara-kiri if she realized people were hungry at a party here."

"Oh, I think she'd understand if it was because we got too distracted to eat...lunch." Selene smiled lazily. "On the other hand, I think we ought to take care of that. If we're away much longer, it'll give everyone time to make score cards."

Nick laughed and handed over her bikini bottom. "Be prepared. I'm pretty sure they have a preprinted set somewhere."

There were no score cards, although there were a few knowing smiles.

There was food and swimming and a game of bocce where no one knew the rules or cared, and at one point, Alison and

Garth both actually sat down at once, which, as far as Nick knew, was a record for a party.

However, there was no more serious conversation.

It wasn't until much later, in the warm, sticky dusk of a hot, sticky day, partway to Selene's place in Somerville, that Selene put her hand on his arm—it had been on his upper thigh, nearly but not quite in his crotch for most of the ride—and said, "If there's anything I can do to help your friend..."

He boggled but did his best to hide it. "Not sure what you could do. First we need to figure out where she is, and then if she actually needs help, and then if she'll admit she does. And you don't even know her."

"That might be useful. I can be more objective." Selene's voice was earnest, different from what he'd heard before, except maybe when she was talking about her studies, her work with battered women. "I'm trained in this stuff. Domestic violence kind of stuff."

"If she went into it voluntarily..."

She nodded. "That's not the question. The question is if she's still there voluntarily. If she's not, we'll get her out. By hook or by crook. And I'll help you figure out how to hide the bodies."

The rest of the ride to her place was very quiet.

Nick stared at his phone when he got home.

Told himself repeatedly that he should call Natalie's mother.

Made excuse after excuse.

Ended up getting a Harpoon Summer Ale from the refrigerator and drinking it as he carefully took down all the pictures of Natalie, wrapped them in newspaper and put them in the back of his closet.

He'd been meaning to do it for months, ever since it had become obvious they couldn't patch things up. He just hadn't gotten around to it—partly laziness, partly the fact they were beautiful, artistic photographs, leaving aside any biases he had about the model. And partly, he admitted it, because he would have been lonely without that familiar face around the place he used to share with her.

Tonight, though, Nick couldn't bear all those copies of her. Tonight, her soft, wide eyes and supple, tattooed body took second place to her air of complete vulnerability.

Each picture seemed like an accusation: *Why didn't you protect me? Why didn't you give me what I craved, make me yours, save me from myself?*

Why didn't you give me the kind of love I needed instead of the kind you wanted to give me?

Chapter Twelve

"How's life in Boston?" Molly sounded like her usual self, a bit frazzled on the surface but calm underneath. Selene could hear one child or the other acting up in the background. Selene's theory was that since Molly had seen so much that was truly bad before turning ten, the little annoyances of life didn't rattle her.

Selene mopped her brow with a tissue and then dabbed between her legs because she was still leaking a bit from simply thinking about Nick and the weekend they'd shared. "Hot."

"Here too, although I've been hearing thunder rumbling up the lake, so it may break soon."

Even though she knew Molly couldn't see her, Selene let loose with her best devilish, sated-woman grin. "Well, yeah, it's about ninety-eight million degrees, and my AC is barely keeping up, but when I say hot, I mean *hawt.*"

Molly sputtered. "You've met someone already? Selene, you haven't even finished unpacking yet. How in the world do you do it? Is he in your program? Please tell me he's not a professor because that's just asking for trouble."

No, I wouldn't do anything that dumb. I went to a meeting for kinky singles and asked a guy if he'd help me fulfill my fantasies about being tied up, spanked and dominated. Isn't that how everyone meets someone in a new town?

No. Not the way she was going to put it.

"Met him at a party and we just clicked. His name's Nick McCutcheon and..."

"Is he employed and relatively sane?"

That was Molly, all right. She knew Selene way too well. "He writes security software, specialized stuff for the government. IRS, I think, not military," she added quickly. As a deacon and would-be minister, Molly was a pacifist, and Selene didn't want to get sidetracked into a discussion of the moral ramifications of Nick's career. "So far, he only seems crazy-offbeat-and-fun, not crazy-crazy. He owns his own place, and it's nice." *And decorated with bondage pictures and has D rings on the bed and walls for tying girls up.* "And Molly, he is gorgeous."

Molly laughed. "They always are, babe. You find hot ones. Crazy ones, irresponsible ones, jerky ones and just plain wrong-for-you ones like Will, but they're all good-looking. If this one doesn't work out, you might want to try someone a little more average. I've had good luck with mine."

"Can I help it if I'm shallow? I keep hoping I'll find someone who's megastud gorgeous on the outside and Devin on the inside."

Molly's Devin was not exactly cover-model material. Short, overweight and prematurely balding, with a round, sweet face and glasses, he was more a teddy bear than a stud. He adored Molly and made her very happy, and if he'd been a two-headed green alien and made Molly happy, Selene still would have thought he had his own kind of beauty.

Color her shallow, though, but she'd take Nick's kind of beauty any day.

"And I hope you do. Ben, don't do that to the kitty! Just a second..." When she returned to the phone, apparently clutching two-year-old Ben, based on some of the noises Selene overheard, she added, "Sorry if I sounded all deacony. All through June, I helped the pastor out with pre-wedding counseling, and some of these kids—though when I say kids, some of them are older than we are, just amazingly immature—were so unrealistic, I know we'll be counseling them through a divorce six months down the road. It's making me cynical. I just want you to find your happy ending, Selene, find someone who makes you as happy as Devin makes me. And it's great that you're having fun, but haven't you ever thought it might be time to settle..."

"Hello, you're talking to almost-got-married-for-all-the-wrong-reasons lass here. Have you forgotten Will already? I mean, I've tried to forget that mess, but I'm surprised you have. Being a deacon and all, I thought you'd remember the major reason I'm probably going to hell."

Molly sputtered again, startling her son into saying "What's wong, Mamma?"

Selene smiled at his toddler mispronunciation. "I'm not even thinking about anything serious until I've figured out what the right reasons are for me and what I need in a relationship. I don't want to put myself or anyone else in that position again. Nick's a great guy, and he's...well, he went through a messy breakup not too long ago himself, so we're not rushing into anything." Well, except bed, but Molly had no doubt figured that out already, and Selene was not sharing even the minor juicies while Molly was cuddling little Ben.

On the other hand, sharing juicy details or not, she wasn't about to lie by omission about what Molly would consider even more important than the best damn sex ever.

Especially not when it had been bubbling up inside her for a few days now. She had to get it out of her system, get a reality check on it from someone who had a history of being smarter and more sensible than she was.

"The thing is, I think he's one of the good guys. The really good guys. Like my dad and Devin. I haven't known him long, but I've already seen that he's willing to go out on a limb to help a woman in trouble—even when it's his ex. He calls regularly, even though we've said we're taking it slowly. And there are other things about him, things that make me feel really secure and comfortable." And others that made her feel nervous in a sexy way, but while those were just as important as the comfortable, comforting parts, they were harder to explain.

Molly made a happily speculative noise, then said, "Sounds promising, and you sound smitten. I hope it works out."

"That's the thing," she said, hoping the edge in her voice would get across her point where her words apparently wouldn't. "I can't fall for him. Not now, maybe not ever. He's made it clear he wants to keep it light. I think he's still on the rebound. If I start getting too serious, I'll either drive him away, or I'll end up pushing him into something he's not ready for like Will did to me."

Not that she thought for a minute he was as weak as she was, as susceptible to being manipulated by someone else's needs. He was a dom, after all, confident and take-charge and sure of himself. He wouldn't make the mistake she had with Will. But she'd heard the edge of regret in his voice when he talked about Natalie, and she didn't want to be a cause for regret down the road. Maybe wistful wasn't-that-fun-while-it-lasted memories, but not regret.

"So anyway," she said, "how are the kids doing?"

Monday started much too early. It always did, and not getting to sleep before two because he was too busy considering the Natalie problem again hadn't helped one bit. Nick needed a gigantic iced coffee. Badly. No way was he going to face the morning without a stop at the coffee shop by the office.

He got in the long line and heard a "hello".

Craig Whittaker was coming right at him. Nick tried to dodge, but there was nowhere to go in the crowded coffee shop, at least not without losing his precious place in line, and dammit, he had his priorities. Craig was to be avoided, but coffee was coffee.

Craig sidled up to him and whispered, "So, you and Selene?

Very interesting."

Nick quickly considered a number of responses. His favorite involved opening a very small black hole and watching gleefully as Craig was sucked into another dimension, but he couldn't figure out how to pull it off.

He opted for a simple, "I think so," but realized immediately it had been a mistake. Even in those three words, he sounded smug, and that would make Craig that much more curious.

Who told Craig anyway? Certainly not Garth or Alison. Alison wouldn't have told Craig where the hose was if his pants were on fire. She'd probably look for marshmallows to roast.

"Bill Moody said you two looked pretty intimate at Garth and Alison's."

Bill had been there? Shows how observant he'd been and how distracted by Selene. As a fine example of the theory that desire makes no sense at all, Craig, the local poster child for rabid and undiscriminating heterosexuality, had provoked a huge crush in an otherwise sensible gay guy. Craig had zero interest in men—lucky for Bill—but he did use Bill as a source for any hot gossip he might have missed.

"We've had a few dates. And that's all the information you're getting."

He tried once more to walk away.

"I'm not asking for details, Nick. I'm surprised, that's all," Craig said. "She's no Natalie."

That pulled Nick up short.

Of course she was no Natalie. That was one—more like five—of Selene's charms. He wasn't about to explain that to Craig, but he was morbidly curious to know what Craig thought he was talking about. "Yes?" he drawled. "Go on."

Craig looked around before answering, making sure the immediate area was clear of their coworkers. "Natalie is an extraordinary creature. So supple, so yielding, so exquisitely trained. No will other than to serve."

"And you'd know this how?"

"We played a few times after you released her. I couldn't offer her the stability she needs..."

Nick nodded in a go-on way, narrowly suppressing the urge to say, *That would be because you're fucking around on your wife.* It occurred to him that Craig wanted him to react in some way, to be upset or jealous or angry that he'd been with Natalie.

To his surprise, he wasn't. A bit disgusted that Natalie had even considered Craig, let alone played with him, but that was just more proof that Natalie craved a different kind of dominance than what Nick wanted to give.

Craig rattled on. "I can't see how Selene could possibly measure up. How could you settle for an inexperienced smart-ass masochist, even a pretty one, after having someone so perfect?"

If Nick had been surprised that he took the goading about Natalie so calmly, he was astonished by the cold fury that overtook him at that remark.

It was one thing to talk about Natalie as if she were a beautiful object. It worked with her kinks. She'd probably take that as a compliment.

Selene was a different matter.

Once again, a number of possible responses to Craig's stupidity flew through his head. Several of his favorites started with punching Craig in the mouth, but that would lead to all sorts of complications, like getting fired and/or arrested and/or barred from his favorite coffee shop; that, Craig wasn't worth.

In the end, he settled for, "For one, I like smart-ass masochists. For two, since when is it settling to choose the most interesting woman you've met in years? And for three, I really do need to get my coffee and get back to work. See you at the next project meeting. Try not to be late this time."

This time, he managed to get away while Craig was doing his fish-out-of-water imitation, and order his iced coffee.

It wasn't until he was back in the office and the iced coffee started working its caffeinated magic that he realized what he'd said—that he'd chosen Selene.

What?

He should have left it at "only a few dates so far". For one thing, it was the truth. Granted, the first one had been a forty-eight-hour date and an intense one at that, but they'd both said no commitments, no romance, just a good time. And sure, he wanted to see her again, but what guy wouldn't when the first few dates had led to enough over-the-top sex that he had sore muscles in odd places?

What made him decide to mark his territory, to rub Craig's nose in the fact that Selene had said yes to him after saying no to Craig? That was just asking for trouble.

What had possessed him to say it?

A little voice tried to suggest that he'd said it because Selene had gotten under his skin more than he'd expected. He drowned it by taking another brain-freezing slug of iced coffee and turning his attention to a particularly knotty bit of code that had left him scratching his head on Friday.

He was so not letting himself go there.

It was the particle physics of relationships.

If he let himself consider the possibilities of a future with Selene, beyond casual dating and great sex, those possibilities would evaporate. The only way he could actually get to those possibilities was by indirection. By not thinking about them. By enjoying what they had and going from there.

Doing otherwise had been his mistake with Natalie.

Natalie, whom he still needed to find.

He'd let her down, hadn't been able to be—didn't want to be—the man she needed.

The more he brooded about that, the more he realized the many ways he'd screwed up there. What he'd given her had been so far from what she thought she needed, she'd bolted and ended up vulnerable and alone, open to the first asshole who claimed to offer her what she needed. Did that make it his fault? He'd been her master, however briefly, so wasn't he responsible for her?

Not too many people were in the office yet. It was the kind of summer morning when people moved slower, lingered in the coffee shop a little longer before heading back to the hot street and to the office, or sat by the fountain in the park sipping an iced latte, soaking up any passing breezes and trying desperately to pretend they were at the beach.

He got out his cell phone. Just like he hadn't gotten around to taking down Natalie's pictures at his house, he hadn't deleted a few Natalie-related numbers from his cell.

Her old office. Just as he'd feared, they said she'd quit months ago and no one knew where she'd gone. Maybe they wouldn't say, but Nick sensed honest ignorance rather than following the dictates of a privacy policy.

Debbie's studio. No one was there, which wasn't that surprising. Debbie did a lot of night and weekend shoots, so she wasn't exactly an early-morning-at-the-office girl. He left a message, asking Debbie to call, saying it was about Natalie without going into details. He had no idea if Debbie would even call back. He'd never been close to the photographer, and he had a feeling that he might have come off poorly if Natalie had told her only her side of the breakup.

Nat's mother.

He got as far as highlighting the number, hesitated.

Probably nothing was wrong, and Nat had just decided to cut her losses in Boston and immerse herself in a new life. In that case, he'd scare Mrs. Sherman into heart failure if he didn't phrase his questions just right.

But what if she really was in trouble? A long time ago, he'd promised Natalie he'd be her knight, protecting and cherishing her. Just because that hadn't been what she wanted, just because she thought she wanted the sexy villain rather than a slightly tarnished white knight, didn't mean the promise was invalidated.

Nick thought it through as he poked and prodded at the code, trying to let his subconscious find the right words to ask a mother if her daughter was safe without actually saying it in so many words.

What happened instead was that the coding solution came to him.

Well, his boss would be happy, anyway.

It wasn't until evening that he finally worked up the nerve to call Mrs. Sherman. Some large part of him was praying that she wouldn't answer the phone, that the number he had for her was wrong.

Maybe he'd get lucky and a great crater would swallow Jamaica Plain whole and spare him the awkwardness of a heart-to-heart with his ex-lover's mother.

He wasn't that lucky. Mrs. Sherman answered the phone on the second ring, with an almost breathless, eager quality that vanished as soon as she realized it was Nick.

After far more pondering than he'd really needed to do, Nick had just decided to go for the easy, straightforward, non-alarmist method. "Hey, it's Nick. I've lost Natalie's new number. I was hoping I could get it from you. I found some of her stuff in the back of the closet and need to know what to do with it."

Mrs. Sherman snorted, and somehow the snort sounded bitter, even though it was brief and essentially toneless. "I hope you have better luck reaching her than I have. I never seem to catch her when she actually has time to talk, and it always takes forever for her to call back. I haven't heard from her in a few weeks myself."

"She must be busy. New job, new home, new boyfriend." Nick hadn't meant to ask, but he couldn't resist. "What's he like? I know it's none of my business, but..." He wanted to come up with some lighthearted, teasing way to say it, but what came out was, "I may not be involved with her any more, but she's still my friend, and none of us have heard much about him."

Other than a few things that made him and everyone else wary, but again, not something Mrs. S needed to know.

A long silence, a silence of the kind that Nick didn't like to hear from anyone female, especially not someone his mother's age—a considering-whether-or-not-to-cry kind of silence, the kind where someone's holding her breath, thinking so hard he can almost hear it.

Finally Mrs. Sherman spoke, her voice iron gray and distant. Hurt, definitely. Angry too, but mostly hurt. "I haven't met him," she said. "Natalie never brought him home, and she hasn't invited me up to visit. I even asked, because some of us girls were going up to the outlets in North Conway, and I thought I could take a side trip and see her, not that it's all that close. She's in some tiny little place that doesn't even have its own post office. Her PO box is in another town. I offered to take her out to lunch, if her house isn't ready for entertaining. I know how long it can take after you move into a new place, and how fussy she is. She said no."

With that, whatever steps she'd taken to control herself slipped, and Nick heard her voice catch. "It's just not like her, Nick. Maybe you can figure out what's going on. It seemed like she always listened to you, even after you guys broke up."

If only you knew, Nick thought sadly as he ended the call.

After that conversation, he didn't expect an answer when he called Natalie, so he wasn't surprised when he didn't get one.

He was surprised when he heard a man on her voice mail, not a phone-company prerecording, but just a guy. Pleasant-enough voice, slightly self-conscious, like most people sounded doing their voice mails: "Natalie can't answer the phone right now. Leave a message, please, and we'll get back to you."

Innocuous enough, but Nick was primed to hear anything out of the ordinary as suspicious. Why would the guy need to record her phone message for her?

It was one more small way someone could take control. Natalie had a phone, but he suspected her dom kept it, let her make calls only occasionally, maybe screened the calls and told her whom she could contact.

Kind of creepy. Nick was pretty sure that Selene's domestic-violence-counselor side would be all over it as a danger sign, even if her kinky-submissive-chick side understood the appeal on some level. Hell, Nick understood the appeal. Controlling someone who wanted to be controlled could be fun. But the way this guy was doing it seemed over the top.

Natalie probably loved it, at least in theory. She'd always craved the kind of micromanaging that some people in the scene found hot and Nick found at best annoying and at worst unhealthy. How she liked it in practice, when she realized she was losing touch with her friends and even her mom, might be another story.

One he was determined to find out.

Nick left her a message. "Hi, got this number from your mom. Everyone misses you. Give me a call sometime when you get a chance." Like that. Simple, basic, innocuous, nothing that would scream to her new dom that he was the old one, if the guy didn't already know.

And now he'd wait to see if she called, and if she did, what she had to say.

If she were happy—well, he'd have a drink in her honor and hope for the best. Let her go, let her be happy in her own way with someone closer to her ideal. It didn't need to make sense to him as long as it did to Natalie and her master.

If she wasn't happy—not sure what he could do there. God knew he couldn't be what she wanted. Just like she'd said at the end, he wasn't a hardcore master. He was a bedroom dom

109

who wanted a sub between the sheets but an equal partner in the streets.

A kinky boyfriend, she'd put it, withering scorn in her voice but something wistful underlying it as if she'd wished one of them could be different.

Unfortunately, neither of them could.

He'd been asking himself ever since Natalie left if they could have found some compromise between her needs and his. If he could have loved her enough to give her the kind of structure and restrictions, tasks and punishments she seemed to need.

If he could have loved her enough to treat her without tenderness except on special occasions, as a reward.

Or if they could work out something more like Garth and Alison's master/slave relationship, stricter than what he wanted, looser than what she craved, but with a mix of love and discipline that perhaps they could both live with.

He'd managed, in a bored single man's active fantasy life, before he'd met Selene, to convince himself it could work if he could see Natalie again under the right circumstances. Basically grab her by the hair, say he was going to punish her for leaving, see if she melted, and if she did—which, in the fantasies, of course she did, in exquisite, wet, moaning detail—set about proving he was boss, and that meant she had to accept his kindness as well as his harshness, compliments as well as criticisms, kisses as well as pain. A wedding ring as well as a collar. Because he said so.

Not exactly romantic by most people's standards, but he and Natalie weren't most people.

Would rescuing her from an out-of-hand relationship be the right circumstances, the catalyst that could pull them back together?

And if it was, would he still want to try?

He remembered how amazingly sexy Natalie looked, tied in some seemingly impossible yogic position, her skin oiled and glistening by candlelight, weights hanging from the rings in her nipples, her sex wet, held open with ropes for his pleasure, and, while she had a hard time admitting it, hers. Remembered how she responded to being spanked or flogged, how she'd beg for more, then half the time apologize for the "greed" and "selfishness" he so enjoyed. How she sucked his cock as if she needed no greater reward than to taste his hot sperm, to feel him shoot down her throat.

But she'd never come from sucking him like Selene did.

And in the two years they'd been together, she'd never offered her assistance with a real problem. Oh, she took good care of him in all the small ways, Donna Reed in black leather, cooking for him, refilling his drinks, rubbing his feet, cleaning his condo whether he asked her to or not, and sometimes it got to the point of freaking him out. Being waited on was nice, but she'd look hurt if he got his own drink, and downright confused if he got her one while he was up.

But the times when something potentially big came up— thankfully those occasions had been rare—she'd sat back, glad to do whatever he suggested in the crisis, but not offering any ideas of her own.

Selene, on the other hand, had jumped right in when she heard Natalie might be in trouble. Offered to help. Offered concrete suggestions. Hell, offered to hide bodies and, if necessary, to create them.

That might be the kind of thing that would lose her the Perfect Sub Seal of Approval from the Craigs of the world, but it was reassuring in a lover.

A playmate, he corrected himself. They'd agreed to keep it strictly friendly and playful—and for all he knew, she'd respond as poorly to a hint of romance as Natalie had, for her own reasons.

But even if you were saying playmate, that implied friend— and he was all for a friend who could react like a grown-up in a crisis.

Especially if she also had a gorgeous ass, a very dirty mind and a kinky streak a mile wide.

He let himself drift from his worries to the more pleasant topic of Selene naked, red-bottomed and smiling, either awaiting his next command or...hell, it was Selene, and she wasn't that passive... suggesting something hot to try next.

That his cell phone buzzed just then was a pleasant coincidence.

A text message from Selene: *Thinking of you. V. wet & hot. Thx for great weekend, sir (or shd that B Nick?)*

Grinning like a Cheshire cat, or maybe like an idiot—he preferred Cheshire cat, but idiot applied equally well—Nick texted her back: *Busy 2night?*

He could practically hear the pout in her response. *Must do wash. Have no clothes.*

Naked is good. Not 4 class, tho. Call when yr home alone. B naked. We'll take care of wet&hot problem.

Not quite an hour later—not like he was timing it or anything—Selene called.

Chapter Thirteen

Nick would so laugh at her if he had any idea how crazy this phone-sex date was making her. Good crazy, as in wet pussy, rock-hard nipples and a brain full of lusty ideas, but also crazy with nerves and more anxiety than the more rational bits of Selene's brain figured the situation merited. It was humiliating to realize her hands literally shook as she stared at the phone, contemplating what she'd say when Nick answered.

She couldn't believe she was doing this.

Couldn't believe she'd actually texted a new lover to tell him how turned-on she'd gotten thinking about him.

Couldn't believe she was calling him now for what was obviously going to be phone sex, and, while it was his suggestion, she'd certainly instigated it with that text message. She'd never even thought of such an outrageous—

Okay, that was a lie. She'd *thought* of things along these lines plenty of times: naughty e-mails, text messages that would brighten a guy's day in a very below-the-belt sort of way, phone sex to while away some of the time she couldn't spend in a lover's company, in a lover's bed. But she'd never done anything hotter than slightly suggestive e-mails or texts, flirting over the phone but nothing explicit. She was afraid of making a fool of herself, of sounding slutty or too eager in new relationships, and once you really got with a guy, that almost desperate sexual edge faded.

At least it always had. She had a feeling that with Nick, it wouldn't. This was going to be all about the fun, the sex, the kink, not the mundane stuff that, while necessarily part of a serious adult relationship, tended to drag said adult relationship down with its weight.

Maybe knowing that was why she felt free to be more outrageous than usual.

It was embarrassing to realize at this late date how conventional some parts of her character really were.

But that was going to change, damn it. She wanted to be the daring, sensual creature she felt like on the inside, and Nick was going to help. Had already helped. She'd spent all day distracted by erotic reveries, her breasts aching to be touched, bitten, maybe bound with ropes, her panties intermittently damp as the memory of Nick's cock intruded on whatever professional, workplace- or classroom-appropriate things were supposed to be ruling her mind.

Those thoughts had led to the text message, even though she hadn't dared to send it from work. And the text message had led to her staring at her phone as if it were a wild animal that might turn on her.

What if she made the call and then couldn't do it? Clammed up in embarrassment or started laughing or got a complete brain freeze and couldn't think of a thing to say? Or what if her roommate came home early from waitressing? Nick had left it in her hands. She could just not call, or call to say something had come up and she couldn't talk long, if it scared her that much.

If what she was discovering about herself scared her that much.

That was what it really came down to, didn't it? She both loved and feared the sexual being Nick was helping her unearth from layers of convention. Backing out of this small thing would mean defeat on some level. A step back into the ordinary, vanilla world, the one where she knew she was safe enough but also didn't want to live full-time.

Damn it. Damn her introspection. This wasn't her whole

life on the line here. It was just talking. Sexy talking, but just talking.

If she was attaching so much importance to something so noncritical, she needed to lighten up.

A little phone sex that would probably lead to laughs and lust in equal measure sounded like a good way to do it.

She took a deep breath and picked up the phone.

And as soon as she heard Nick's voice, she knew everything was going to be all right.

The combination of heat, tenderness and command in his voice when he said, "Hello, Selene. Are you naked like I told you to be?" drove all the stupid fears and worries out of her brain.

And replaced them with a different, albeit more fun, one.

In the flurry of getting home, getting her laundry together, finding quarters and her detergent and hauling the first load down to the laundry room in the basement—not to mention angsting about things that now seemed pointless—she'd forgotten the *be naked* part. How could she have been so distracted? So...so dumb?

"I...uh...I'm not wearing a whole lot," she said, frantically trying to peel off her tank top and running shorts as she talked. "I don't *have* a whole lot to wear that isn't in the laundry. Even threw in the bra and underwear I'd worn to work."

She managed not to drop the phone as she peeled the tank over her head and let it fall, a faded purple blob on her bedroom floor.

"But you were wearing something when you called. Bad Selene." Nick didn't sound upset. If anything, his voice was rich with amusement. But it was edged with something: Heat. Erotic cruelty. "I was going to see how many times we could make you come. But maybe I'll just get you all worked up and get myself off instead, listening to you getting closer and closer, knowing I'm not going to let you get there." He was practically purring. "Yeah, I like that idea. I'll tell you stories, tell you what to do, and when you get close to coming, I want you to say 'edge'. Then I'll decide if I'll let you come or not."

She cursed. After a long day lost in erotic fantasy, that sounded like the most frustrating thing imaginable. But when Selene pulled off her shorts, they were moist with her juices, more so than they had been moments before, as if in perverse response to the idea of not being allowed to come.

Fine, if she was already in trouble, even if it was fun trouble, she might as well make it worthwhile. Make Nick sweat a little bit to come up with an appropriately dominant response over the phone if she was going to be left on the edge. "I could have just lied and told you I was naked."

"Could you?"

She only had to think about it for a second. "No. I'm still figuring out all the rules here, but that would have been cheating. And I'm a lousy liar anyway."

She didn't say that she didn't think she could lie to him at all, at least not in the context of their erotic games. Maybe to hide what she'd gotten him as a birthday present, assuming they got to the birthday-present stage, but not anything else. "Might have been more fun, though."

"Really?"

Damn, he could read her way too well, even over the phone where he couldn't see what she could feel—the straining nipples, the damp thighs, the undoubtedly wide eyes, the flaming cheeks, the actual God-help-her trembling with a combination of arousal, anticipation and nerves. "No, it wouldn't. It would have been more fun if I'd remembered to take my damn clothes off...but since I didn't, I'd rather take whatever evil consequences you have in mind. And that doesn't make sense."

Nick laughed, but not mockingly—almost caressingly. "Oh, yes it does, beautiful. You like the idea of me controlling your orgasms, just like you like the idea of me tying you up or telling you how to suck my cock. You like the idea of rewards and punishments."

Did she? The throbbing in her pussy told her the answer. "Yeah, I do—as long as they're sexy and fun. I wouldn't like you to actually *punish* me for real, in anger." Honesty compelled her to add, "I don't think, anyway. I've read some hot stories about it, but they scare me, even when I'm masturbating over them."

Nick's voice seemed to drop an octave as he said, "They should scare you, Selene. Serious rules and serious consequences are a whole different thing from what we're doing. That's not play so much as a way of shaping your life around someone else's will completely, or shaping someone else to your will." He paused, seemed to think for a second. "I bet you just got wetter, didn't you?"

She managed to let out a pathetic squeak that must have gotten the point across.

"I know because I got harder, thinking about putting you under that kind of control, making you into a slave who lives by my rules and faces my wrath if you don't. A little naked pleasure slave, just waiting for me to use her and make her come, or to hurt her in exquisite ways."

She wasn't touching herself, but the sound of his deep, purring voice and the image of herself as naked, collared, maybe branded like in the ridiculous but arousing Gor novels about barbarians and their slave girls that she'd read as a teenager, made her pussy flutter and clench around nothing. "Edge," she hissed.

"I didn't tell you to play with yourself." There was such a bite of erotic menace to his voice that she saw herself as that pleasure slave, wearing nothing but a collar and maybe some strategically placed jewelry, begging for mercy from her master.

"Please, I wasn't touching myself, sir." She added the sir instinctively, although he hadn't asked for it. "It was just the words...the idea of the pleasure slave...and your voice...and everything." She hoped he wasn't secretly scoring her on how much sense she was making, because to her own ears she sounded ridiculous.

And a little pathetic, as if each word were begging.

Again, the image of the poor imaginary pleasure slave— she'd be terrified, knowing she might be whipped bloody or sold to someone horrible, or worse. And yet, in her familiar place at her master's feet, she'd probably have an idea or two what she might do to get out of her predicament.

That thought gave Selene a few ideas on how to get out of her less serious and far funnier situation.

She tried not to crack up as she said, "Please, sir, you have to believe me. I'll do anything!"

There was a second's hesitation at the other end of the line, as if Nick were gauging her mood and/or figuring out what to say next in a script that was evolving as it went along.

Then he chuckled, a warm, liquid, evil chuckle that sent shockwaves into her cunt. "So you say, slave, but you've already disobeyed me once. We'll see how you obey from now on. Get on your knees."

Selene hesitated. Surely he didn't expect her to really drop to her knees—all by herself, alone in her undecorated, box-cluttered bedroom? That wasn't sexy. It was just silly.

The image of the slave girl came back to her mind. Kneeling, wearing nothing but a pretty, jeweled collar, knees spread to show a pussy that was wet and slick despite the panic in her eyes.

Kneeling on an Oriental rug in an exotically decorated room. No, not a room, a tent, but nothing like a common camping tent. Silk hangings and piles of pillows and a low bed covered with furs and embroidered silk covers, and in the corner a whipping post or something. And her master—Nick, of course—but Nick bare-chested, in leather breeches and high boots. All she could really see from her position without raising her head more than she ought to would be a delicious stretch of well-worn black leather encasing calf and thigh. Yum.

With that in mind, she could kneel, shutting out the messy room and the fact that Nick was on the other side of town, not here where she could smell the leather or at least his warm, masculine flesh, feast her eyes on him, hope to feast her mouth and cunt on him.

Yeah, that was more like it. The carpet, a shade of brown she wouldn't have chosen but hadn't had time even to think about replacing, vanished. The piles of boxes in the corners, blocking the mirror, vanished. Everything vanished but Nick's voice and her arousal.

"I'm kneeling, sir."

"Master. Have you forgotten so quickly you should call me Master?"

But he hadn't said...

He was playing with her head. It was all part of the game. She breathed a quiet sigh of relief that she hadn't screwed up for real. Then she realized she was wetter and more open from that second of panic.

When this was over, she was going to have to have a long talk with herself about preserving some basic common sense. Natalie sounded like a nutbar, but already Selene was starting to grasp how easy it would be to fall too far into the fantasy, lose touch with the fact that outside of the unusual relationship with Nick, the world continued to operate on its normal rules, and she still had all her normal rights and responsibilities in it.

"Master," she said, trying to put a world of yearning and yielding into the one word.

What would come next? Well, ideally, she would ease the throbbing that had spread from between her legs and threatened to take over her entire body, but that was not to be.

She cast her mind back over things she'd read, things she'd fantasized. Things that had made her come even though, at the time, she wasn't sure she'd ever have the courage to do them. Still wasn't sure, in some cases. But that was the joy of phone sex, wasn't it? You could play with your further-out fantasies safely.

"How may this slave earn your forgiveness, Master?" Then she added, in a slightly different tone of voice—the narrator, "Picture me arched over, like the child's pose in yoga, kissing your boots."

"My boots?" His voice was amused but throaty, aroused.

"Black thigh-high boots. Very pirate."

"They're a bit dirty," Nick said. "Not nasty dirty but dusty. Maybe a little grass stuck to them."

"I still lick them. You feel the pressure of my lips through the leather. My tongue licking off the dust. My arms around your legs, clinging to you. And in between kisses and licks, I look up at you as if waiting for instruction."

This was the corniest thing ever. So how come she was actually leaning forward as she was describing? How come she was imagining the scene so vividly, smelling the leather and Nick's unique scent layered with it, tasting the leather and the hint of dust?

How come she was grinning like a very turned-on fool?

"Do you like that, slave?"

Selene thought for a second and was surprised by her own reaction. "Yes. I'm dripping, and when my nipples brush against the carpet, it almost hurts, but in a good way."

"Your nipples are that sensitive?" Damn, from the barely suppressed glee in Nick's voice, she was in for some nipple pain. Although why that was a *damn* situation, she couldn't say, because her pussy was clenching at the thought, and she liked it when Nick treated her nipples roughly. "Do you have nipple clips?"

"No, Master." She'd always meant to order some off the Internet but never had, figuring they wouldn't be nearly as much fun without an appreciative partner.

A laugh. "That was actually Nick asking Selene, but I like hearing you say *Master*. If you had clamps, I'd tell you put them on. Instead, pinch your nipples, slave. Hard. And don't stop until I tell you to."

"Oh yes, Master." Now that was an order she was glad to obey. She sank her fingernails into the plump, sensitive flesh, imagining jeweled clamps, in keeping with the exotic theme the fantasy was taking. Heat roiled from her nipples outward, sunbursts of pleasurable pain radiating out, filling her body. Experimentally, she rolled and twisted, gasped in pleasure, eased up a bit because some small fragment of pride didn't want to mewl *edge* again so soon, confess to how hot this silliness was making her.

"Does that feel good, slave?"

"Yes, Master." Think. He couldn't see. She needed to describe. "Feels wonderful, even though it hurts. Better than a light touch ever did, Master. I used to think there was something wrong with my nipples because I wasn't that crazy about having them played with, but I've figured it out. I need pain." She twisted again, letting him hear her sharp intake of breath.

"Good to know. I want you to get some old-fashioned clothes pins as soon as you can for emergencies like this. You'll need your hands later. And we'll have to go shopping soon, get you some toys. Would you like that, slave? Some toys of your own?"

For a second, she broke role completely. "Cool! Are there good places in Boston to get stuff like that? My vibrators could use some company."

"Yes, but I won't say where. Don't want you going without me."

"I wouldn't. Besides, aren't I kept in a cage or something when you're not using me?" She couldn't keep the sly amusement out of her voice.

Or the arousal out of her body. She could see the fantasy slave's cage, see herself behind the bars, staring out at her hunky master, aching for his sweet cruelty.

"I never should have mentioned the cage to you, should I? I've hit on a fetish."

She laughed. "Not a fetish. A fantasy. When you made that joke, my logical brain said, 'Holy shit! He's crazy!' and my pussy said, 'But wouldn't it be fun?'"

"Very well, then. You have a cage. Quite spacious and comfortable, with furs and pillows, maybe something to read, and definitely sex toys to entertain yourself—and me—with but securely locked. Once you're in there, you're trapped. At your master's whim. Waiting to be let out and used."

"Maybe I don't need to be let out to be used. Maybe it's set up so I could suck you through the bars, or be fucked. Would you like that, Master? Having me locked up and secure but still fuckable? Would you like to fuck me through cold steel bars, knowing I was your prisoner?" Between the nipple-play and the graphic images spinning out of control through her mind, Selene was barely in control, her cunt contracting around empty air in futile hope it could satisfy her.

He groaned. "Jesus, yes! You are making me so fucking hard and hot, Selene. I love your dirty mind." In a more controlled voice, the voice of the evil master, he added, "I'm putting you back into your cage, slave girl, to think about your behavior, and when I come back, you'd better be ready for me."

"Yes, Master." Selene snuck a hand to her pussy, a quick, cautious caress. She was liquid, fiery, probably leaving a stain on the ugly carpet, and she bit her lip to fight the urge to bring herself off.

"Play with yourself, but don't you *dare* come. I'll be back shortly." Then Nick's voice changed. "Although, I'm actually not going anywhere. Tell me what you're doing."

"I'm lying down in my cage—well, really, on my bed. Is that okay? I'm not used to kneeling this long."

"Go ahead. I only want to break you in fun ways. And you can stop playing with your nipples while you're getting settled."

She scrambled onto the bed. "I'm lying in my cage, my legs spread wide."

"Are you playing with your nipples again?"

"Not yet."

"Then do it. Pinch them. Pinch them hard. Harder than you were before. Imagine it's me, and I'm punishing you by torturing your tits."

She complied. "I'm squeezing them, pinching as hard as I can, using my nails and thinking about clips. Some really nasty ones I've seen pictures of, with weights...don't know if I could handle them, but I'd like to..." At the image that flashed into her mind—her breasts bound tight, swollen from the pressure of the ropes, ornamented with evil yet pretty weighted clips—her breath caught, and for a second, she lost track of what she was saying. "Edge," she confessed.

"And still not playing with your pussy?"

A desperate whisper. "No, Master."

And an even more desperate one. "But I need to. Please..."

Nick laughed, a rich, evil chuckle that Selene thought sounded a little strained. "You won't come until I tell you to, slave. And I may not. But go ahead. Play with yourself. See how many fingers you can stuff into that hot, hungry cunt of yours."

Her hungry cunt. Yeah, that was what it was right now.

"I'm not even going to bother with one, Master. I know I need more." She slipped two fingers inside, feeling her inner muscles tighten, milking them. Tight but not full yet. Not what she knew she could take.

She pulled them partway out, worked a third in with them. "Three, Master."

"Does that feel good? Does it fill you like my cock would?"

What a question! "Feels wonderful..." She pumped in and out, feeling her juices slipping out, still kneading and pinching at her nipple with her other hand. "Not like your cock, but..." She opened her eyes, stared at the disorder surrounding her, let it distract her from the building wave of sensation. "Really, really good."

"Can you take more?"

Could she? "Oh...my God. Yes! Four fingers. So full. And the angle is perfect. I'm getting my clit too and it's...wow."

"More?"

"Can't, Master." But damn, it felt good to try. Dirty and depraved and wonderful.

"Imagine you're in your cage, doing what you're doing now. I come into the room, catch you at it. Watch for a bit, stroking my cock."

"How?" It was all she could do to get the word out. The room was fragrant with girl juices, and it no longer felt like pretending she was in a cage in her master's luxurious tent. With her eyes closed, she was there.

"Lightly, up and down the shaft. Not trying to come, just enjoying the sensation. Enjoying the greedy look on my slave girl's face, knowing how much she wants the cock inside her."

Selene's brain wasn't functioning at peak, but that was a cue if she'd ever heard one. Besides, it fit in well with what was going through her mind, the only thing she could focus on. "Please, Master. Fuck me. Fuck me hard. Let me come...please."

"Edge?"

She nodded frantically, forgetting in her frenzy that he couldn't actually see her. But he seemed to understand.

"Not yet, slave. Present yourself to me for fucking."

She tried to think what she'd do, could form the mental image of herself on all fours, pressing back against the bars, positioning her pussy just right for him to penetrate her, but couldn't get the words out. "I do."

Again, he seemed to understand her situation. "Good girl. Good slave. I get behind you, fit as much of my hands through the bars as I can so I can dig my fingernails into your ass. Can you feel that?"

She used the tit-torturing hand to dig into her own butt instead, astonished how good it felt. Normally, if she'd tried to do that while masturbating, it would have been distracting. Under orders, though, it worked.

"Yes, Master."

"And the cold bars against your skin?"

"Yes, Master."

"And my cock, driving into you, hard and fast?"

"Yesss..." Her voice trailed off on a wail. "Edge."

"Keep going. Don't stop. Think about me fucking your slave cunt. Because you're *mine.*" The word came out as a roar, followed by rabid-animal sounds.

Between the noise and the idea of Nick shooting off on himself and the idea of pirate-booted-master Nick shooting into her, Selene didn't stand a chance.

She had just about enough wits left not to scream her release directly into the phone, but she had no doubt he heard her incoherent stream of "NickNickOhMyGodNickcoming!"

"Keep going," he urged, his voice harsh. "You might as well enjoy yourself now. Come for me, Selene. Come all your greedy pussy wants to come."

She did, fucking herself, playing with her clit, arching up as if Nick lay over her and she was meeting his thrusts. Came until she was a limp noodle of a woman, drenched with sweat despite the humming air conditioner. All the while, she heard Nick murmuring encouragement.

Chapter Fourteen

The first coherent thing she said afterward was, "Oops."

"Oops what? Got the neighbors checking to see if you're okay?"

"Oops I wasn't supposed to come until you said I could, and I started without permission."

Nick laughed. "I'll let you in on a secret. Sometimes I like to set up challenges that I don't expect you to win. If you do, you get rewarded. If you don't, you get punished." She could practically hear the quotes around *punished*. "But either way, it'll be fun for both of us. It'll give you something to look forward to, besides the toy shopping."

"Really?" Her rational mind had suspected as much when he'd set up the conditions in the first place, but her rational mind had gone pretty far away for a while and wasn't fully back yet.

"Really." She could picture his lazy, post-orgasm smile. "Another secret, although you've probably figured this one out already: I love making you lose your mind like that. There are a lot of ways to dom someone, and some guys get off on rationing their sub's orgasms. I can see that for a short time, like we did today."

An aftershock ran through her, and she shivered pleasurably. "It made me come extra hard when I finally let go."

"Point. But the whole chastity-belt thing isn't for me. Very boring. I've always figured the best way to get control over a woman isn't with deprivation and isn't with pain—except the fun kind. It's by melting her brain on a regular basis."

"Damn," Selene breathed, boneless and content, "I knew I liked you for a reason."

Later, after a needed potty break and a chance for Selene to deal with her laundry, Nick called her back. "How did you feel about the fantasy?"

"The fifty-two orgasms and eardrum-shattering screams didn't tell you?" She rubbed idly at her clit through her shorts, not exactly wanting to come again, not sure if she could, but enjoying the warm pleasure.

"No." Nick's voice was serious. "That told me it was a hot fantasy, but is that what you want?"

"To be a caged girl who licks boots? Once in a while as a game, sure, but not as a lifestyle. Living in a cage would be hell on your back after a while, and there'd be no room for my computer and all my books. And I think they'd frown on a domestic violence counselor living in a cage." She wasn't sure where he was going with this, but if he was worried he'd scared her, she wanted to be clear that the answer was no. At least not in the sense he seemed to mean; she was still a little startled with how quickly she was taking to this, still overwhelmed by her response, the depth of her need.

"Do you think you want to be a slave? Like Alison, more or less?"

Oh my God, what was the right answer to that question?

Her brain and her body had very different ideas.

Honest answer, right answer—if he didn't like the honest answer, they had a problem, and better to know it now than later. "I have no idea. The fantasy makes me wet. Always has, even before I had any idea what it meant. But I don't know if I could really live that way."

"Neither do I," Nick said softly.

"Do you mean if I could or if you could?"

His answer was, simply, "Yes."

That reply left her with a lot more questions than it answered, questions she wasn't entirely sure how to put into words.

There was a future implied here, one that she wasn't ready to think about, one that she didn't think Nick was ready to think about either. At least she hoped he wasn't, because that would scare the hell out of her.

Trying to change the subject, she asked, "Any luck tracking down Natalie?" She crossed her fingers as she said it, prayed there was news and it was good, that Natalie had just been out of touch for some commonplace reason.

Instead, Nick sighed, the kind of heavy sigh she could imagine ruffling her hair even through the phone. "Yes and no," he said. "Got a number and a post office box from her mom. She talked to her mother a few weeks ago, but I haven't actually talked to her, and I don't know if I'll be able to. She's not even talking to her mom regularly, and they're pretty close. I think her master's screening her calls and telling her who to call back and when."

A panic alarm went off in Selene's brain. All her counselor training screamed that this was bad.

In the context of what she knew about Natalie, maybe she could downgrade it to suspicious and possibly bad. Natalie might find it comfortable and reassuring to have things be mostly her master and her, without any outside interference. But being cut off from her own mom?

Not cool.

There had to be some way to get through to her, find out what was really going on. "PO box? No street address?"

"She's so far out in the boonies that the PO box isn't even in the town where she's living."

"Give me the number," Selene said. "I think I have an idea.

Something that might get her to call back—and might intrigue her dom-master-whatever enough that he'd be okay with it."

Chapter Fifteen

Her idea was vague, and she spent a long time rehearsing and thinking it through before she came up with the right words, and, more to the point, the right tone to say them in.

A little nervous, a little humble, a little young and drunk on fantasies of the lifestyle, she decided, kind of like the barely-of-age girl from Kinksters, the one who called herself slave kat.

"Hi, Natalie. My name's Selene." She tried to think lower case. "Master Nick...sorry, he said to call him Nick...suggested I get in touch with you about...uh, slave stuff. 'Cause Alison, she's great and everything, but she keeps telling me to take stuff slow, and I know what I need, you know? Just need to figure out how to get there, and it sounds like you have."

There. Suck-up message left. If the guy she and Nick had started calling the Domly Dick was as arrogant as she suspected, he'd like that his slave was the go-to gal for newbies—especially if he was a Craig kind of guy who might like a crack at the newbies himself.

And if Natalie wasn't as tightly controlled as they thought...well, she'd call back, because what woman wouldn't be curious to find out if her ex was actually boinking the ditzy college girl Selene was pretending to be?

July passed into early August. The short summer semester was in full swing, and between that and her part-time job, Selene had been pretty busy. But she and Nick had managed to squeeze in a few more hot dates, a few more afternoons in

Garth and Alison's pool, and plenty more steamy phone-sex sessions.

But no sex-toy shopping trip yet. It had never worked out. Okay, so two times when they'd meant to go, they'd met up at one of their houses first, taken one look at each other and ended up in bed, and the third time, they'd actually been on their way downtown on a particularly sweltering day when Alison called up and invited them to come use the pool.

On a more worrisome note, there had been no calls—for either of them—from the elusive Natalie. It became obvious as the weeks went on that Nick was growing more anxious each day, and that, in turn, made Selene more anxious.

Kind of crazy to worry so much about a woman she didn't even know, but that was her training. Her calling. Her classes were showing that more and more, even though she hadn't gotten involved with a hotline yet in Massachusetts—no time yet, between getting settled and the heady whirlwind of meeting Nick.

Would a hotline still want her?

She expressed that worry to Nick over the phone.

"They don't need to know you're kinky, do they? Though it might be helpful you know the difference between fun rough stuff and real violence, and you might be able to help someone else sort it out." He hesitated a minute. "This really means a lot to you, doesn't it? Helping out women in trouble?"

"Yeah."

"I wouldn't have thought you'd have seen a lot of it where you grew up. It sounds like...like America's Heartland."

Selene gave a dry, sad laugh. "I wish. It happens everywhere. In places like Lodi, the isolation makes it easy, I think, and the whole no-sun-from-November-to-April thing makes people a little crazy. But for all we know, Garth and Alison's neighbors in that big, gorgeous house are in trouble too."

131

His voice was gentle, nothing like his dom voice, when he said, "I guess what I mean is this sounds like more than a passion to do a generally good thing. Is there someone I need to track down and kill?"

She took a deep breath, trying to fight past the lump forming in her throat because she had no doubt that he would go to bat for her, maybe in some ridiculous alpha-male way, just as he was for Natalie. "Not for me personally. My parents have a great marriage, and Mom's parents are the poster couple for senior-citizen love. I've dated my share of jerks, but it was never like that. They weren't abusive, just careless with my feelings."

"But there's someone."

Not her memories. Not her story. Not Nick's business.

It had colored her life, but it seemed too soon to speak of it with him. Going into some of her worst, scariest memories, even if they were things she'd understood only imperfectly when they were going on, didn't have much of a place in a casual friends-with-benefits relationship. Not on her planet.

But it was still sweet he cared so much.

"Persistent little bastard, aren't you?" She tried to make light of the memories and of the way his concern was making her feel. Tried to ignore the warm blanket of protection his attention wrapped around her.

"You can't begin to know how persistent I can be." His voice held an edge of the dominant, a hint of erotic threat that should have clashed with Warm-Nurturing-Guy, but oddly didn't.

She'd analyze that later.

"Answer me, Selene. I'd really like to know."

Her tongue froze.

Why was he prying so much? Why had she even brought it up in the first place?

At her silence, Nick's voice softened to an intimate whisper.

As if he'd read her mind, he said, "I'm not just being nosy, although God knows I am a nosy bastard and I want to know what makes you tick, so I'll ask you a lot of crazy questions. But in this case, I'm asking for specific reasons. One is that it's important for me to know if you have any damage, physical or emotional, that might crop up while we're playing. I don't want to do something that triggers some kind of horrible memories for you, any more than I'd want to tie you up in a way that put stress on an old injury. We probably should have had this conversation a while ago."

That made sense. He'd already asked her a ton of questions that first night—did she have any severe allergies, did she have back problems, stuff like that. Childhood traumas would also be important to know. "Although," she said, continuing her thought aloud, "I probably wouldn't be so interested in kink if someone had hurt me for real."

A dry chuckle, as humorless as hers had been earlier. "You might be surprised. The human brain's weird, and for some people it's helpful. Lets them face the bad stuff in a situation where they have choices and control or something. But I don't know that I'm a good enough dom to guide someone through hell and back like that."

What Nick wanted from her now made sense. He wanted to make sure there was nothing haunting her in ways he might need to deal with later, ways that might crop up and spoil both their fun.

And with that in mind, he deserved an outline of the truth. "When we were growing up, my friend Molly's father was abusing her mother and the kids. They lived next door to us, but next door was about a mile, with a lot of vineyard in between. One night, Molly and her little brother showed up at our back door. They'd run through the vineyard to get help because they didn't dare to use the phone where their dad might hear. It might make him even angrier." She blinked away sudden, hot tears, remembering Molly's white face and wide

133

eyes staring up at *her* dad, hoping that another grown-up could help even though she had no reason to trust any man. Remembering Adam, the bruise across his face from when he'd tried to intervene, as if a seven-year-old could do against a grown man's insane wrath.

"What happened?"

"Mom helped the kids call the police. My dad went over and intervened. He won't talk about exactly what happened to this day, but when the police got there, Reverend Baker turned himself in."

Nick sputtered. "Reverend? That makes it suck even more. But it sounds like it had a happy ending in the long run."

"Mrs. Baker and the kids ended up living with us until she could get back on her feet. She'd been a full-time mom for years, and she didn't have a lot of confidence after living with someone who treated her like shit, so it took her a while to get her head together, let alone find work. It came out all right in the end, but seeing that, and seeing how long it took all of them to get their lives back on track, made an impression on me."

"I bet Molly's not a regular churchgoer."

Selene found herself smiling despite the sad aspects of the story. "Oddly, she's a deacon in what used to be her father's church. She plans to go to divinity school when her kids are older. She says she's clear that it was her dad who was screwed up, not the church and certainly not God."

Hmm, come to think of it, she owed Molly a call. Not that the last couple of calls had been entirely easy. Molly, of course, wanted to know all about Nick, and Selene ended up having to gloss over a lot. Molly got the picture they spent a lot more time having wild sex than they did, oh, going to museums and movies, and she was quietly amused by that, but Selene got the feeling she knew a lot was being left out. "Selene?"

Selene jumped. "Sorry, just woolgathering. Thinking I need to call Molly or at least pop her an e-mail." She thought of something. "Hey, you said you had a couple of reasons for pushing me to talk about this. What was the other one?"

Nick laughed. "Who's being nosy now? Honestly, I can't remember what I was going to say. Probably something about how it's not good to have Big Honking Secrets"—she could hear the capital letters—"between a dom and a sub. Knowing all about you helps me get my claws in deeper and all that."

Then his tone changed. He chuckled evilly and said in that rich voice that sent shivers down her spine, "Speaking of claws, I found the most interesting toy online today—metal claws. I'm sending you the link right now. Let me know what you think."

The change of topic made Selene's head spin, but she had to admit the claws sounded intriguing, and she fired up her laptop. "Ooh, pretty! Very Goth. They look dangerous, though."

"But sensual as well. I wouldn't want to break skin, but imagine how they'd feel just trailing lightly over your skin, tracing your jugular vein or circling your nipple."

She shivered, a mix of apprehension and arousal. "Pinching, maybe?"

"Oh yes, pinching. Scratching, digging into your glorious ass when you're at the peak of arousal so that extra shock of pain pushes you over the edge."

Good grief, how had she gone so quickly from all serious, almost teary-eyed to getting wet and having the most interesting, sexy ideas?

She'd needed the distraction so she didn't get maudlin. And Nick was just that good.

"All my mental images are kind of vampiric and Gothy right now. I see myself in a corset and black velvet."

"Bet you'd look great in a corset, and it would push up your breasts nicely so I could run the claws across them."

She chuckled throatily. "I do look pretty good in a corset, if I do say so myself."

"You own one?"

"Just something from one of those mall-Goth stores, not a real one. I haven't worn it in a few years, but I found it and the skirt that went with it when I was unpacking the other day. I can't imagine why I even kept them. It was a Halloween costume."

"Wear it on Friday. I like the idea of you all gothed out. And I want to take you out to dinner because I think that's the only way we're ever going to make it to the toy store."

"Do you have any idea how hot velvet and a corset is?" People had assured her that this summer was unusual for Boston, but the heat had continued unabated ever since she'd moved. The few cloudbursts had just served to make it steamier.

"Yeah. That's why I want you to wear it." He chuckled deep in his throat. "But, yeah, I guess the velvet skirt might be too much. Got anything else that might go with the corset?"

She mentally scanned her wardrobe and said, "Probably." And if she didn't, a little shopping wouldn't be the end of the world. Life as an IT administrator at a college in western New York had left her with a wardrobe best described as *functional.*

"Too bad I won't have the claws yet," Nick mused. "I bet if you stick those in the freezer, they'd feel really interesting on hot skin."

Selene's breath caught, thinking about something sharp and bladelike and icy cold caressing her. "Wow," was all she could get out.

"We'll have to stick to ice for now." Nick's voice was elaborately casual. "Of course that's not a bad thing. Ice can go places I wouldn't want to put those claws. Speaking of which, go get an ice cube."

And Selene was lost.

Nick hung up the phone and took a deep, jagged breath.

Guiding Selene through orgasm after shattering orgasm over the phone was proving addictive, and the way he came knowing that she was under his hand even when he wasn't physically present was damn addictive as well.

Masturbation was usually a stopgap for him, no comparison to being with a woman. Controlling a woman. So much of sex for him was about the control, the connection, the power exchange, that the pure physical sensation of stroking his own cock didn't do a lot.

Selene could make him feel that power exchange over the phone—her excitement, her yielding, her pleasure in temporarily giving him the reins.

And she was open to so much. The way she'd responded just to the idea of the claws—not to mention to pushing ice inside her as she made herself come—was incredible.

A hot woman with a good heart and a sharp mind.

But as his head cleared, he wondered at himself. What in the world had prompted him to go from talking about domestic violence, a serious and seriously unsexy topic if he'd ever heard of one, to heavy phone sex? Sure, they'd needed to lighten the mood, but something had thrown him, had prompted him to make the transition a little awkwardly. He'd meant to save the link with the claws for when they were together, so he could watch her reactions. Had really just meant to talk with her this evening, find out a little more about what made her tick. How had he gotten sidetracked?

Then it came to him.

She'd been asking him for the "other" reason he'd been so adamant about finding out why she felt so strongly about domestic violence work, and he'd had to change the subject quickly before he tried to explain it.

Tried to explain that at the very thought that she might have been abused, he felt a surge of red rage. Not the urge to help a friend in trouble, like with Natalie, not the "someone needs to do something and since I'm here, it might as well be me" reaction he'd probably get if he realized anyone, even a complete stranger, was being abused. It was something far more primitive and possessive, an urge to eliminate anyone or anything that threatened what was his. Never mind that he was a mild-mannered, civilized Bostonian code monkey better suited to wars of words; the images that came to mind were decidedly caveman.

First of all, Selene might laugh at cracks about "someone needing to die", might even make them herself but probably wouldn't be thrilled with actual violent instincts, especially not after what he now knew she'd witnessed.

And she didn't need to know that his inner caveman, the part that lurked in the deep recesses of his hindbrain and occasionally made trouble for the civilized, evolved guy, had decided that Selene was his personal possession.

They were supposed to be taking it slowly, just having fun. It was too soon for reasonable adults to have such crazy ideas. Especially when he knew damn well that if things did get serious between him and Selene, the caveman and the civilized guy would end up at war over how to treat "his woman"—and everyone would lose, just like with Natalie.

Chapter Sixteen

Thunderstorms were rumbling over Boston by Friday evening. They still hadn't hit, but a slight breeze with a green hint of rain had taken the temperature from sweltering down to merely sultry by seven o'clock when Selene met up with Nick at an Ethiopian restaurant in Boston's South End.

As Nick had requested—okay, ordered—she was wearing her pseudocorset. It was too hot for the sweeping velvet skirt that went with it, but it looked good with a black silk broomstick skirt with narrow lace insets, and she could get away with wearing cute flats. If you looked closely at the corset, you could see it was shoddy velvet and the kind of satin better used for linings. But the looks she was getting as she walked from the South Station T stop to the restaurant suggested that male people, at least, were primarily noticing its flattering burgundy color, its figure-enhancing properties and the way her breasts seemingly attempted to escape. It made her self-conscious, and she was glad that a few blocks from South Station, more and more of the male passersby seemed to be with each other, and not just in the going-out-for-drinks-with-the-guys sense. The neighborhood was an arty one with a big gay population, and if a lot of these guys stared, it was either critiquing her fashion sense or wondering if they could find something similar in their size.

At least no one could tell she wasn't wearing panties.

Normally, the attention would make her feel like her skin didn't fit quite right. But today, while it did make her self-conscious, it was in a good way, warming her up for the scrutiny she knew she'd be getting from Nick.

Even with the bit of breeze, she was sweating by the time she arrived at the restaurant, the silk skirt clinging to her legs. A hostess in what she assumed to be traditional Ethiopian clothes smiled graciously and led her down a flight of stairs to a blessedly cool room where Nick was waiting for her.

Oh no. Nick was waiting for her.

He rose when she came in—the seating was low to the ground here, at small round tables made of wicker—buried his hands in her hair and kissed her, heedless of the hostess and the other guests, heedless of the dark lipstick she was wearing, the closest she could get to a Goth look with the makeup she had on hand.

Fever from her lips down to her toes.

And something pressing on the back of her neck, something cold and metallic.

Not sharp, but definitely cold and metallic. Had he gotten those claws already, had them Fed Exed or something? Or did he have something else devious in mind to torture her with?

The mystery, as much as the sensation, made her shiver.

When he pulled away from the kiss, his face was stern, although the effect was somewhat spoiled by the fact he was wearing some of her lipstick, making him look disturbingly pretty.

"You look beautiful," he said in a voice that rumbled against her clit. "Go into the bathroom and put these on."

He palmed something to her. She uncurled her hand, glanced down nervously. Nipple clips, or maybe tit-jewelry designed to slip around the nipples, adorned with delicate dangling faux rubies.

She let out a soft meep. "Am I in trouble? I know the train was slow, but I didn't think I was late enough I needed to call."

He smiled and brushed his fingers over her curled ones

that concealed the clips. "These are just to get you in the right mood for shopping. Don't make them too tight. I want you hot but not bothered."

Instead of a dreadful, frightening weight in her hand, they felt like gems. She walked to the bathroom with a spring in her step.

Dinner passed in a blur, a wet, horny, very fun blur. At one point, she found herself asking, "Can we come back here sometime without nipple clips?"

"Don't like the clips?"

"Love the clips. But I think I'd love the food, too, if I wasn't so distracted!"

They didn't linger over coffee.

Thunder still rumbled in the distance but no rain fell, though the air was so moist it might as well. Fully dark now, the night was stagnant, sticky; the pleasant breeze of earlier had died altogether. "It's only a few blocks," Nick encouraged, but his sexy voice seemed wilted by the heat.

Every step was a fight between arousal—the nipple clips tugging at her bouncing breasts, the weight of need cupped in her pelvis—and sheer sweaty discomfort.

Selene thought the discomfort had won when they reached Eros boutique a few blocks away. Sweat was pooling between her breasts because the cheap fabric of the bodice didn't breathe at all, and while she figured the way the silk clung to her legs might look enticing, it felt like she was smothering in a wet parachute. She barely looked at the items in the small, barred display window—a chap-clad mannequin dangling a set of purple leather cuffs from its truncated wrist, a bondage Barbie and Ken set, and an elaborate leather mask. She didn't even want to go in at this point. She wanted to get back to Nick's place with its central air...

And take a shower. A nice, long shower, with a shower gel called something along the lines of Cool Peppermint or Ocean

Breezes.

After a shower and a few cold drinks, maybe she'd be able to think about sex. Right now, even with over-stimulated nipples and a moist, open pussy taunting her, sex sounded uncomfortably warm and sticky.

She'd opened her mouth to suggest the retreating-back-to-A/C plan when Nick pushed the door open and took her arm. "Let's go shopping!" he said, childish glee on his face.

The glee was contagious, and she found herself grinning despite her discomfort. "I've never heard a guy that excited about shopping before—not even for geeky electronics or tools. Maybe a car. Or where I grew up, a new tractor."

"Sex toys may be the only thing better than electronics and tools for getting guys to shop. How many times can you give someone a present you'll enjoy at least as much as she will?"

At that point, curiosity—and the cool though rubber-scented air coming from inside—got the better of her.

Selene had never been in a sex shop before. Sure, she had Good Vibrations and Blowfish.com bookmarked because a girl never knew when the Rabbit Pearl might need company. But being in an actual store was different.

Very different.

Very hot and also a little intimidating, as they climbed narrow stairs lined with posters for various fetish and gay events and entered a store full of leather, rubber, latex and gleaming chrome.

"I'm not even sure what some of this stuff is," she whispered, brushing her lips deliberately against Nick's ear to make her embarrassed confession more sensual.

He whispered back, "Honestly? Me neither. That's either a fucking machine or a really funny-looking ergonomic chair." He pointed toward a curious black piece of furniture that did seem to have a place to hold a dildo but looked at least as much like some weird office furniture. "And that? I don't know and I don't think I want to know."

Selene stared at the offending item curiously. Rings and metal spikes. "I think it's a chastity belt for a boy."

"I said I didn't want to know!"

She patted him soothingly. "I promise I'm not interested in trying it."

Not on Nick, certainly. But, she admitted to herself, if not to her lover, that once she figured out what it was, she got the most fascinating image of a faceless but very good-looking guy wearing nothing but one of those and a strained smile, enjoying the torturous yet exciting sensation of needing to come and not being able to.

She didn't think she wanted to put a guy in that position, but she could see why someone might. She could definitely understand why the guy would go for it. It would feel so good going along with it and feel even better when he finally earned his release from some delightfully evil, elegant domme or burly leather-clad master.

"I've never seen so much latex in my life." She grimaced. "That's got to be sticky."

"No trying on latex tonight. Maybe in cooler weather."

Selene drew a sharp breath. *Cooler weather* implied a future. She'd been trying so hard to enjoy the moment and not think ahead, not assume anything, that Nick's words set off a jumble of conflicting feelings. Warm pleasure and chilly panic, comfort and fear.

Then she internally mocked herself. She was reading way too much into a few random words.

Nick pulled one dress from a nearby rack and she let the movement distract her from her silly ponderings. It was certainly eye-catching: a full-length cobalt-blue gown with a tulip hem, floor-length in back, slit to well above the knee in front but with a graceful line that made it look elegant as well as dead sexy.

"Oh yes!" She didn't think latex would ever be her thing—give her silk, velvet and leather any day—but she could see the appeal of being poured into a dress that would mold to her every curve and show them off to best advantage.

She could get lost just in the clothes and lingerie for hours. Not that she could think of many places to wear these clothes, but that didn't mean it wouldn't be fun to own them. But that wasn't what they were here to shop for.

They were here to look for toys.

Thinking about that went straight to her clit.

The atmosphere in the shop didn't help, or maybe it did, depending on the definition of help. Bondage gear everywhere, faceless mannequins in leather masks that made them look like sexy aliens, the pair of attractive young clerks, both with facial piercings and funky haircuts. The guy was eying Nick, and she was pretty sure the girl was too, but was also checking her out. Even the somewhat claustrophobic space with the barred windows and the smell of rubber and leather—it all conspired to make her aware of the clips distending her nipples, drawing them out to tortured, exquisitely sensitive peaks.

Was that why the girl was staring at her? Could she tell that Selene had clips on her nipples and a great well of moisture between her legs, making her move as if she carried a heavy weight with her pelvis?

Without thinking about it, Selene ran one hand lightly over her nipple, shuddered at the sensation. She shuddered in a different way when she realized what she'd done. But they were alone in the store except for the clerks. The male clerk, she suspected, wouldn't have noticed boobs if they were on fire and waving under his nose, not with Nick and his fine ass in the room anyway, and the female one just gave her a nod and a mischievous grin, as if to say, *Glad you're having a good night.*

Emboldened, she grabbed Nick's arm. "Let's look at the toys!"

He laughed and said, "Patience, little girl," and made a show of allowing himself to be dragged to the display case, but from his smile, and more importantly the impressive bulge at the crotch of his khakis, she could tell he was into it. "I'm looking for nipple toys for the lady," he said grandly.

The female clerk, grinning knowingly, pulled out an array of nipple clips and spread them on the glass countertop. Square ones that operated like a vise. Ones with an elaborately engineered design that, the young woman explained, as casually as if comparing the advantages of two different sets of speakers, allowed a very firm grip so you could hang weights from them or use them as tie-down points for bondage. "And of course there are the alligator clips," she said, displaying something that looked for all the world like small versions of the toothy clamps on the end of a jumper cable. They looked like they could draw blood.

Selene felt her eyes widening as she stared at them, trying to imagine how that level of pain on her delicate nipples could be pleasurable. Her grip on Nick's hand tightened. "Not for you." Nick stroked her bare arm reassuringly, as one would pet a frightened cat. "Not yet, maybe not ever. I wouldn't want to risk spoiling those lovely nipples. No, what I want for the lady is something lighter. Tweezer clips, or something more like this one..."

He reached inside her bodice, and for a second Selene feared, or hoped, or both—her pussy hoped; the rest of her was fiercely undecided—he was going to pop her breast out of its confinement. It was so close to spilling over the top of the corset anyway...

Instead, he pulled off the earring-like clip to show to the clerk.

She had about a half-second of indignation.

It drowned in a flood of sensation—hot pain as blood rushed where it had long been denied, followed by hotter pleasure as waves of arousal shot from her liberated but still-aching nipple. Sensations flooded her brain as well, threatening to short-circuit it—Nick's casual possessiveness, the near exposure, the behavior that skirted the line of completely inappropriate, yet seemed all right in a late-night sex shop with the male clerk's eyes devouring Nick and the woman's devouring them both.

It was all too much.

Her hips swayed forward, and her pussy clenched around nothing, and Nick's dangerous fingers found their way back inside her bodice again, to brush the throbbing nipple as he whispered, "It's all right, Selene. You may come."

And, face flaming, she did, knowing that both Nick's eyes and those of the pretty little clerk were devouring her pleasure, and the young guy was probably getting a vicarious kick out of the casual display of dominance and maybe wishing it was him instead of her.

They came away from Eros with a set of delicate tweezer clamps with bells on them and a slightly sturdier set connected with a chain, as well as a new dildo and butt plug for her, and a toy for Nick that made her giggle with nervous glee—a paddle that left an impression of the word NAUGHTY on the spankee's ass. It looked like it might really sting, but there was something so tongue-in-cheek about it, so playful, that she was more charmed than anxious.

The threatened rains came on the way back to Nick's car, dancing in to the accompaniment of thunder and lightning. "I love sex during thunderstorms," she told him as they poured their drenched selves into the car.

"Funny," Nick said, pulling her almost out of the seat with his kiss. "So do I."

Chapter Seventeen

Of course there were no parking spaces near Nick's place. By the time they'd run two blocks, squealing with glee at particularly bright lightning bolts and occasionally stopping to kiss because they were going to get soaked one way or the other anyway, and Nick fumbled with the complicated series of locks on the outside door of his building, Selene was drowning in drenched silk and soggy poly satin, and Nick's khakis had soaked up enough water to irrigate Arizona. She kicked off her sodden shoes as soon as she walked in the door, felt her slick bare feet squelch against the hardwood floor.

They left streams of water behind them as they ran up the stairs, laughing all the way.

They were still laughing when Nick, neglecting his own clothes for the moment, pulled down her skirt, letting it fall into a puddle on the floor. "I want you naked," he said, fumbling with the wet lacings of her pseudocorset. "Naked and slick like a water goddess."

Because the warmth of his breath made her shiver, because her nipples were still swollen and aching, echoing her swollen, aching clit—and because the pseudocorset, not the most comfortable garment to begin with, now felt like she was wearing a boned wetsuit—she took pity on him and, while he was still working on the lacing, she liberated herself using the hidden zipper in the back.

For a second, or an hour, he stared at her reverently in a dim room strobed by lightning flashes. "A water goddess," he repeated, reaching out to stroke between her breasts and down her torso. "Pearl skin and mermaid hair."

"Mermaid hair?" she sputtered. "Is that a poetic way of saying my hair's a disaster?"

"Your hair style's a disaster. Your hair is glorious, all damp and curly. And your skin... I want to lick those rain drops right off you."

"Why don't you?" she purred. Partly because she liked the idea, partly because the way Nick was talking sounded perilously romantic.

He didn't mean it that way, she told herself, or maybe he did in this rain-soaked moment with lightning flashes illuminating the room.

Nick followed up his words with delicious, distracting action. He came around behind her, lifted her sodden curls and traced a rivulet of water down her spine with his tongue. Worrying about the future was *definitely* overrated when a gorgeous man was doing something like that to her. This relationship might grow into something more than sex or it might not, but now, she'd enjoy the sex.

The bag of toys sat neglected in the foyer as they licked and nibbled and stroked the rain from each other's skin, tasting the lightning that trembled inside them. But as the storm picked up—the rain drumming like Niagara Falls, violent thunder following right on the heels of white-as-day lightning—Nick fumbled in the bag just long enough to open the new box of condoms, then bent her over the couch. "This way, we can both watch the storm out the window while we make love." His voice was low and intimate in her ear.

Too low. Too intimate. Too scary, and not the roller-coaster scary of his evil-dom voice. She could fall for a man who wanted to watch lightning while they made love.

He'd never said "make love" to her before. Must be the storm getting to them both.

"Let's try the tweezer clips while we fuck," Selene

suggested, maybe a bit too brightly and eagerly. Nick hesitated a second, his blue eyes dark and stormy.

Then he grinned. "Now why didn't I think of that?"

Nick's hands were hot on her breasts, the clips and the chain between them delightfully cool. Selene almost regretted the suggestion as he adjusted the clamps on nipples already tender from the jewelry she'd worn earlier. The weight, when he let go, was startling, tugging at her sensitive nipples painfully.

When he bent her over the leather sofa again and positioned himself behind her, though, the sensation changed. Just as painful in some ways, but it made her more aware of the cool, smooth leather, of the hard heat of Nick's body and his hands firmly grasping her hips, of her own arousal.

He thrust into her. The movement jarred the clips, tugged on the chain, but now the pain mingled with pleasure and was good. No, great.

With each thrust, her need built. The thunder and lightning added to the sensation, making her head swim, making her body thrum.

"Edge," she gasped, although Nick hadn't actually said anything about telling him when she was about to come. It just felt right.

"Good girl." Supporting himself with his strong thighs only, he slipped one hand between her legs, used the other to yank on the chain between the tweezer clips.

Selene exploded like the sky overhead, and Nick was close behind.

Then a hot shower, a glass of wine, and round two, because the storm's unabated force was still making Selene's clit quiver.

She refused to let herself consider whether emotion might have anything to do with that quivering.

The sound of a ringing phone woke them. Drowsy, lulled by

the sound of rain still falling on the roof, by memories of last night's sex and by Selene curled against him, Nick was inclined to make sure Selene let voice mail get it while he got on to the far more important business of discovering just how tender Selene's nipples were this morning.

One good suckle and she began to moan. Pretty tender indeed. He gave a light slap, just enough to make the soft but firm flesh jiggle enticingly. "Hey!" she exclaimed, not sounding upset. "Is that fair?"

He was about to expound on the meaninglessness of the concept of fair in the context of their peculiar relationship when the answering machine began to spew forth a message.

"Selene? Please pick up if you're there. Please. This is Natalie, and I need you to get a message to Nick…"

At the sound of Natalie's voice—at the edge of tension, even fear in it—Nick froze.

Selene pushed him off her and in the general direction of the phone. He grabbed it before Natalie had gotten much further. "This is Nick, honey. What's up?"

A sob, quickly suppressed. "I've screwed up. I thought I wanted this. I really did. I do want it, but not like this. I've given Master everything, and he still wants more." Another sob. "And when your new girl called like I was some kind of role model, I just knew… I've been trying to call, but it took a while to get permission. I guess I'm not a slave. Not the way Master wants. I don't know if I can do this, and I just wanted to talk to you. I'm so confused."

"What do you need? Try to stay calm." Selene had picked up the other line, her voice calm and soothing. For the first time ever, Nick was glad that the cell reception was iffy enough in his condo that he'd kept a landline.

Natalie drew a deep breath. "Are you Selene? You don't sound…"

"Yeah, it's Selene. Long story. Are you in danger? Can you

get to a safe place?"

Another deep breath, the kind that was definitely holding back the urge to fall to pieces. "I don't know. I don't think I'm in physical danger, but I'm in way over my head. I'm scared, I'm losing my mind and I can't leave. I don't have a car. I don't even have a license anymore. I don't know anyone up here except for Master, and he's not going to let me go, and we're in the middle of fucking nowhere. I'd try walking to town, but it's six miles, and my only shoes have five-inch heels."

"What? You had fifty pairs of shoes, and most of them were flats."

"He threw them away when I moved up. He wants me either barefoot or in really high heels. Same with most of my clothes. The people in the grocery store must think I'm a hooker. It's probably good I don't get to go out too often."

The professional tone in Selene's voice cracked. "He threw out your shoes and clothes? Girlfriend, that's not quite like killing your cat, but it's pretty high on the seven-warning-signs-that-you-should-run list."

Natalie laughed bitterly. "Someone should have sent me that list before I hooked up with Master."

"We tried," Nick said. "We all tried. I know I did, and I know Betsy did too."

"But it was what he wanted. I tried to give him everything. I tried. I tried to do the right thing. But I'm a failure. I don't know if I can live this way. I know I should be able to if I'm a real slave, but I guess I'm not. I've failed him, but he won't let me go. Says he's going to make it work, but I can't take it. I don't *want* to take it. I know that's not my choice anymore, but I don't know…"

"Can't you talk with him?" Nick asked, trying frantically to put the concepts into terms that Natalie could accept. "Explain it's too much, too soon, see how some of the rules might be modified?"

"I've tried. He'll let me talk, but he does what he wants to anyway. All it does is prove to him that I need more discipline, which I suppose I do."

"Do we need to get you out today?" Selene asked. Nick felt a thrill he couldn't quite place at Selene's assumption of *we*.

"He won't harm me. I'm his property, and he values me. I don't know why I called. I need this. It's what I always wanted, isn't it? I'm just having a bad day. Lonely, I guess. It just gets so boring sometimes stuck in the house by myself, and when Master gave me permission to call Selene..."

"Stuck in the house?" Nick had to ask, although he suspected what the answer would be.

"He's eased up," she said. "For a while, I was locked in the closet with a camping potty when he wasn't home, but he decided I needed to start doing housework and besides I was getting too fat and soft because I wasn't moving around enough. But I can't go outside without him."

Yup, that was what Natalie had always wanted, being half house pet, half object.

"Yes, you can!" Selene said, her voice a little strident. "You made the choice to follow his rules. You can make the choice not to follow them or to leave. That's in your hands. It's always in your hands."

"No, it's not," Natalie said quietly. "Not anymore. I gave that up. The last choice I made was to be with Master. You don't understand, do you, Selene? This is the real deal. I'm property. No rights, no privileges. The only reason he can't just kill me is that he wouldn't want to deal with the consequences. This isn't role-play, and at the moment, it's not fun, but it's my life. That's why I had to call you, to say to listen to Alison when she says to take your time and figure out what you really want and need, because this isn't for everyone."

Natalie took a deep, sobbing breath, then went on. "Nick...I miss you. You might not have been the right master for me, but you're a great guy. I just wanted to say that. And Selene, I don't know if you're really as much of a newbie as you came off as in your message, but in any case, you've got one of the good doms. Hold on to him because there are a lot of ass..." Suddenly Natalie's tone changed completely. "Slave must go now. Slave's master is home. Good-bye, Selene, and remember what this girl told you. This girl would love to chat again sometime when her master permits."

The phone went silent.

"Oh shit." Nick buried his head in his hands. "She is *so* in danger, whether she can admit it or not. What do we do now?"

Selene walked in from the other room and put her hand on his shoulder. "That's the suck. We can't do anything yet except worry and try to keep in touch. She hasn't actually asked us to help. She's not happy, but she's still trying to make it work, although I can't tell if that's because she wants to or because she's scared not to."

"With her, it could be the same thing. Natalie...well, you heard her. She's not dumb in the usual sense, and I don't know that she's mentally ill, but she's extreme. Hardcore. She wants to give her all to someone."

"Maybe it would be all right with someone who'd take good care of her, but this guy sounds like a prime grade-A asshole. I see what you meant about a sex nun. Only she's like Sister Mary Fruitbat who thinks she's seen Jesus on a taco shell."

Guilt and regret washed over him, leaving him queasy. He'd tried, or thought he'd tried, but his efforts hadn't been good enough. If Natalie destroyed herself or let this still-nameless so-called master destroy her, would it be his fault? She'd been willing to give him control of every aspect of her life.

What if he'd taken it, then made her take some of it back? Pushed her but in ways that would have been healthy for her? Pushed her to get back into doing photography instead of contenting herself with being a model? Made her get some counseling and figure out if she really wanted the complete surrender she thought she craved or if she was running away from something—responsibility, adulthood, mortality?

Could he have turned her around when they were together?

Could he do so now, if he had the chance?

And should he? It would wreck the fun he was having with Selene, but they were friends and play partners, in lust, not love. If Natalie needed him, if he could help the woman he'd loved and lost, wasn't that more important than hot monkey sex with someone who, with her good looks, sexual curiosity and level head, could find another playmate at the drop of a hint?

Selene sat on the bed and snuggled next to him. Her body was soft and delicious and should have been tempting, but when he pulled her closer, it was more to enjoy the comforting contact.

"Besides," Selene added, breaking into his reverie, "we're still not sure where she is, so even if we're convinced she needs rescuing, we can't just sweep in and do it. We have to wait for her, and that sucks."

"Sure does."

Damn, he needed to stop thinking, needed a distraction. He pulled Selene down onto his lap and began to spank her idly. Focusing on her lovely ass under his hand, the curve of her spine, her brown curls still wildly tangled from the rain, spread out on her back and the bed, let him breathe again.

At first, she was obviously going along with him for the same reason he'd started it—because it was better than worrying about a situation they couldn't affect. After a while she softened and relaxed into it. Her ass started to rise up to meet his hand, and her yips were punctuated with gasps. "Harder, Nick," she begged. "And then let's try out that new butt plug. I need to stop thinking."

Nick couldn't agree more. "You get the butt plug; then I get your mouth on my cock."

Chapter Eighteen

For a few weeks, Natalie remained as absent as she had been before the bizarre phone call.

And for a few weeks, Nick managed to believe that he wasn't all that worried about her. Concerned, sure, but as Selene had said, since Natalie hadn't let him know where she was or what she needed in the way of help, there wasn't much he could do.

By dint of spending a day repeating it to himself until it sounded true, he convinced himself that while she'd gotten herself into a situation most people wouldn't like, it might work out for her in the long run. She longed to give absolute submission, after all, had wanted it enough she'd left him to find someone who wanted to take complete control.

Actually being in that situation, though, must require a huge adjustment, and it wasn't surprising she'd have days when it seemed like she couldn't handle it.

After work, it was easy not to think about Natalie. Without ever discussing it, he and Selene had fallen into a pattern of getting together most evenings, except when Selene needed time for homework. Their explorations of BDSM, dominance and submission pretty much wore him out, let him sleep without waking in the night wondering if Natalie was okay.

During the workday, he threw himself into the latest project with a vigor and enthusiasm that he himself recognized as avoidance. Selene's school was too far from his office to grab lunch with her regularly—only on Tuesdays did her class schedule allow her to meet up with him. But he made a point of going out with his coworkers when he could.

He kept telling himself that it was just to get away from his desk, from work that could otherwise eat his brain completely. It was healthy to see the sun occasionally rather than his cubicle walls and his computer screen, good to talk to his colleagues about something other than the project—or even to talk to them about the project over halfway decent Thai food instead of in the office.

And good, he reasoned, to avoid the temptation to spend his lunch hour sending Selene the sort of text messages that would at best leave them both distracted all afternoon and at worst eventually get one or both of them in trouble at work. The kind that directed her to go into the bathroom and play with herself but not come, or to take a picture of her pussy with her phone and send it to him, or to do a little striptease in an empty classroom so she ended up panty-free, not trying to let others see her but not caring if they did, either.

Okay, he wouldn't really ask her to do that quite so publicly. But that didn't mean he wouldn't threaten her with it.

Yeah, he had it bad. He was getting turned on just thinking about naughty text messages. Not even writing them, just pondering what to write. Then again, Selene had that effect on him. She didn't need to be doing anything to him to make him hard; she just needed to respond to his verbal banter and he'd want her on the spot.

He needed to remind himself there was life besides work and kinky sex. Remind himself that there was life beyond Selene, Selene's curves, Selene's insatiable curiosity and willingness to try just about anything once, Selene's sexuality. That there were people in his life other than her.

Selene was the one who brought up another theory. "You actually went to lunch with *Craig* today?" she asked, her face incredulous and a little concerned.

"A group of people that included Craig. I was feeling

restless, needed to get out."

"Was it a really good lunch?"

He shrugged. "Just the deli. Nothing special."

They were already holding hands across the restaurant table—they were waiting for their sushi—but she covered his hand with her free one and squeezed. "You're worried sick about Natalie." He didn't answer right away, just stared at Selene, wondering why she'd been able to see so quickly what had been hidden to him. Wondering how he could squirm away from things he didn't feel like contemplating when he'd much rather be contemplating a good dinner and the prospect of better-than-good sex.

"What are you thinking?" she finally said.

"What I did to deserve to meet someone who's wise as well as beautiful and sexy? And how I can be sure to keep doing it so you'll stick around."

Unfortunately for him, the wisdom he'd mentioned wasn't derailed by his flattery. She just rolled her eyes and said, "Nice attempt to change the subject, Nick."

"I *was* thinking that...among other things."

"And those other things?"

What he'd been thinking, or more accurately feeling, wasn't the kind of thing he normally admitted to women. At least not to women he was dating, women who preferred to see him as dominant and in control, women he wanted to impress with his self-control.

Selene was stable, though. Sensible. She could handle his imperfections and still want him. Maybe she'd even have a good idea about the situation.

He opened his mouth to speak.

When he'd tried to talk to Natalie about self-doubts and fears, she'd become convinced that she'd failed him, that if she were good enough, submissive enough, loyal enough, he'd be completely confident, one hundred percent dominant male, undiluted by weakness or worry. Or a trace of actual thought, perhaps, but that wasn't the point. The point was he'd blown Natalie's illusions and it had scared and hurt her.

He closed his mouth again.

How could he let Selene know how helpless he felt, how frustrated...how impotent?

She seemed like she'd be able to distinguish between the in-control dom and the human being who didn't always know what to do. But he didn't want to risk blowing her fantasy and destroying her interest in him.

He didn't want to take that chance. At the same time, he couldn't pretend he wasn't concerned about Natalie. She'd think less of him if he didn't worry.

"I'm half tempted to start driving around the North Conway area with a picture of her, asking questions," he finally said. That sounded strong and decisive, or at least tough and ready to take action.

Selene's smile clearly said, *Better to laugh than to cry.* "I understand the temptation. But there's a lot of territory to cover up there, and if it's anything like the area I grew up in, half the roads don't have signs. The post office probably won't give you a street address to go with the PO box, and if she's staying home as much as it sounds like she is, people in the nearest town may not recognize her."

He sighed. Getting hit with the wet haddock of reality was never pleasant, even when it was administered by an attractive woman. "I bet if anyone did recognize her, they'd decide I was a psycho stalker ex-boyfriend and lie. Certainly what I'd do if some stranger came poking around asking questions about a cute female neighbor." He considered his audience for a split second. "Or any neighbor, although I'd be more suspicious if it were a cute female one. If they were asking about the odd mobsterish guy next door, I'd probably think *undercover cop* rather than *crazy ex,* but I'd still put them off until I saw proper ID."

"Would you like me to try calling her again? Who knows if she'll answer or call back, but at least there's a chance...."

"Please."

He knew he should be glad Selene was willing to jump into the breach, willing to take action, but it just served to underscore how little he could do for Natalie.

After he'd helped push her into her current situation.

Craig caught Nick at the coffee shop the next day, before he was awake enough for dodging assholes.

"So, how's it going?" Craig asked in a manner that layered all sorts of swarmy meanings into the simple question. "Haven't seen you"—a slight, significant hesitation—"outside of work lately."

Meaning Kinksters munches and meet-ups, because he and Craig didn't see each other in any other context. He and Selene hadn't been bothering to go. They saw Alison and Garth and some of the other Kinksters socially once in a while, but given the choice between going to a munch and talking about kink and *doing* kink with a beautiful, eager woman, the choice was crystal clear.

"Been busy lately." Nick took a swig of coffee to avoid the temptation to say more.

"Good busy?"

The obvious fishing pushed one button too many. Nick nodded and flashed the best approximation of a shit-eating grin that he could produce with a mouth full of iced latte.

"Ever hear anything from Serena or Serendipity or Serenity or whatever her name was?" It was painfully obvious Craig not only remembered Selene's name but also every detail of his smashingly unsuccessful attempt to flirt with her. "I wasn't sure how committed she was, but I'm kind of surprised I haven't seen her around. Still, I suppose that crowd doesn't suit everyone."

Nick swallowed his coffee and with it the urge to say something along the lines of *I don't think we're really in the same crowd. You're a wannabe, and everyone knows it.*

He couldn't, though, resist the urge to say, "I'll tell Selene tonight that you were asking after her."

Craig made a face like a fish out of water.

Nick's mouth started working before his still-caffeine-deprived brain could stop it. "If she doesn't make me forget anything half so mundane within thirty seconds of seeing her. We're still at that can't-keep-our-hands-off-each-other stage."

This time, the sated grin, unhampered by coffee, was probably obvious enough that everyone looking in his general direction realized Nick McCutcheon was a happy man.

"I've been a bit busy too. Very nice summer and fall. Met a few interesting young ladies and one of them seems to be shaping up promisingly."

Well, the world was full of idiots, and Craig did seem to find playmates easily enough. Keeping them might be another matter, but his smutty talk, dominant posturing and slightly used good looks seemed to work in the short run. People said guys thought with their dicks. The fact that Craig managed to get laid on a regular basis was proof that women weren't immune to the same problem.

"Glad to hear you've met someone. Do she and your wife get along?"

"Very funny."

When he saw the look on Craig's face, Nick wished he'd fought off the urge to gloat.

It wasn't the annoyance at being asked about his wife. Nick expected that. Hell, he deserved that for being deliberately obnoxious. But a grown man shouldn't look that nakedly needy and envious, like a toddler who wanted his brother's toy. At least not in a coffee shop at eight thirty on a Thursday morning.

There was a certain cheap satisfaction in knowing that someone wanted what, or in this case, who, you had, and sometimes when someone was macho-posturing at you, it was impossible to resist the temptation to posture back, bigger and badder. But by rubbing Craig's nose in his own happiness, he'd only made the tension between them worse.

That was the last thing either of them needed, considering they had to work together until the IRS decided it was satisfied with their current project—which, at the rate things were going, might be a long time.

Chapter Nineteen

"So, how are things going?"

As she dried the glasses that Alison handed to her, Selene shrugged. "All right, I guess. School's great, and the contract web work is a lot better than being locked at one company full time. But I don't feel like I'm connecting to anyone except you guys and Nick. Are people in Boston not very friendly?"

"So it's been rumored. Or maybe it has something to do with you getting a new boyfriend so soon after moving here? Like maybe you're a little distracted?"

Selene laughed. "Yeah, Nick's definitely distracting, though he's not exactly a boyfriend."

Before she'd said it, the thought hadn't been disturbing, just the matter-of-fact truth that was easy to accept when she wasn't in Nick's arms. As the words came out, though, she felt like she'd swallowed a stone. She'd been calling him a boyfriend to Molly, not sure how to describe the relationship that wouldn't make Molly's head explode, but that wasn't what he was, was he?

She reminded herself firmly that when she'd gotten in the relationship, she'd been clear she wanted to keep it casual, for all kinds of reasons that still applied.

Besides, even if her feelings had changed, Nick's hadn't.

Alison glanced toward the kitchen door before she answered, a very conspiratorial look accompanied by a smile to match. "So, what would you call him?"

"Hotter than hell?"

"Well, duh," Alison said. "I've been at enough play parties with him to know that."

The wave of jealousy—completely stupid jealousy, since it had to do with a time when she hadn't even known Nick, let alone been dating (or whatever the right word was) him—almost dragged her under. She tried to fight it and mostly succeeded, but apparently not quickly enough to hide it from Alison's quick eyes.

"Are you sure *boyfriend* isn't the right word? Because I saw you turning all green-eyed there, and your eyes are definitely brown."

This time, it was Selene's turn to look at the kitchen door, not to give a sense of *we're all girls together,* but to be sure there was no possibility of Nick walking in on them and overhearing.

"I don't know what he is. With boyfriends, you go to movies and play mini-golf and go grocery shopping and sit around on Sunday morning in your pajamas drinking coffee and reading the *Globe* and argue about whose family you'll see at Thanksgiving. Normal, everyday stuff."

"And with Nick?"

"Mostly we have sex. Amazing sex. Best sex ever. And I wear a collar while I'm doing it and I call him sir, and then I take the collar off and I call him Nick and...then we usually start having sex again anyway. So maybe he's my fuck-buddy or play partner?"

"Lover?" Alison suggested. "That covers the super-hot-sex part."

Selene shook her head, wondering why she was suddenly feeling down about a situation that, until she'd started analyzing it, had seemed pretty much ideal. "Too romantic. We decided going into it that this wasn't a romance. It was about a good time and about me learning about BDSM. No mushy stuff allowed. So to get back to your original question, I guess dom's the right word. But it seems pretty specific, and I think there's more to it than that. I'm just not sure what."

"No mushy stuff, huh?"

"Nick doesn't think it mixes with BDSM."

Alison let loose a very unladylike snort. "Since when?"

Oh hell, that hadn't come out right, had it? Alison and Garth mixed the two just fine, that much was clear, and she certainly didn't want to sound like she was disparaging her new friends' relationship or that Nick was. Especially not when Nick and Garth were so close. "I mean," she backpedaled, "that he doesn't think it works for him. Obviously it does for you and Garth, but Nick doesn't think he can keep the right balance if we get too attached."

Put that way, it made Nick sound like an asshole. "Don't get me wrong," she insisted, carefully setting the last crystal wineglass onto the counter. "I'm not complaining. I was the one who brought it up first, about not getting too serious. I didn't want to get in over my head. This has been such a learning experience for me, but I was scared of getting overwhelmed. I didn't know..."

She stopped and stood there, wringing the dishtowel, unable to continue.

Alison put an arm around Selene's shoulders. "I'm sorry I said anything," she whispered. "Nick seems so happy, and so did you, until I asked."

It took Selene a while to corral her wild thoughts and force them into some kind of reasonable order. "It is going well. Too well. Do you know how hard it is not to fall in love with such a great guy when you're having this much fun?"

"Yeah, I do," Alison said. "I was convinced when I was first involved with Garth that a real master would never fall in love with a slave—I'd read too much bad erotica, I guess—and at the same time, I'm human. I still have pride. Didn't want to be the pathetic girl who fell in love with someone who'd never love her."

"So what happened?" Selene could feel her eyes get wide. What woman didn't like a good love story, especially one that involved hot, taboo sex?

Alison laughed. "Basically he kidnapped me up to Maine in the middle of winter—with my enthusiastic consent, of course, but it was still the middle of nowhere, with nothing much to do other than eat, sleep and have sex—and alternately beat and fucked me until my brain and my pride melted, and I admitted I was madly in love."

"And?" She pretty much knew what the punch line was. It was written all over Garth's face every time he looked at his wife and the air of good-humored reserve he usually wore dissolved into complete and unabashed adoration.

"He said something along the lines of, 'Thank God!' and apologized for not telling me how he felt sooner, but he'd wanted to force me to admit what I was feeling, at least to myself, before he did. He didn't quite say that it would have been too embarrassing to pour out his heart to someone—his slave, no less, whose role was to act like he was God—and have her be all 'meh, that's nice', but I could tell it was what he'd been scared of. And then he asked if I'd wear his collar permanently. When I said yes, he proposed."

Selene shivered with pleasurable envy. Happy endings always made her feel that way, delighted for the people enjoying them but also wishing for her own someday.

Once she figured out what her version of a happy ending would be—a cuddly, supportive husband, a harshly erotic master, or someone in between, someone who could slip from one role to the other as mood demanded.

"I can't exactly do that to Nick," she said, smiling but only half-joking.

And if she could lock him up and have sex with him until his brains ran out his ears, could she actually trust anything he said? Or would he be doing to her what she'd done to Will? Saying what she needed to hear, making her happy because it seemed like the right thing to do.

Garth and Nick were doing complex things on the grill involving pineapple, bananas and some sort of rum-laced marinade. Ideally—Nick had glanced at the recipe, which was something Garth rarely deigned to do—the fruit should have soaked beforehand and then patted dry, but Garth had forgotten that step and was drizzling the marinade on as they went. It kept threatening to catch fire, not an uncommon occurrence when grilling with Garth. Meticulous about safety in some areas, he was like an unattended small boy around flame.

Over the sound of sizzling, Garth said, "Selene's good for you, Nick. Try not to fuck it up."

"I don't plan to, this time. We're keeping it light and having a great time." He'd wanted to convey some mixture of *drop it* and *if you have actual advice, I could use some.*

Things were going great with Selene. He just didn't know where they were going or where he wanted them to go—other than bed. How the hell did you figure something like that out when you'd gone into things resolved to keep it casual? He didn't want to get into some deep talk with her only to find she wasn't ready for anything serious, or maybe he really wasn't. But he didn't want to ignore the whole question, because that was a bad idea too. He glanced at Garth, hoping he'd either say something profound or forget the line of conversation.

Garth flipped the pineapple rings, then stared at the sear marks admiringly before he responded. "Selene's not Natalie, and probably the best way to screw things up with her is to forget that. Hey, hit these with the sauce."

When the sauce dripped and flared, he'd never been so glad for Garth's fondness for dangerous cooking.

It wasn't that Garth was wrong. It was that Nick wasn't ready to consider the implications of what Garth had just said. Be careful what you wish for. He'd wanted profound words of wisdom—but he really hadn't.

The grill flare-up was conveniently timed.

"I have an idea," Nick said as they flailed at the flaming fruit. "I'll go to the store for ice cream. And you can explain to Alison why the fire department's on its way."

The fire department didn't need to be summoned, and butterscotch-swirl ice cream topped with cooked-down rum sauce and the few surviving bits of fruit proved a more than satisfactory dessert. Nick forgot the conversation with Garth in a wash of good food, a glass of dessert wine and the pleasure of sitting in the screen room with Selene, apparently taking a cue from Alison, sitting at his feet. Not kneeling or anything, just sitting cross-legged, casually, leaning against his bare leg. He couldn't tell if in her mind it was submissive or just comfortable, and while he planned to ask her later, he didn't see that one answer was more "right" than the other. Either way, he still got to enjoy the pleasure of her soft brown hair against his thigh, her hand casually tucked around his calf. He got to stroke and occasionally tug at her hair, got to glance down and get a lovely view of her cleavage and gloat to himself, *Mine! All mine!*

Yeah, life was good.

At least it was until Selene's cell phone rang with a ringtone he'd never heard before. Aretha Franklin singing "Rescue Me".

If that hadn't made it obvious, the look on Selene's face and the speed with which she excused herself to go outside with her phone did.

Nick's body tightened. A rush of adrenaline pumped

through him, readying him for action, whatever action might be useful. At the same time, the lovely meal formed an uneasy lump in his stomach and the sip of wine he'd just taken soured in his mouth.

Quietly, he excused himself as well and followed Selene. Did his best not to hover over her, did his best not to eavesdrop. Failed on both counts. But pacing up and down the back deck helped the queasiness and the jumpy urge to do something even if it was wrong.

The call took only a couple of minutes, but it seemed he paced for hours in the summer dusk while Selene made notes on a piece of scrap paper from her purse and occasionally made soothing noises into the phone.

Finally, Selene folded her phone back up, came to him, and buried her head against his chest. Nothing sexual there, just a creature seeking warmth and comfort, and he gave it back in the same spirit.

"She's ready," Selene said at last. "I'm not sure what the last straw was. She was having trouble being coherent enough to give me directions, but she's ready. And apparently he's not coming home tonight. Something about teaching her to appreciate him, but it's convenient for us." She pulled away then, and Nick saw resoluteness in her face, focus. Zeal, even.

As Selene left a phone message warning her boss at the temp job that she was sick and would most likely miss work the next day, Nick went to make excuses to their hosts.

It was no surprise that Garth and Alison both immediately offered to help.

Nick flailed, not answering immediately. His instincts told him no, that this was his job, but he was pretty sure that was his inner caveman talking, or maybe his guilty conscience, not anything reasonable. "Ask Selene," he finally said. "She's the professional here. I'm just the muscle."

"Thanks, but we need stealth and speed. I don't trust that

this guy won't come back, so the sooner we get on the road…"

Garth handed Nick his car keys. "Take the Denali. There's room for her stuff, and room for people to stretch out in the back and nap. It's going to be a long night."

Garth ran out to get large iced coffees from the nearest Dunkin' Donuts while Alison raided her closet for flip-flops and clothes for Natalie. Fifteen minutes later they were on the road in Garth's big navy blue Denali, heading toward New Hampshire.

Nick fidgeted in his seat, wishing he hadn't had that last glass of wine. At the moment, Selene was behind the wheel, but if he could focus on driving, he'd have some distraction from the ugly fears in his head.

What if the guy came back?

What if they were too late?

Chapter Twenty

Silence surrounded them like a pall as they headed north. Usually Selene and Nick had no trouble bantering about sex, talking about life in general, but Selene found she didn't have the heart for casual chatting and certainly not for sexual innuendo, and while Nick kept his hand on her thigh as she drove, resting it at the line where skirt and skin met a few inches above her knees, it didn't seem to burn into her skin like it usually did.

She didn't know if he'd shut down that channel of fierce, erotic possession between them in the face of Natalie's troubles or if she was just too anxious to feel it.

Had Natalie been quivering with excitement and anticipation and the thrill of a new relationship when she made this trip the first time, followed the long, dull snake of Route 95 onto New Hampshire Route 4? She must have been, since she'd been going to move in with the master of her dreams.

Who turned out to be the creep of her nightmares.

Selene had had her own fantasies of late, not the stock harem girl or barely-clad-slave-girl-with-big-brawny-mercenary fantasies that had haunted her since before she had a clear idea what the barely clad couple might be up to.

Very specific fantasies involving a tasteful collar like Alison's, a place at Nick's feet, calling him Master and obeying him not as a game but for real. She saw herself more like Alison than O in *The Story of O*, still having a career but submitting, serving and enjoying regular floggings, spankings, bondage and all the other hot games with pleasure and pain, control and release, to which she'd become addicted since meeting Nick. Nick's, full-time and forever.

Suddenly those fantasies seemed scarier than they had before.

Oh, they'd always seemed scary, but in the roller-coaster way, not the serial-killer way.

Now, thinking of that vibrant, beautiful girl in Nick's photographs and the broken, defeated woman she'd heard on the phone, they just seemed creepy, not quite suicidal but akin to morbid, depressed fantasies of attending your own funeral and seeing who bothered to show up.

The fact that she knew Nick was nothing like Natalie's asshole only made it so much better.

She'd gotten lucky, meeting him.

As she drove, she stole occasional glances at his pensive profile, his gaze locked out on the dull scenery off the highway. Yeah, lucky to be sure. And that had already been putting her in a quandary because she was starting to care far more than he'd want her to.

If on top of that she became nervous about playing, needed to pull back from the control games and the rougher sex for a while, would he still want her, or would he drift away?

When they got off the highway, the little town at the exit was black and quiet except for the flickering light of televisions in a few windows and a cluster of older teens hanging out in the parking lot of a blessedly still-open convenience store.

Even more blessedly, the woman behind the counter actually had some notion where Chapman's Township was, because the GPS didn't. Between Natalie's somewhat garbled directions, the clerk's advice and a map detailed enough to show the back roads, they were able to piece together what looked like a viable route. Nick didn't know this part of New Hampshire well, but he'd been to North Conway several times, which was better than Selene could say, so she let him take the wheel.

In their rush, they hadn't grabbed Nick's iPod out of his car, and the few CDs floating around the SUV were Baroque classics too mellow for a tense night drive. Selene fiddled with the radio until she found a station that came in halfway decently on the mountain roads.

Predictably, it was country. "Reminds me of home," she muttered. That got them onto the subject of radio stations and from there to music in general, the good, the bad and the just plain wacky.

Somewhere along the line, Nick exclaimed, "I had no idea you liked Freezepop too!"

Selene said, "I think the whole 'which bands do you like?' conversation was one we skipped in favor of you spanking me or introducing me to butt plugs or something. Not," she added quickly, "that that's a problem. Just an observation."

"I hope it's not a problem. Because when this mess is settled and Nat's safe somewhere—and we've had some sleep—I'll want to take the paddle to your sweet ass until it's pink and tender and telling the world just how naughty you are, and then see if you're ready for a bigger butt plug. I do love fucking you when you've got something in your ass. It makes you even tighter, and you get so wild..."

"Nick, I'm not sure..."

He paused, turned to look at her, although he probably couldn't see all that much in the darkness. Suggestions and shadows, just like she could see of him. "I can't believe I just said that," he said. "I mean, with Natalie and everything, I really wasn't thinking about sex. At least I wasn't thinking about it as much as I normally do when we're together. But all you had to do was say the word spanking, and there I was. Hard. And I'm sorry. It's probably inappropriate, but talking about how much I want you seemed better than worrying."

It took Selene a while to answer, a while in which she

squirmed in her seat, shifting her thighs against each other and forcing herself to be honest. "No need to apologize," she finally said. "I feel weird about it too, but I'm wet now. Wet enough that I want to pull over somewhere and beg you to spank me under the stars—and extra points if we attract a state trooper. And I feel really, really shallow. I mean, poor Natalie's in trouble because of kinky sex..."

"Stop right there! Nat's in trouble because I wasn't what she needed, so she hooked up with someone who turned out to be a nutcase. It's not BDSM. It's people."

Her first thought was that he made sense, that vanilla people got into screwed-up, even dangerous relationships too. Violent loons and the people who unfortunately loved them were everywhere, and most of them weren't prettying it up in the guise of consensual kink.

Her second thought, though, was the one she actually articulated. "You can't blame yourself, either. It's obvious to me you loved her. She did what she thought was best for her. She was wrong, and it sucks, and you're doing more than a lot of people would do for an ex."

She snorted, trying to ignore the sinking feeling around her heart as she thought about just how much Nick was doing for this particular ex—this exceptionally hot, slender, flexible, experienced-sub ex. "I can't say I'd go rescue any of my exes like this. Then again, I can't imagine any of them ending up in such a bad situation. Their mistakes are more of the point-and-laugh variety, not the..."

She bit her lip to shut herself up. She didn't want to say *not the life-threatening variety.* Maybe Natalie was exaggerating. A relationship could be miserable and not, strictly speaking, abusive or dangerous.

Maybe this was all part of a clever plan to win Nick back.

Oh, Natalie probably *had* started dating the Guy from Hell after Nick dumped her. Rebounds could be a bitch like that.

First guy out of the gate who talks a halfway good game and suddenly you find yourself in bed with someone who likes NASCAR when you like opera or vice versa, or who still lives in his mom's basement and conveniently forgot to tell you. And sometimes when you're on the rebound, you're even crazy enough to move in with Mr. Not-So-Right and then realize you're stuck living with his unwashed dishes, stinky unneutered ferrets and unresolved Oedipus complex.

But come on, would any woman really move in with someone who'd made it clear he planned to throw out her wardrobe, including her shoes? Hell no. That was a level of weird that would push its way past any amount of good-looking-and-fun-in-bed and scream at you to run, do not walk, and don't look back whatever you do. She *must* be exaggerating, either to get Nick back or simply to get a hand out of an awkward situation.

Selene mentally shook herself and called on her training as a domestic violence counselor. She wasn't being fair to Natalie, and she knew it. Smart women got into stupid relationships all the time—God knows she'd had her share—and sometimes they turned ugly instead of merely embarrassing. There was no reason to think it hadn't happened to Natalie, especially when she'd been looking for a hardcore Master/slave relationship and an overeager would-be slave would probably find it easier than the average woman to wind up with a man who crossed the line between consensual non-consent and dangerous abuse.

Selene understood this. If she doubted, she was reacting to the regret in Nick's voice and that was just borrowing trouble. Of course he'd have some second thoughts about breaking up with someone who then got into a disastrous new relationship. Guilt, maybe regret, possibly wishing that things had gone differently.

But that didn't mean he'd want to get back together with someone who'd been so clearly wrong for him.

At least not if Selene had anything to say about it.

Selene's mental picture of the Domly Dick's home had alternated between a dark, brooding Gothic manor and a crazy mountain man's log cabin, complete with a half-starved hound tied on the front porch, probably next to Natalie. She'd known either one was unrealistic, a cartoon drawn by her brain to distract her from more important and scarier subjects, but the sheer normality of the house threw her for a loop. In the dark, it looked no different from the basic cookie-cutter house you'd see anywhere: white with dark shutters, two-story, probably built in the past few years. The only odd thing about it was that it was several miles from its nearest neighbor, set in a clearing in the woods, when it would have looked more at home in a suburb with a picket fence around it.

At the moment, much to their relief, the driveway was empty. Still, they approached the house cautiously, going around to the back door as Natalie had instructed.

Selene's only mental image of Natalie came from nude photos, so it wasn't such a shock having her open the door naked. And for someone in a Master/slave relationship, bruises, a stainless-steel collar and matching manacles might be a sign things were going great. But the bruises on Natalie's rib cage and face, and especially the black eye, didn't look like the result of anything fun or consensual.

As Natalie hurried them in, Selene saw more disturbing signs. In all the pictures she'd seen, Natalie had been slim and muscular—healthy-looking. Now she was gaunt and flabby at the same time, and her skin tone reminded Selene of mushrooms. The long, fair hair from the photographs was gone, replaced by a badly shaved head with a few haphazard longer chunks. Her scalp looked scarred.

How had such a beautiful woman gone to hell so quickly?

Nick stepped in the door and folded Natalie into his arms,

and Selene found she had to look away. Too much pain on both faces, too much confusion.

She closed the door behind them, not sure what to say.

After a silence that seemed to last for several months, though, she was the first to speak. "Do you have your things together?"

Natalie nodded and pointed to one pathetically small messenger bag. "Everything else is Master's. Derrick's. I have to get used to calling him that. I never have, not even to myself."

"The cuffs and collar?"

"It's an Allen key. I know where it is, but I can't manage the collar myself, and I was too scared that Derrick might..." Natalie took a deep breath and then made the oddest face Selene had ever seen. Despite the seriousness of the situation, Selene couldn't help thinking that if Natalie had been a cartoon character, she'd have been hit by something labeled "Clue by Four".

"No," Natalie admitted. "I couldn't do it. I know it's not working and that what he wants from me is hurting me. I need to leave, and I tried to tell him that and do it all like normal people, but he wasn't having any of it, so I know it has to be like this. But taking the cuffs off myself... I've worn them almost constantly since Master claimed...since Derrick and I first got involved, and when they've needed to come off, he's been the one to do it. I couldn't bring myself to do it, even though I can't exactly leave with them on."

She started to look teary-eyed. Selene reminded herself that Natalie was entitled to be weird under the circumstances, and that if Nick were to believed, she'd been a little weird all along. Calling upon reserves of patience she didn't know she had, she asked, "Where's the key, honey?"

"Derrick's bedroom, in the bedside table. Top of the stairs to the right. I'm not allowed... Oh, the *hell* with it! I have to get past that."

They followed behind Natalie as she stomped up the stairs and into a large but rather grim bedroom with one mirrored wall and a beige carpet that was several years past due for replacement. "Derrick's room?" Nick asked. "You didn't sleep with him?"

"I slept in the closet. Once or twice he let me sleep at the foot of the bed, as a treat."

"Guy's a fool," was all Nick had to say as he got to work on taking off the collar and manacles.

Selene had to look away so she didn't start crying.

What was the point of being with someone if you couldn't snuggle at night?

And would she sink to that point if she weren't careful, that point where she'd sleep in the closet because someone told her to?

Nick seemed to know what she was thinking. He turned around, shook his head at Selene and said, "Don't worry. No closets or floors. I like being able to reach out and touch you."

"Besides, I'd kick your ass from here to Chicago if you suggested it. Closets are for clothes. And repressed people, but most of them are trying to get out."

Natalie looked from Nick to Selene, her expression scandalized but reluctantly entertained.

"Clothes," Selene said, handing over what Alison had grabbed in those frantic fifteen minutes. "I remember you saying you didn't have much anymore."

Natalie looked at the little bundle of clothes and the pair of flip-flops. Her lower lip began to quiver. "Alison... Does Alison know how badly I've fucked up?"

"No, hon," Nick reassured her. "She knows how badly Derrick did."

"We were at her house when you called."

"You were at Master Garth's? So he knows too?" She began

to cry in earnest. "I'm a failure as a slave, and no one will ever speak to me again because I betrayed my master. Maybe I'm better off staying with Master and trying harder to be what he wants. I..."

"Oh, snap out of it! I'd slap your face like they do to hysterical women in old movies, but you might like it."

Natalie blinked away her tears and stared first at Selene, and then at Nick. "Are you sure she's a slave?" she asked her former lover.

"I'm not a slave," Selene said blithely, sounding rather more sure than she was on that complex question. "Bottom definitely, submissive with Nick, but not a slave. But even if I was one, I'd be tempted to slap you silly right now, which isn't fair to you. It's natural to have doubts and fears when you leave an abusive relationship. Probably more when you'd voluntarily put a lot of your choices into his hands before things got ugly. But it's after midnight and we have a three-hour drive ahead of us. Put some clothes on, and let's get you the hell out of Dodge before Derrick gets home. Once you're away from here and have a few days in a bed, wearing clothes and generally acting like a human being again, you'll start thinking more clearly, and then you can start working through things. For now, we need to move."

Natalie blinked twice, owl-like, and obediently began putting on the shorts and T-shirt that Alison had provided. Petite though Alison was, they hung on Natalie's skinny frame.

Once the clothes were on, her expression changed subtly. She still looked as lost and confused and sad as Selene would expect under the circumstances. But she looked like a lost, sad, confused woman, not a kicked puppy who was likely to wag her tail at the one who'd kicked her.

They were walking out the door when they heard the sound of a truck coming up the road. Natalie cursed. "Quick! That's got to be him! He said he was going to be out most of the night, but sometimes he'd lie just to get me to screw up. What are we..."

Nick grinned. "Selene, you grew up in the country. Ever do any off-roading?"

At the grin and at the teenage memories it unleashed, the heart-pounding panic changed into an endorphin rush. "Sure did. Buckle up, Natalie. Things may get exciting."

With their lights off, they backed out of the driveway and sped up the quiet side road, away from the approaching truck—and from the main road that would take them back to Boston. By the light of the full moon, it was possible to see the road winding ahead of them, its twists and turns through the mountains. But where trees blocked the moonlight, it was the kind of dark that brought out primitive fears of monsters and things with saber teeth. That just made it more fun.

By the dim dashboard light, Selene tried to make out the map. "Right turn, just a ways ahead." Nick switched on fog lights long enough to make the turn, careening from low-grade pavement to what seemed to be dirt in a way that made Selene wince for the Denali.

Natalie, huddled in the big backseat, was silent except for the occasional yelp. When Selene glanced back, all she could see of the other woman were the whites of her wide, frightened eyes.

Selene was biting back on the urge to whoop with glee.

This was dangerous and crazy and potentially even more dangerous and crazy if Derrick caught them. Sure, this looked like a dead-quiet road, but you never knew who might be heading home from working the late shift. And out in the boonies, there were always deer and other critters—possibly moose or bear this far north—not to mention that the narrow dirt road itself was risky when lit only by moonlight.

Still, her heart raced more with excitement than fear.

She remembered doing this kind of stupid shit when she was a teenager, racing around on the twisting, narrow back roads between Seneca and Keuka Lakes, cutting along the even smaller and bumpier roads through tracts of state land. It wasn't something she'd admit to most people she'd met since leaving Lodi. But she glanced over at Nick and saw he too was having a teenage flashback.

"I thought you grew up in Nashua," she said.

"I did. But you don't have to go very far out of Nashua to be in the middle of nowhere." He hit a bump, and the SUV became momentarily airborne. "Yee-haw!"

"Is he behind us?" Natalie asked. "I can't look!"

Selene looked in the rearview and saw headlights coming over the rise. "Natalie, where does this road go?"

"I don't know. But it looks like there's a place up ahead for hikers to pull off and park. If we go in there and keep the lights off and wait, he'll miss us. Figure we headed straight for town and go that way."

Nick grunted his agreement and pulled off into the rutted little spot marked with a trailhead sign. "Looks like we're on the edge of a state park or something."

A vehicle sped past them, going too fast on the dirt road, its lights low, though not entirely off.

"That's his truck," Natalie confirmed, her voice quivering.

By the dim dashboard light, Selene studied the map. "If we turn around and go back to the road we just left and keep heading away from the house, there'll be a left coming up that's an actual road, not a glorified logging trail. If we take that, then a right, then another left onto...it looks like Bear Creek Road...we should be able to get back to what passes for a highway without running into Derrick. I hope."

At that moment, Natalie's phone rang. She apparently hit Ignore, because it stopped, but it started again immediately as if whoever was on the other end—it had to be Derrick—was determined to keep calling until she picked up. She switched it to silent or maybe turned it off, because the ringing stopped. Still she kept staring at it as if it might bite her, trembling, looking like she wanted to answer it but had just enough sense not to.

Finally, she asked them, "Tell me it's okay to litter in a good cause."

Selene, understanding instantly, said, "It's okay. Isn't it, Nick?"

"Sure is. Go for it."

The phone went flying out the window at seventy miles per hour. "Waste of a nice phone," Natalie said, "but I was going to wear down. I know as soon as I talked to him I'd find myself agreeing to anything he said, even if I knew it was the worst thing on earth for me."

"Phones are easy to replace," Nick said. The implied *and you're not* was clear.

After a series of twists and turns on the back roads, they finally felt safe they'd lost Derrick. They hadn't seen headlights behind them for a while. Selene couldn't help half hoping that the moose they'd seen ambling into one dark road behind them had done a public service by having a close encounter with Derrick's truck, though it would be a shame about the moose.

Two hours or so later, after making their way to a state route with an actual number they could find on a map, they passed through a town with an all-night diner. Selene and Nick looked at each other, and groaned, "Coffee."

Nick pulled into the parking lot and he and Selene climbed out. Natalie stayed in the backseat just long enough for Selene to think she'd fallen asleep. Then Nick said, "Come on, Natalie," and she hopped out as if she'd been waiting for permission.

Natalie, looking very small, almost childlike, huddled in the slick red booth, shivering in the air-conditioned chill. She stared at the specials list written on a distant whiteboard without saying a word until Nick said, "Do you want something?"

"May I? Please?"

He took her hand as gently as he would treat the child she resembled. "You don't have to ask, Nats."

She took a deep breath. "It seems like it's been years since I could go into a restaurant and order what I wanted to eat. I know it hasn't been, but it feels weird."

"Good, though, I bet," Selene said.

Natalie shook her head. "Yes and no. Mas...Derrick has some strong opinions about food. Like, he's allergic to tomatoes and potatoes, so they must be bad for everyone. I wasn't allowed to eat sugar because he thought I was getting fat, and slaves can have red meat only from Master's hand. I got used to it, but I tell you, I've dreamed of a burger and fries, and I was always more of a fish and veggies girl before. I could sit here all day just trying to choose between the steak and eggs and a piece of pie."

Selene looked at Natalie's sticklike figure. "That's easy. Both, with hash browns. Not like you can't afford the calories. And tonight's dinner's got to be prime rib and ice cream. Girlfriend, you've got months of deprivation to make up for."

The eastern sky was turning pale with predawn light by the time they finally limped back to Boston, the navy blue SUV grayed out with dust and mud from unpaved roads and badly in need of a trip through a car wash.

"We'll worry about that in the morning. The real morning," Nick declared, and they staggered up the stairs into his condo.

Selene, fighting sleep, went to pull out the sofa bed in the living room for Natalie, but she waved her off. "Just a pillow's fine," she insisted, and both Nick and Selene were too tired to argue. They managed to get her to take a light blanket as well.

Selene figured she planned to crash on the couch, which looked like it would be a comfy bed for someone as small as Natalie. But the last she saw of her, she was curling up on the floor like a dog, nested in the blanket. "Nick, we can't just..."

Nick put his hand on Selene's arm. "It's what she's gotten used to. Maybe what she's comfortable with. Some people feel it's a slave's place." Nick's tone made it pretty clear he didn't agree.

"But she's not..."

Selene stopped herself, suddenly understanding. One of her mom's friends was a painter who'd developed arthritis in her hands. She couldn't hold a brush long anymore, but she painted when she could and did whatever she could to remind herself that she was still an artist. It was who she was, Lila always said, and if she let it go completely, she'd just fade away.

Everyone had something too precious to let go. For Lila, it was painting. For her, it was her work with battered women. For Natalie, it was being a slave. That was her core identity, and she was clinging to it to help her through a rocky time.

It had never occurred to Selene that you could be a slave without a master. Could someone need to submit so badly that it didn't much matter to whom she submitted?

It seemed strange. Maybe it was just as weird to have chosen Nick as a dom without being in love with him, but that was different. Wasn't it? She'd just been trying to learn.

Nick was asleep almost as soon as he hit the pillow.

Selene, on the other hand, lay awake, watching light fill the room and listening to Jamaica Plain bustle to life outside. Dealing with Natalie had shaken her on a deep level, and she wasn't proud of her own behavior. Despite her experience as a domestic violence counselor, she'd slipped into anger with Natalie as much as with Derrick, found herself questioning whether Natalie was "really" abused.

But even if Natalie had wanted a more extreme Master/slave relationship, Derrick had crossed a line into non-consent, into risking her health and safety. When Natalie had tried to confront him within the rules of their particular relationship, he'd refused. Every abused woman started out thinking she wanted to be with her abuser, and many of the ones Selene had worked with in Rochester were, like Natalie, torn between self-preservation and lingering, misplaced loyalty.

So the problem wasn't really that Natalie's situation was ambiguous, but that Selene was having problems being objective. Maybe it was Natalie's past with Nick. Maybe it was the way Natalie's ugly situation seemed like a funhouse mirror of her own wilder fantasies.

What did it all mean for her chosen career, or, for that matter, her relationship with Nick? BDSM wasn't likely to lead her down the same dangerous path it had Natalie, but it could still screw her life up if she wasn't careful.

It might be smarter to run away, to go back to a vanilla world in which the sex might not be as good, but at least the line between right and wrong, play and abuse, consent and rape, was clear.

The problem was, Selene didn't want to run away.

Because while tonight had raised a lot of tough questions about her vocation and her ability to be kinky and still do domestic violence advocacy, it had made one thing painfully clear.

Nick was a genuinely good man, strong and caring and willing to go out on a limb for people he cared about.

And God help her, Selene loved him.

Which was not the thing to figure out on a night when everything she *thought* she'd figured out about herself seemed up in the air.

Chapter Twenty-One

Selene got to Nick's house that night before Nick did. She'd known he'd be a little late at work tonight, but he'd said to meet him in Jamaica Plain. Natalie should be home to let her in. It still seemed weird to think of Natalie being "home", but she'd been crashing on Nick's couch for over a month, temping whenever she could get work. It made sense from an objective point of view. Her mom lived in a small town where work was scarce, and the commute to Boston was too long to justify for a temp job. But in the one-bedroom condo, it wasn't the most convenient arrangement. More often than not lately, Nick had been going to Selene's place.

When they'd been getting together at all. The fall semester had started a few weeks ago, and Selene had thrown herself into her studies, determined to find her way back to her vocation. Between that and the volunteer position she'd taken on at an abuse hotline, their dates had tapered off to once a week or so.

Selene kept telling herself it wasn't a totally bad thing. Okay, it sucked, but it helped keep her cravings for pain and control—and her feelings for Nick—in perspective, as a fun part of her life but not its center, nothing that should derail her work or her emotions.

Most of the time it worked.

Tonight, she was in JP because Kate from upstairs was doing a reading at the bookstore on Centre Street. Everyone from the house was going. And Natalie be damned, tonight she was staying with Nick.

The door was unlocked when she arrived, so Selene breezed right in. Natalie sat folded up on the couch, doing something on her laptop. The laptop, it had turned out, had taken up most of the one small bag she'd had with her when she escaped Derrick. In a rare burst of practicality, she decided that since she'd bought it long before Derrick had claimed it, like everything she owned, as his, she was taking it back.

Natalie emitted a muffled shriek when Selene entered. "Oh my God, I'm sorry. I didn't... Oh, hi, Selene, it's you."

Selene wondered briefly what she was apologizing for. Nice girl, but very weird. Then again, she supposed that after what Natalie had been through, she had a right to be weird, whether or not she'd been a bit odd to start with.

The speed with which she'd shut down the laptop offered a hint. Probably she'd been watching a movie or playing a game or, for all Selene knew or cared, surfing for porn, not job hunting. Selene figured even the most dedicated job hunter had a right to take a break, but Natalie seemed to feel she'd been caught goofing off.

Natalie actually blushed as she unfolded herself from the couch. Like a cat, she could get herself into seemingly impossible positions, and, like a cat, she seemed to find them comfortable. Selene imagined a man would enjoy watching the process, especially considering what Natalie was wearing.

Or wasn't wearing, more to the point—a tiny cotton-knit camisole in a baby blue that brought out her eyes but was too sheer to really hide her nipples, with matching boy-short panties.

Hell, Selene enjoyed the view herself. She wasn't attracted to Natalie, not the way she was to Alison, but other than still being too skinny, Natalie *was* nice to look at. Even the shaved head looked good now that it was a soft fuzz rather than a concentration-camp buzz, as if Natalie was some kind of cutting-edge artist or rock star.

The blush made Selene curious. Natalie always jumped and apologized if she'd been "caught" taking a few minutes for herself, but the blush suggested the other woman had been up to something particularly fun and maybe even frivolous. It was a good sign that she could goof off again. "What are you up to?"

"Got bored. A girl can't job hunt all day, the house is clean, I don't have enough money for retail therapy, and I'm joining the crew for Cambodian tonight, so there was no point in cooking. So I was just... Well, want to see?"

Pleased at the friendly overture and admittedly curious about Natalie's brain-candy choices, Selene nodded. Natalie opened the laptop cover, and the machine sprang back to life.

Selene looked over Natalie's shoulder, blinked slowly. Felt heat flare in the pit of her belly and rise up her body until she was sure not just her cheeks but her entire torso were flaming. "Please tell me that's Photoshopped," she said, looking at the picture of the intricately bound, intricately bruised and battered woman. It wasn't the bruises that bothered her so much as the apparent blood. Bruises could be fun to get, but the model looked like a rope-wrapped road accident.

"Don't tell me Nick hasn't used the singletail on you yet?"

"N...no."

And if that was its effect, he wouldn't be. Selene liked a few bruises, but something that seemed to remove chunks? Thanks, she'd pass. "That's like something out of a costume drama. You know, where the hero's flogged by the evil ship captain? Always kind of turned me on," she admitted, "but not...for real, you know? I always figured that for real, it would hurt like hell in a bad way."

Natalie smiled dreamily. "Oh, you'll love it. It's the most beautiful kind of pain I know. Kind of like being stung by a thousand bees, only erotic. I can't explain it right, because that sounds horrible."

"Yeah, it does. It looks horrible too."

"Too bad they have her tied so you can't see her pussy. I bet she's wet as anything, just off in a world of her own, waiting for her master to use her. I know I would be."

There was something odd in Natalie's manner that Selene couldn't quite put her finger on. She was so dreamy, clearly off in happy fantasyland, putting herself in the place of the bound and whipped woman, who, on second glance, was either a very good actress or was enjoying herself. At the same time, Selene sensed a challenge in her words, a kind of one-upsmanship. Damn it, they both knew Natalie was far more experienced. Natalie's most recent experiences had been seriously nasty, but not all of them had been.

Not the ones with Nick, for instance. Selene knew those would have been wonderful. Nick was very, very good at what he did.

She took another look at the picture. Okay, it was hot in a purely theoretical way, but she was so not ready for that level of pain play yet, if she ever would be. The only time she'd be up for voluntary bloodshed would be if she needed surgery. The ropework, though, fascinated her.

"I like the bondage," she said, surprised to catch such a wistful note in her voice. "It's so pretty with the different colors of rope, and I do like being restrained. We haven't tried anything that elaborate yet," she added. It must take a lot of time to rig someone up like that in a confining but elegant gown of rope that accented the breast and waist so temptingly. Time and attention. How would it feel to be the center of that much focus, that kind of artistry? "I'd like to." She caught the dreamy tone slipping into her voice.

"The fancy stuff's not Nick's favorite thing. He mostly likes simple restraints," Natalie said, as if that settled the matter.

"But if I asked him..."

Natalie's jaw dropped, as if Selene had calmly suggested flying to the moon under her own power. "You can't just ask him for things. Don't you know anything?"

Apparently not, because she had been asking for things—and more often than not, Nick was delighted to try anything she suggested.

"Slaves don't get to ask, except maybe once in a while when we've pleased our master." Selene could hear the capital M. "We exist to please our masters. It's not about us. We get our pleasure from pleasing." She had an evangelical quality to her voice, someone who had Seen the Light™ and wanted to share it with anyone who was willing to listen or didn't get out of the way fast enough. She put one small, bony hand on Selene's arm, very gently. Even though it was warm for September, Natalie's hand was like ice.

"It's all right," Natalie added, and again Selene was reminded of a passionate preacher, except the one actual preacher she knew, Molly, was a lot more discreet about it. "It takes a while to understand it deep in your bones. Learning not to want is the hardest part of being a slave. Because we do need and want. We can't help it; we're human. Slaves just have to learn to fight it, to focus on our higher purpose."

At this point, Selene had to correct the misapprehension. "I've told you before, I'm not a slave," she said, not sure why the admission embarrassed her when it was a simple statement of her truth.

"Oh. Right." The missionary had just been told no, thank you, we're happy with our own religion. "That's different. Perhaps that will be all right for both of you. I thought Nick wanted a slave, but perhaps he's changed. Nothing wrong with just being a sub if that's what you like." Her tone suggested the opposite. "It's good to take the time to figure out what you are, what you and Nick are together. But it's a hard balance. I know he let me go when he started getting too attached. It's hard to be a partner and a sub at the same time, and it almost looks to me that that's what you guys are trying for. Neither fish nor fowl."

189

Selene swallowed a sudden lump in her throat—tears, queasiness, some combination of both.

She and Nick were just friends and play partners, right? She'd known how he felt about love and kink, known this wasn't a forever relationship. She'd thought she was okay with that, really she had.

So why did she feel like a little kid who'd just been told Santa didn't exist?

Then a fierce determination took hold of her.

Relationships were made up of people. They weren't things unto themselves, with inalienable rules of their own beyond those created by the people involved. What hadn't worked for Nick and Natalie might work for Nick and her, because she wasn't Natalie. She already knew that some of the problem with Natalie had been Natalie wanting to be too much the picture-perfect slave, to the point that she stopped being *her*. Well, at least Selene wouldn't need to worry about that particular mistake.

But she did get a bit of a shiver—okay, more than a bit and more like a clench, a surge of heat and wetness—thinking about being more under Nick's control. Not like Natalie's last crazy relationship, but like Alison with Garth, loved but controlled, with status and respect but with rules and rituals to follow.

Alison could answer a lot of her questions, and Selene couldn't imagine her red-haired friend putting the fun into dysfunctional with the same gusto that Natalie could. On the other hand, Natalie was here, and at the moment, Selene's curiosity was piqued enough to risk asking the potentially dumb questions. Natalie might be a bit out there, might have made some mistakes—even before she wound up with a toxic man—but it was important to know what didn't work too, right?

"So," she asked, screwing up her courage, "I'm new to all this. I'm still trying to figure out where I fit, and the idea of being a slave is scary. Sexy but scary."

Natalie smiled like a punk Mona Lisa. "It's supposed to be scary. Giving up your control, your independence, giving all of yourself to a man... If that doesn't scare you, it should."

"Sounds like being in love to me. You give up something of yourself, and it's scary but worth it."

Again that smile. "Like and not like. The scary-but-worth-it part, yes. But it's not giving up something of yourself. It's giving up just about all of it." She shrugged. "Of course, some masters—Nick was like this—will give a lot of it back to you, let you make decisions about everyday stuff that doesn't matter much to them. Not everyone is like Mas...like Derrick, wanting to control every bite you eat, every time you pee, how you think, how you pray. He took it to an extreme that was hurting me. I know that now. But being a slave means someone has the option of that kind of control, and you hope they're careful with it, but they don't have to be. After a while, you can't imagine doing certain things without their permission, including coming. And you have no idea how strong that makes your orgasms." She grinned dreamily, and Selene wondered which master she was thinking of, Nick or Derrick.

"We've played that game." And God, it was hot. A couple of days of directed playing with herself, without orgasm, and when she saw Nick again and he let her come, it was like a nuclear detonation.

"It's not a game. That's the difference. For you, now—for a part-time sub—it's a game. A really great, intense game."

"And how!" Selene laughed, fanning herself, making a joke out of it so she didn't let on how hot the memory was making her, how deliciously moist and open and tender she felt, how much she regretted that Nick wasn't home yet and that it might be in poor taste to drag him off to the bedroom immediately with Natalie there. Not that Natalie had any illusions as to their chastity and propriety, but they'd been trying not to be downright rude about it.

191

"As a sub, you still have the 'fuck you' option. You can always say, 'Fuck you, that's not fun.' Might get into a fight about it, might get 'punished'"—she made air quotes—"but it's not a deal-killer."

"But you can always safe-word if things are going really badly."

"No." Natalie's voice was uncharacteristically firm. "*You* can. A real slave can't. I mean, Nick was nice about saying I should let him know if anything was dangerous, like if my circulation was getting cut off. But that's optional, your owner's choice. Otherwise, you don't get to stop scenes. You can only stop the relationship."

"I'm not sure I understand. Why would you want that setup?" And why would Nick, or any dom, set up rules like that? Control was one thing, but that was way too much responsibility for someone else's life and safety, like having a perpetual toddler. How could the dom ever relax?

"That," Natalie said pityingly, "is because you're not a slave at heart. If you're meant to be a slave, submission isn't a game, isn't something you do in the bedroom when it amuses you both. It's a state of being. You'd hear this and know you'd found your way home."

Half of Selene felt like smacking the smugness out of Natalie's voice, except she might enjoy the smacking. As far as Selene knew, Natalie was straight, but she was bored too and had obviously recovered enough from her ordeal to be horny again.

The other half felt something click in her brain. It was partly anger, the implication that she was somehow lacking, not good enough, *incapable* of being a slave.

And partly recognition that she wasn't nearly as appalled by the concepts Natalie presented as she'd like to be. She'd toyed with the idea of being someone's helpless plaything— treasured property, but property, for most of her adult life. But it didn't seem like a feasible fantasy, too much trust to put in one person. After seeing what had happened to Natalie in her eagerness to fulfill what she seemed to feel was her destiny, talking about it in general terms was damn scary. There were dangerous people out there, and others who might not mean any harm but shouldn't be trusted with the responsibility of a goldfish, let alone another person.

But Selene was weighing the idea of being *Nick's* slave, and that was an entirely different story.

And if that level of yielding was what it took to make their casual relationship into something more committed, she could learn to do it.

"Tell me more," Selene begged.

"I'm not the most articulate," Natalie admitted. "I get too emotional. Let me point you at some websites."

Nick heard a murmur of female voices as he reached the front door. He couldn't make out any words, but it was definitely Selene and Natalie, chatting away.

Good.

There'd been some strain between them. No surprise there, but he was pleasantly surprised there hadn't been more. The ex and the current were bound to be a little judgmental and harsh toward each other, each wondering *what does he see in her?* And they were very different people. Selene, for all her submissiveness in some areas, was strong, a go-getter. Natalie, he realized more than ever, needed to get her act together before she could survive outside "captivity". She could be struck by lightning and turned vanilla as a vanilla bean, and she'd still feel like she needed someone to guide her, help her make decisions.

Maybe they'd be good for each other.

He opened the door as quietly as possible, then stood in the doorway to watch the dark head and the fair bent together.

Over a laptop, he noticed.

Cool. Selene must be helping Natalie job hunt. He'd been hesitant to help much, afraid he'd pull her back into depending on him for too much. Perhaps a woman would be safer, a good example rather than a crutch—especially another submissive woman.

So good to see his women getting along so well.

His women? Ha! Nice thought, but his inner caveman needed to take it easy.

Natalie wasn't his anymore. She still had a place in his heart, though, as a dear friend and someone who'd taught him a lot, including lessons he was pretty sure she'd never meant for him to learn.

Like he was a dominant but not a master, that he loved the sensation of possession and control in the bedroom but didn't want that kind of full-time responsibility over another adult human. Hell, he hadn't even been settled enough to think about owning a pet until recently. Why had he thought owning a slave would work for him?

And Selene wasn't his yet. At least not that either of them had admitted.

But she would be. Sure, they'd both started out talking the no-commitment talk, but he knew by now that he wanted more, and he was pretty sure she did too. He wasn't sure how to define where he saw them going together. Not master and slave, more than playmates and definitely...kinkier...than most lovers. Dom and sub, sure, but there was more to it than that.

He wanted to come home every night and find her on his couch, laughing with a friend or curled up reading. He wanted to wake up next to her every morning. Maybe get a cat, or a big goofy dog if they got a bigger place. Both, even, if the cat and dog could get along.

Wait a minute.

They. Place. Together.

Joint mortgage?

He poked at the idea.

Yeah.

And that, more than anything else, made him realize what was going on.

Good kinky sex could be just good kinky sex, simple and basic and wonderful as that. Waking up together? Well, good sex led to infatuation, which led to wanting to spend more time with your lust object, and he'd been writing it off as that for a while.

But a joint mortgage? That was serious commitment.

If you trusted someone enough to consider that...

Yeah, better face it. Nick was in love.

And he wasn't quite sure how or when to tell her.

Luckily, for the moment, he was off the hook thanks to Natalie's presence.

They still hadn't noticed him. Must be one hell of a conversation. He could only catch a few words—dedication, skills, opportunity. Yup, talking about work, though in a way that was making them both smile a lot.

He coughed, and they looked up. Natalie looked like a deer in the headlights—probably some holdover from life in hell with Derrick. Sitting equals slacking or something.

Selene, on the other hand, looked positively radiant.

"Your lord and master is home, ladies," he announced, expecting Natalie to look bewildered and Selene to giggle.

Natalie did exactly as he expected—she looked as if she wanted to genuflect or something but knew he was teasing and resisted the impulse.

Selene didn't.

Instead, she blushed, a rose-red veil spreading over her cheeks. She dropped her eyes, looked away, but before she did,

195

she let her gaze linger enough to set him smoldering.

Maybe the girls hadn't been talking about job hunting after all.

Or maybe, just maybe, Selene had been contemplating more permanent arrangements as well.

If their plans for the evening hadn't included other people, he would have changed them to include wining, dining, crazy-yet-tender sex and then a deeper conversation than they'd had until now about future plans.

Unfortunately, there was a cast of thousands involved, all planning to meet at the Cambodian place on Centre Street in about twenty minutes.

A cast of thousands that included Natalie, the last person on earth, other than his mom, he'd want anywhere in the vicinity when he and Selene tried to negotiate the tricky terrain of moving from lovers to people in love.

Chapter Twenty-Two

The evening air held a hint of autumn, but it was still warm and soft, scented with honey-sweet alyssum planted in containers scattered around the roof deck. Nick and Selene had the whole triple-decker to themselves tonight. Natalie was at her mom's, Kate and Stephanie were off at another of Kate's readings, this one in Provincetown, and Mr. and Mrs. Figueroa on the first floor had left in the morning for their daughter's in New Jersey.

With no other plans for the evening, and no one who might disturb them, or be disturbed by them, Nick and Selene were planning a pleasant evening in.

Chicken marinated in lemon and basil on the grill, a bright Riesling from Selene's old stomping ground of the Finger Lakes in a glass, nipple clips on her nipples, and their latest sex-toy purchase, a silicone device shaped like two eggs joined at the ends, inside her pussy, sending low waves of lust through her every time she shifted on her knees.

Because she was on her knees at the moment. It would be a few minutes until Nick needed to attend to the chicken, so he was sprawling back in his Adirondack chair and sipping his wine. She had been sitting and sipping too, until about a minute ago, when he'd smiled like a cat and told her what he wanted.

It was good to be alone in the house.

Now she knelt on a seat cushion between his jean-clad legs, her white T-shirt pulled up to expose her clamped breasts, her short, pleated schoolgirl skirt flipped up on itself, tucked into its own waistband to expose her ass and cunt, and Nick's glorious cock was in her mouth. The musky taste of him was a perfect appetizer, salty and rich and a bit like brie, only a thousand times better. With each sloppy, wonderful slide of her mouth along his hard length, Selene could feel herself getting wetter, feel herself clenching around the balls inside her. They were weighted somehow, and with each movement, each clench, they shifted, teasing at her G-spot.

It wasn't enough to bring her off, not by a long shot, but enough to make her pelvis feel heavy with heat and blood, make her clit hard and eager for attention, make the cock in her mouth taste that much better. Add to that the silky feel of his shaft between her lips, the pressure of the tweezer clips on her nipples and the rude joy of being bare-breasted and bare-assed in the open air if not exactly in public, sucking a cock as if she were some kind of back-alley whore (or a naughty, thrill-seeking exhibitionist, which was more like it), and she could feel hot juices slicking her pussy lips and trickling down her thighs as she engulfed his cock, sucking at various rates to offer different sensations.

She swirled her tongue around the head, toying with the sensitive little opening until she tasted his rich, salty pre-come, teasing around the ridge. Used her tongue on the shaft, swirling and licking as if he were made of chocolate ice cream.

No hands, that was the rule tonight, or at least for the moment—he was known to change such rules when the mood struck him. She wasn't very practiced at that, and she let his cock pop out of her mouth a few times, half-gagged herself at others. Her bright rose lipstick was smeared all over Nick, and no doubt all over her face, and she was, to her own embarrassment, drooling.

It didn't matter. Not to her, and not to Nick either, based on the noises he was making, the way he was muttering, "Oh, good girl. Good, good girl. Good, naughty girl. Sucking me so nice," as a constant litany, almost prayerful in its heartfelt, throaty intensity.

She felt his body tensing, his cock twitching as if getting ready to surge and fill her mouth with his come. She looked up, hoping he'd read her gaze and tell her whether to continue. She couldn't imagine that he'd want to stop now, close as he was, but sometimes, she swore, he liked to torture himself as well as her, holding off his own orgasm until he was crazy with need. She'd learned not to make assumptions over which it would be on a given night.

Her answer came in the form of strong hands buried in her hair, moving her, forcing her rhythm.

She felt the pressure as if he touched her between her legs, adding to her excitement. Just as he groaned and filled her mouth with his hot come, he pulled off the nipple clips, sending shockwaves of pleasurable pain surging from her tender nipples through her swollen, bared breasts, shooting down her body into her pussy. She fought against the urge to bite down as she fluttered and clenched on the toy inside her and waves of orgasm washed over her.

"Hope I didn't spoil your appetite with that little snack," Nick said over the rush of blood in her ears. He pulled her up onto his lap, sprawling awkwardly in the Adirondack chair, and cuddled her until they both had enough wits to remember the chicken.

It was a bit overcooked, but neither of them gave a damn.

Especially not after Nick cooled her flaming nipples with ice from the ice bucket and then put the nipple clips back on her.

Especially not after he told her what he intended to do after dinner. "I'm going to tie you up," he said, falsely casual. "Not just the simple ties we've been doing, but a bit of serious ropework. Once you're wrapped up in rope, unable to move, I'm going to paddle you and whip your breasts with the light suede whip, because I know they're already tender and that will make them hurt so beautifully for me. And then I'm going to cane you."

She set down her newly refilled wineglass so abruptly that wine sloshed over the sides.

Then she picked it up again and took a nerve-soothing slug. Criminal way to treat a decent wine, but her nerves were all aquiver with a combination of arousal and anxiety.

Mostly arousal.

"Wow," she said, then collected herself enough to admit, "I'm nervous, but I've been looking forward to trying that. A lot."

"Me too. A lot. I just wanted to wait for the right time, and since we have the place to ourselves tonight…"

"Yay! I like Natalie, but it does kind of put a damper on things when she's in the next room. It's hard enough listening in when you're just the single roommate. It's got to be worse when you're single because your last lover should have come with a warning label."

"I've been concerned about that too," Nick admitted, "but on the other hand, it's nice having Natalie around in some ways."

"I'm sure. She's still running around as close to naked as she possibly can."

As soon as she said it, Selene bit her tongue, wishing she could take back the snark.

For one thing, while you'd normally think a woman wouldn't walk around semi-undressed in front of someone else's lover, their relationship was hardly a standard one. If they weren't precisely sure where they stood, no surprise Natalie was clueless.

And it wasn't like Selene minded Natalie's skimpy outfits most of the time. Hell, she kind of enjoyed them too sometimes. But other times she thought Nick enjoyed them a little too much.

But being snarky at Nick while he was in full-on dominant

mode was asking for trouble.

Interesting trouble, probably; trouble that made her clench up a bit and wiggle in her seat, causing the weighted silicone toy inside her to shift. That, in turn, made her clench a little more.

That toy was evil in the best possible sense of the world. When she'd first tried it, at the recommendation of the cute clerk at Eros, she'd been disappointed. It felt teasingly good, made her achingly aware of her sexual needs, but it wasn't enough to let her come.

The first time she tried them with Nick around, she realized that was precisely the point.

This toy was all about the tease, about knowing you were out in public with your pussy stuffed full, about needing to get off for so long that it seemed like burning desire was your natural state.

In a public place, the toy was exquisite torture. In a semiprivate one, like Nick's rooftop deck, it was even worse.

Because Nick could do what he'd just done—lean over and tweak her now painfully sensitive nipples.

Okay, she was going to pay for being a smartass, but it would be fun payback.

Nick gave an evil laugh. "Actually, I was thinking more about help with the housework. She's taking it a little far, and I need to talk with her about it, but I'm also lazy, so I keep putting it off." He grinned like a big cat and leaned toward her, his mahogany hair, loose from his usual ponytail, swinging forward over his cheekbones. "And yeah, the half-naked's all good. I'm a guy, okay? I like half-naked women."

He cupped her breasts, swirling his thumbs over her inflamed nipples, making her gasp and arch her back. His eyes turned a deeper blue when he was aroused, and at the moment, they were shading toward cobalt, looking intensely into Selene's. "But I'll let you in on a secret. The Natalie eye candy is nice, but I prefer seeing you half-naked. Or fully naked. She's a little skinny for my taste."

"Sure." It was hard to keep a sarcastic tone when she was getting so turned on, but she somehow managed. "And that's why you were with her for years. Because she was too skinny."

My God, what well of feminine insecurity was this garbage coming from? She'd promised herself up and down that she wouldn't be like this, that she wouldn't let herself push Nick for a commitment in any way, that she would be totally understanding of his decision to let Natalie stay with him because it really did make sense.

Yet she couldn't keep her damn mouth shut.

Natalie would have, had their positions been reversed. Good subs didn't act like this. Good slaves certainly didn't. Natalie was always gentle, always soft-spoken, always respectful.

Considering Natalie had been with Nick for years, that was probably what he liked long-term, not her own brasher ways. Hell, good girlfriends didn't even nag like this, leaving the whole submission question aside.

Pulling his hands away, Nick sighed. "Do we really need to have this conversation? We have a fun night planned."

Selene shivered. She knew Nick wasn't like Derrick, knew it with an instinct deeper than reason. And she wasn't like Natalie; she wouldn't let a guy get away with crazy, dangerous behavior, like shaving her head and beating her bloody because she'd spoken out of turn.

But for a second, all she could think was that he was going to punish her, inflict some kind of painful consequence for her flare of jealousy.

She inched away, wanting to be far away from his touch but at the same time wanting to throw herself at his feet and beg for mercy. "I'm sorry, sir. No, sir. I won't..."

"Stop it!" The anger in Nick's voice made her jump. "Don't

cringe at me, dammit. I've had to put up with Natalie cringing and apologizing and making herself small all the time. Don't you start."

Fine. He didn't want cringing and small, he'd get what he wanted. "You don't want me to cringe? Don't yell. I don't deal well with yelling."

"And I don't deal well with being made to feel like a pig or a cheater for wanting to help a friend get back on her feet. You're supposed to be the big advocate for battered women. Can't you see she's not ready to strike out on her own?"

"I agree she's not, and it's a good thing to help her. It's another thing to have her cooking for you and cleaning and acting like a 1950s housewife. Serving you, like she was your slave."

Nick blinked. "She's not serving me, not in that sense. She's being a good...housemate." His voice trailed off on the last word. "Do you think I'm taking advantage of her?"

"I think it's more the other way around." Selene held up one hand and started ticking things off as she ranted. "She makes dinner every night unless you actually tell her we want a night on our own. She cleans the goddamn bathroom, and trust me, a woman does not clean a grotty bachelor bathroom unless she thinks she's getting something for it. Maybe that's just trying to pull her weight when she can't pay rent, but I think there's more to it. Her posture changes when you're around. She lowers her eyes and raises her tits. Maybe she's not even conscious of everything she's doing, but on some level, she wants you back. Or at least wants to serve someone, and you're here."

Selene bounced to her feet. The movement tugged on the nipple clips, but this time it didn't feel good. This time it was just pain. "Someday she'll wind up in bed with you, and it'll seem like she's always been there! You'll let her because you can't see how she's just trying to get herself with someone more dominant because she can't deal with taking care of herself.

She has to learn to stand on her own, and you're just encouraging her to cling to you."

"Do you honestly think that's what I'm doing? Trying to lure her into being my sub again?"

Selene had to stop her rant and think about the best way to answer that. She wasn't convinced the way she came up with was particularly good, but it was less whiny-jealous-unreasonable-girlfriend than the first few things that came to mind. "I don't think you're trying. I think she's trying, and you're not telling her no. It's flattering to have someone want you, and hell, if someone wanted to cook and clean for me and spoil me rotten, I'd find that pretty seductive. Extra points if it was a hot half-naked guy doing it."

"To repeat myself, a half-naked you is seductive. Random half-naked women, not so much."

"But she's not a random woman. She's someone you slept with for years. Someone you loved."

"And I still do, as a friend. But I wouldn't want to...she doesn't want to, and even if she did..." She could see Nick taking a deep breath. "Damn it, listen to me. I don't want her. I want you. I love you. Do I have to be any clearer?"

No, he was crystal clear.

Crystal clear that he was angry and probably confused by the way the hot, sexy evening had suddenly taken a left turn into relationship hell. Crystal clear that he was at the point where he'd say anything to get her to shut up. Even tell her he loved her in a totally unconvincing way, at a moment when, even if he did love her, he would have been thinking, *Oh, for God's sake, shut up!*

She shook her head, fighting back the tears that threatened to overwhelm her.

She'd opened her big stupid mouth and pushed him, just like Will had done to her. And Nick had said what he figured she needed to hear, just like she had with Will.

No one would possibly say *I love you* for the first time in the middle of having a remarkably stupid argument. In this context, it was the last resort of a guy who didn't know what else to say to appease an angry woman.

She wanted to believe he loved her, wanted to with all her heart and soul and body.

She didn't dare.

Selene pulled herself together, forced back the tears she wanted to shed, the damn female tears of someone who yearned to believe herself loved but couldn't. "You don't need to say that stuff about love. You want me. I want you. That's good enough. And I'm sorry I'm getting frustrated with having Natalie around. I've gotten spoiled. A week or so without a good beating, and I get all grouchy and weird."

He still looked dubious, concerned, but he managed to laugh as he said, "Maybe I have spoiled you, but that's the kind of spoiling I want to keep up."

She wrapped her arms around Nick's neck, pressed her body against his, trying to will herself back to the state of mindless desire he could usually get her into with a glance.

"We'll take advantage of the privacy, then." Nick pulled her close, rubbing against her so the movement yanked the fine stainless-steel chain connecting the nipple clips. His voice became molten, dark chocolate laced with whisky, and his eyes darkened to something close to navy blue. "You can scream all you want tonight. And I'm going to push for it. See how much you can really take."

God, she wanted that, wanted erotic pain and hard use to turn off her overly busy brain, wanted to come like a banshee and lose herself and her worries on a tide of red-hot pleasure. Wanted to lose herself in Nick and what Nick could do to her so she wouldn't obsess about what that careless declaration of love really meant.

"Yes," she said, shuddering, rubbing against him like a wild thing. "No mercy. Break me. That's what I need tonight, Nick. Sir. Please."

His only answer was a slap on her cheek. More a tap, really—it didn't even sting—but it did something very strange to her already muddled brain.

She felt as though she were divided into two.

Half of her was just plain pissed. It made her feel small. Lesser. Like a kid who'd been smacked for sassing her grandma.

Humiliated.

Nick's games of sex and power had embarrassed her in the past, in a way that made her blush and squirm and flood with arousal, but had never humiliated her. She understood on an intellectual level that some subs craved humiliation, but she'd always been sure she wasn't one of them.

Now she wasn't so sure, because the other half of her had been rocketed into another world, a world where Nick was her dark god and she was a small creature whimpering at his feet. A world of nakedness and pain and lust where he ruled and she obeyed. Where she was unworthy but honored that Nick would deign to claim her. Where she knew she would take whatever he gave her, however unnerving, however brutal, because she was his toy and nothing more.

The rational, pissed-off half didn't think much of this half. It seemed broken, pathetic, a little too much like Natalie at her worst moments, or like an abuse victim rationalizing her situation because she was too cowed to escape it.

Nick grabbed a thick handful of her hair and dragged her to her feet. "Inside. Now," he barked, handling her as if she were either a sturdy parcel or an unruly kitten.

"But I haven't finished eating."

"Yes, you have, because I've said you have. Are you questioning me?"

Obviously she had been, but it struck her as unwise to

continue doing so. "No, sir," she said, trying to make her voice sound respectful and humble, but not the small and cringing that Nick hated—even though she felt like cringing at this harsher side of Nick. "I'm sorry, sir."

"You will be." Somehow the menace in his voice didn't sound as enticing as it usually did. "And tonight, call me Master. It'll be good practice."

Was this the face of Nick Natalie had craved? The one she apparently hoped to see again?

For the first time with Nick, Selene felt frightened rather than pleasantly nervous. She remembered the lingering bruises on Natalie, her stories of what had happened when she angered her former master.

Still, she let Nick half drag her to the door from the roof and push her inside, still trotted ahead of him into the apartment.

Obedience had become, if not instinct yet, at least habit.

And some traitor part of her, the part that had utterly meant it when she begged him to break her, wanted to experience whatever he had in store.

She might love it, she might hate it—but at least she'd know if she could take it.

She might, on some level, scorn Natalie as confused and weak, but she suspected the little blonde could handle and enjoy levels of pain that would make her dissolve into a whimpering wreck.

And being wimpy would be no way to win Nick's heart.

She had to show that she had Natalie's depth of submission, Natalie's ability to take pain, as well as all the qualities that Nick admired in her that Natalie lacked.

Only that combination might convince him that love and BDSM could coexist, with the right woman.

With her.

Chapter Twenty-Three

Nick was doing his best to ignore it, but he was pretty sure his heart was breaking. Cracking, at least.

He'd just told the most incredible woman he'd ever met that he loved her, and she'd told him he was talking bullshit. Told him that she wanted hot kink and plenty of it but didn't exactly want him. She wanted him as a hot-and-cold-running dominant, a playmate who would hurt her exquisitely and use her and make her feel both trapped and free—but would never show her his heart, show her anything but the storybook master.

Just like Natalie.

But damn it, he wasn't going to make the same mistake he had with Natalie. If that was what she wanted, he wouldn't force his feelings on her. He'd do his damnedest to give her what he *could* give her, what she needed, and maybe in time she'd learn to care.

At the very least, she, unlike Natalie, would be safe with someone who treasured her.

Even if he had to push all Selene's limits—and his own—to keep her that way.

Earlier in the evening, when he'd first threatened to tie her, he'd had in mind something like a rope bra and her hands secured behind her back, something more sensual than stringent.

But his plans had changed.

Now he wanted her to be pushed, to feel not just the

security and sensuality of ropes but the strain of holding a challenging position.

"Lie on the bed," he commanded. "Face up."

Then he started arranging her.

Arched her over so her thighs rested on her chest.

Made her hold herself in place with her arms.

Tucked a pillow under her ass to keep it raised.

Tied her that way, ass in the air, pussy open and exposed, muscles straining. Helpless. Her eyes were wide, glancing about frantically like a panicked animal, but her labia were swollen, her pussy slick.

Just as he'd suspected.

"You love this," he said, and it wasn't a question

"Yes," she replied in a small, confused voice. "Yes, I do." She sounded like she didn't quite believe it herself.

Slap to the face. "Yes what?"

This time, to his own surprise, he left a pink handprint on her cheek. He hadn't meant to give her more than a tap, but apparently his hindbrain had different ideas.

Her eyes screwed shut, and for a second, he thought she might start crying. This was harder than he'd pushed her before, harder than he'd wanted to push her. Maybe harder than she could handle being pushed.

Part of him wanted to cradle her in his arms and beg forgiveness.

But that wasn't what she needed, wasn't what would win her over.

And to be honest, it wasn't what he needed or wanted at this minute. He needed to prove to her that, whether or not she was ready to call it love, Selene belonged with him.

Belonged to him.

"Yes what?" he repeated, letting all the hurt he was feeling transmute into harshness, arrogance.

Selene took a deep breath. "Yes, sir," she said. After a slight pause, she corrected herself. "Yes, Master."

"Very good." He forced an evil smile, found as he did so that he didn't need to force it. Despite his mood, there was definitely something to be said for a beautiful woman, securely bound, at his mercy and not sure whether to be more aroused or alarmed.

The fear in her eyes was painful to him, because it looked like it was approaching real panic.

But she should trust him by now, should know that he wouldn't harm her. Even knowing she didn't care, didn't give a damn about anything but the sex, the kinky games, he still loved her.

And even if he didn't, he wasn't Derrick the Dick.

Just a man who needed to make a point.

He picked up the NAUGHTY paddle from the bedside table, admitted to himself as he did that, hurt or not, angry or not, he was also hard, despite his recent orgasm, straining against his fly at the thought of what he was about to do.

Nick had never been comfortable with dishing out the level of pain Natalie craved, but that didn't mean he hadn't enjoyed it. On the contrary, he'd enjoyed that aspect of things a little too much—and that was what scared him, that he might go too far, might step over the line from good pain to damage, and, wired as she was, Natalie would just take it.

Selene had boundaries, though. He could trust her to let him know how she was doing, to use her safe word if it were more than she could handle.

If she was ready to heat things up a few dozen degrees, then he'd give it to her.

With pleasure.

Usually he'd warm her up with light spanking until her bottom was rosy, then work up from light, percussive pops with the paddle, interspersed with lots of stroking and kissing, pinching at the tender places, tracing the letter imprint and then soothing the hurt, playing with her plump nipples and fingering her juicy pussy until she was panting and slick and begging for more.

Only then would he strike her more heavily, knowing that she was ready to transmute pain into ecstasy.

Not tonight.

The paddle cracked down on her lovely ass.

Selene shrieked, bit her lower lip, then glared at him.

And while she was still glaring, he struck again. Several more whacks followed in rapid succession. Selene stopped shrieking after the third but continued to gasp with each blow.

After about eight, Nick stood back, studied the red effect of his handiwork, "Naughty" repeated several times in bold white letters against a rosy ground. It was starting to get hard to read, though, from overlapping blows. Before long, he hoped it would be illegible.

"Should have gotten the SLUT one," he growled. "Or better yet, CUNT. That's what you are, isn't it? A cunt."

He smacked her again. "Isn't it?"

When she didn't answer, Nick grabbed a handful of her hair, pulled her head back roughly. "Answer me when I talk to you."

"Sorry, Master," she said, her voice gloriously meek and quavering. "I...I couldn't catch my breath." She breathed in and out a few times before answering the question he'd asked—but not the way he'd expected. "No. I'm not a cunt." A second's hesitation. "Master. I have a cunt. But I'm not one."

Nick felt like Jekyll and Hyde. *Cunt* was a word that women reacted to strongly—it made them either hot and bothered or just bothered, and part of him loved Selene for saying how she really felt instead of giving him the pat answer he'd expected, under pretty trying circumstances.

His inner caveman growled in frustration, and at the same

211

time, in arousal. She'd begged to be broken. He wouldn't break her, not really, but he'd be happy to bend her. Soften her up. Make her yield.

And by the end of the night, she'd agree she was a cunt or any other damn thing he suggested—because by then she'd want to.

"You're not a cunt?" He ran two fingers along her slit, scooped away some of her juices, moved so he could show the thick slickness threading between his fingers. "What other kind of woman gets wet when she's tied up and paddled?"

"A wanton one. A sexual one. A horny one. A slut, even." Selene hesitated, then added, "One who wants you very much, Master."

The inner nice guy, the one who'd fallen hard for Selene, wished she'd said *love* instead of *want*.

The inner caveman crowed at the admission of how much she wanted him.

"Do you want me? You'll have me, little one. But first you have to admit you're a cunt." There, that ought to set up a nice little dilemma in her mind, the kind of thing that should turn her brain to Jell-O by defeating any effort to think logically. "Admit you're a cunt and take whatever I choose to give you. But I know you'll do that, because you love it, and that's why I say you're a cunt." He didn't give her a chance to answer, just started paddling her again.

She didn't seem to know how to react. Her eyes were bright with tears that she wouldn't shed, and she was biting her lip to keep from screaming, and her ass looked like it was on fire. But still her nipples were hard, her pussy gleaming.

And still she would neither safe-word nor call herself what he wanted to hear, either one of which would have stopped the pain and let him give her the sound but tender fucking his cock ached to administer.

Wet pussies didn't lie, he figured. And in his experience,

neither did Selene.

If she wasn't using the safe word yet, she must be all right. Soon it would be time for the cane.

Chapter Twenty-Four

Selene's ass was ablaze and so was her brain.

She'd asked for this, begged for it. Begged Nick to break her.

That meant she had to take it, didn't she? Otherwise she'd be a wannabe, a smart-ass masochist who topped from below, a poser, all those terms Natalie had thrown around, scarcely bothering to hide that she was talking about Selene.

Besides, she deserved it. Deserved to suffer for pushing at Nick's emotions, forcing him into a declaration of love he wasn't ready to make.

Worse, she wanted it. Needed it. Nick was right about that, although she wasn't sure she could admit it to him even if she could get her brain and her lips in synch.

It wasn't fun pain, but it balanced the pain inside, the pain of knowing how badly she'd fucked up.

And for non-fun pain, pain that shouldn't have been any more enjoyable than having a root canal, it was making her awfully wet.

Not the pain, perhaps, but the yielding. The knowledge that she'd put herself completely into Nick's hands, that intense as this scene was, her only choice now was to trust him and endure.

Trust. That was why she was enduring, why she wanted him to break her open, to get past the fear and doubt and emotional blackmail and back to the trust.

Every muscle in her body cried out for release, relief from

the challenging position he'd put her in, and her ass was on fire, and open as she was, the paddle sometimes caught still more tender areas—her anus, her swollen pussy lips.

Then she'd scream.

But she wouldn't use her safe word. She refused to use her safe word, to admit her wimpiness. It was only a paddle, dammit. Not a singletail, not a riot whip, not a knife, not any of the implements Nick had used on Natalie when they were together and that Natalie had described to her in breathless, wet detail. This was nothing. Just a paddle, used harder than usual.

Dimly, as the pain built, as the paddle cracked down again and again on her tender ass cheeks and reddened thighs, she knew she was dripping.

And why shouldn't she be? She was a cunt in the sense that Nick meant.

But she couldn't bring herself to say it, not after hearing Molly's father shouting it at Molly's mother, not once, but often, usually coupled with *worthless.* She hadn't known what it meant then, just knew instinctively it was a terrible thing to call someone.

Nick didn't mean it that way. He meant a woman who liked sex, who gave herself shamelessly to pain and pleasure, and she certainly was that. He just wanted her to say it in the starkest, most embarrassing way possible. And she couldn't.

This was beyond the level of pain she thought she'd wanted, but she found she could take it, take joy from knowing she was taking it. Each blow made her tense her buttocks—and each time she did that, she tightened around the toy inside her and felt surges of pleasure rippling out to meet the surges of pain.

Finally he stopped, ran a hand softly over her hot, tingling bottom. The touch soothed her, and when he smiled a smile of sweet evil and whispered, "Good girl. Good, brave girl. That was new for you, wasn't it?" she swore the pain melted into waves of... Well, her ass was still throbbing and sore, but it was a good kind of throbbing and sore, the kind she didn't ever want to stop.

And when he ran his fingers over her slick, swollen pussy, smiled approvingly, then ever so casually circled her aching clit...she surged, tried to arch to meet his touch against the chafing rope, cried out her pleasure as she convulsed around the toy inside her and some of the almost-unbearable tension melted away on a river of bright pleasure.

Interrupted by a slap on her inner thighs and pussy lips.

The slap itself, in her erotic haze, was sharp ecstasy, just one more strong sensation that would push her toward another orgasm.

Nick's words were what made her plummet back down to earth. "Who said you could come, you worthless cunt?"

Several things—all very bad ideas to say at the moment—flashed into her mind. *You never said I couldn't* and *Mother Nature, asshole. It's what happens when you play with a woman's clit* featured prominently.

But what actually came out of her mouth was, "I'm not worthless. Never call me worthless. Ever. Especially not a worthless cunt. Or I walk."

Everything slowed to a creepy, horror-movie version of slow-motion. Nick's eyes went wild, and Selene thought he looked as panicky and miserable as she felt. He opened his mouth, and for a second that might have lasted ten minutes, she thought he might apologize, untie her, cuddle her, start things again from a different, better place.

Then a layer of ice seemed to form over his beloved features. She'd seen him do the cold, distant act, though never for long, but it was definitely an act; beneath the detached mask, he'd been engaged, eager. This time he seemed to go somewhere else, leaving a stranger—a handsome but cruel stranger, frightening yet paradoxically seductive to Selene—in his place. He was still fully dressed, which wasn't his usual habit when they played, and that made him seem even more a stranger.

"Maybe not worthless," he said. "But worth more with stripes."

He turned around, grabbed a thin, flexible rattan cane from the antique umbrella stand near the bed.

For a second, Selene was grateful he chose a thin one. Surely it would hurt less than some of the ones in the collection—the heavy Lucite, the fiberglass rod that looked like a conductor's baton and that had left a narrow but deep bruise on her thigh when she'd surreptitiously tried it on herself, the metal one.

He whipped it through the air a few times, making sure she heard the whip it made, making sure she saw how it flexed, eager to strike.

"Get ready, cunt," he barked.

She heard the cane, felt the wind of its passage, prepared for a new sensation—a frightening yet seductive one like this new, harsher face of Nick.

The cane crashed into the mattress beside her. Out of the corner of her eye, she could see the dent it left in the sheets.

Tension she hadn't realized she'd been holding left her body. He wasn't going to back out—it wasn't that kind of night—but he wasn't going to hit her that hard, either.

And then he did.

She screamed, not a cry of pleasure but the furious and frightened bellow of a wounded animal. Somewhere underneath the fiery pain was the possibility of pleasure, but it was too distant to reach right now, just like Nick was too distant, not meeting her eyes when she looked at him, trying to get his help transmuting this agony into something she could bear because it pleased him.

"Had enough?" he asked. "Do you need to use your safe word?"

Selene gathered a breath around the remains of the scream, around the shocking line of fire across her ass, around the tears that she refused to shed, tears less of pain than of confusion and fear. The safe word danced on her tongue, ready to be spoken, ready to save her from more lines of fire, more of Nick's humiliating words and weird, distant, angry attitude.

Then she remembered Natalie and decided to tough it out. If that little bony thing could take this—and while that Cirque du Soleil body of hers was sexy, it had absolutely no padding to absorb blows, unlike Selene's ampler form—so could she. Take what Nick wanted to give her. Show she was tough but yielding.

Not worthless, but worthy.

Biting her lip to keep the safe word—and/or a really ill-advised taunt of *do your worst*—inside, Selene shook her head.

Five more stripes, and with each, Selene held on with tooth and claw, with pride and determination, with a fierce need to prove something to Nick, although by the second blow she couldn't have possibly explained what that something was anymore.

On the fifth, though, she flinched hard enough that she managed to wiggle away slightly.

But not in the right direction.

The cane, already in motion again, caught her not across the fleshy curve of her ass but across the thighs and the clit and labia.

A hand-slap there was intense but arousing.

This was unbearable. Knifelike intensity, fire radiating through her lower body. She was sure she must be bleeding.

At the same time, she was sure the wetness she felt was pussy juice, because despite the pain, despite the shock, or maybe because of it, she felt herself convulsing around the balls inside her as if he'd done something exquisitely pleasurable instead of exquisitely painful.

"Too much," she sobbed. "Too much."

He positioned the cane as if he planned to use it again.

"No!" she begged. And then, meeting his eyes, realizing what she had to do, "Red. Red, goddamit, red!"

As he threw down the cane, Nick's demeanor changed from distant to intensely, dangerously present, from cold to...she wasn't quite sure what. A mix of concern and something negative.

Probably disgust at her for safe-wording.

But she couldn't tell because she couldn't really see through the tears.

She'd cried during scenes before, but it had been a catharsis that left her feeling light and clean. This felt different, wrenching sobs that welled up from inside her, threatened to choke her, threatened to keep coming forever.

It wasn't from pain, although it had started with the involuntary, unfightable tears that sprang to her eyes when he'd caught her vulva.

She'd fucked up.

Natalie's dictum, *"Slaves don't have safe words,"* echoed in her brain like thunder. And if she couldn't handle being Nick's slave, even on a trial basis for one night, and he didn't really want a girlfriend, where did that leave her?

Alone, that was where. Without the man she'd come to love.

Maybe she was better off that way, because she was a huge wimp who couldn't take what Nick obviously wanted to do as a dominant. Couldn't take a little paddling and caning. Got pissed off at a few measly dirty words. Made an ass of herself. It had been fun while it lasted, but clearly she wasn't cut out for this lifestyle.

Wrapped in her misery, she hardly noticed Nick cutting the ropes off her—hurriedly but gently—with the EMT shears he kept on the bedside table.

Hardly noticed when he briefly left the room.

Flinched when she felt pressure on her still pulsing clit but relaxed when she realized it was a soothingly cool washcloth—relaxed, at least, to the extent she could, which meant pulling back behind her walls of shock and misery.

So she hardly noticed him lying down beside her and cradling her in his arms. Good dom behavior, she registered briefly. Nick was a good dom.

And someday he'd find a good sub again, but it wasn't going to be her, not after tonight's debacle. He wasn't going to want to deal with her, and she wasn't sure it was a good idea for her to deal with him. He'd injured her by accident. The real hurt, she'd done to herself.

That meant it was time to get out. In the worst cases of abuse, the victim learned to do the abuser's work for him. And while Nick wasn't being abusive, that didn't mean they might not both be harmed by the mess they were making together.

Nick held Selene close, listened to her sobbing as if her world had fallen apart, wished he dared to say how much he loved her.

Fat lot of good that would do now. If she hadn't wanted to hear when everything was going more-or-less well, she certainly wouldn't now when he'd fucked up so grandly.

It wasn't the missed stroke. That must have hurt like a bitch, and he felt bad about it, but occasional accidents happened to even the most careful doms.

It was the whole damn scene. He'd pushed too hard, too fast. He'd played with things they'd never really talked about, edgy things like face-slapping and humiliation, springing them on her out of the blue when she was already off-kilter.

And he'd played while he was angry and upset, something he'd promised himself he'd never do. That way lay madness, or at least stupid accidents and emotional minefields, both of which had happened tonight.

At least she'd had the sense to use her safe word, although he guessed after the fact that she'd been tempted to long before she did. He should have been paying more attention. He knew how hard it was to admit something was too much, especially for a proud woman like Selene, and how just plain hard it could be to think when you were caught up in a heavy scene. A responsible dom kept a little bit of detachment so he could see if his sub had reached the point where she couldn't manage to say the safe word because her brain had stopped working. But he'd been too rattled to keep that detachment.

He only hoped he could repair the damage he'd done to their relationship in his stupid pride. Maybe she wasn't in love with him, but she'd liked him a lot until now. With luck, she still did, and maybe when she calmed down, they'd be able to talk this through and be all right. At the moment, though, she seemed happiest pretending he wasn't there, and he wasn't sure he blamed her.

All he could do was hold her shuddering, sobbing form and whisper almost inaudibly into her hair, "I'm so sorry," and "I love you."

When she finally stirred and rolled onto her back, he breathed a sigh of relief. When she opened her eyes and looked at him, he breathed another one.

"Hi," he said, knowing it was feeble. "Can I get you anything?"

"Another cold cloth and a glass of water. Please."

He padded off to the kitchen.

Over the sound of running water, he heard the door slam.

With the faucet still on, he ran back to the bedroom.

Selene's play collar and the toy, still drenched with her juices, lay on the bed, the collar surrounding the balls.

But Selene was gone.

Chapter Twenty-Five

Half naked on the roof, Selene watched him run outside, calling her name. He pelted down the street toward her usual bus stop, a madman in the dark, calling her name.

Then she took her cell phone and called for a cab to meet her at a T stop several blocks away in the opposite direction, finished putting her clothes on, and headed back down to the street.

She walked briskly, though not without looking back. The brisk was because some of the area between Nick's place and the T stop wasn't the nicest neighborhood, not dangerous but rundown and depressing and more so in the dark.

The looking back... She couldn't decide if she hoped Nick wasn't following her or hoped he was.

She hated leaving like this, hated running away, but she knew if she tried to talk to him now, even about something like why she needed to go home and clear her head before they tried to talk about what had happened, it would make the current mess even worse.

She needed to be calm, to face up to her failures like a rational adult so they could end the relationship in the measured, friendly way they'd begun it.

Because it would have to end after tonight, wouldn't it?

She couldn't imagine Nick would want anything to do with her after a debacle of emotional blackmail, hysteria and safe-wording.

And that thought was bleak and lonely enough to make a

seedy Jamaica Plain side street late at night look cheerful and bright by comparison.

The cab ride home gave her all too much time to think, but not in a productive or calming way. Different voices echoed in her head. Molly, pointing out she'd been nuts to be there in the first place and would be better off without Nick—and had she considered therapy for that self-destructive streak? Natalie, mocking her as a day-tripper into the land of BDSM, unable to hack the reality. Her mother, sad and sympathetic about a promising relationship fizzling without beginning to understand what had happened. Alison and Garth, annoyed that she'd done a number on their friend. And her own inner voice, the one she'd use if a friend told her a similar story, pointing out that Nick wasn't lacking in fault here, that he'd been sending mixed signals, then he'd pushed her boundaries, taking her deep into unknown territory without talking her through it first, without his usual care to make sure she was okay with things.

And her other inner voice, troubled and troubling, reminding her that she'd come like the Fourth of July while he pushed her, that her body still trembled with desire, that her thighs were still sticky with moisture. *That* inner voice suggested, not gently, that the situation was even odder and more confusing than it appeared on the surface.

Her cell rang three times during the relatively short ride, but each time she saw Nick's number and ignored it.

She knew she and Nick needed to talk, but not yet. Good God, not yet, not when her mind was still such a muddle. Not when her body still throbbed from pain and her pussy still throbbed with an aching need for Nick, Nick's body, Nick's cock, whatever it took to send her to space and then bring her safely back again. Not when she couldn't decide if the things they'd done had been awful, blissful, or both.

The emotional turmoil? Awful, definitely awful. The cane slip, ditto. That was the kind of pain you should only have to experience in, say, the course of lifesaving medical treatment;

otherwise, she'd pass, thanks. But oh, she wouldn't mind feeling a cane again under other circumstances, feeling that delicious helplessness of being bound so tightly, being pushed past the point where things gave pleasure in any simple, straightforward way but came in layers. Pain and pleasure and pain and the pleasure of knowing she pleased...

The phone shrilled again. Really, she needed to shut it off.

But as she fumbled in her purse for it, she realized it wasn't Nick but Alison.

She was ready to ignore that call too. There had been brunch plans for the morning. Let Nick explain why she wouldn't be joining them.

Then she decided she owed Alison an explanation for why she'd be dropping out of sight for a while—or maybe permanently.

The first words out of Alison's mouth were, "I just got a really weird call from Nick. He called me, said about three words, then hung up. Now he's not answering. Is everything okay?"

"No," she choked out. "No it's not. I've ruined everything and... Oh Alison, I know you're Nick's friend more than mine, but you're the only person I could possibly talk to about this. Molly just wouldn't understand. Can I call you tomorrow?"

She dropped her voice abruptly. It probably wasn't the first time the cabby had driven a passenger who wasn't having the best damn night of her life, but he didn't need to hear everything.

"No time like the present, sweetie. That's what friends are for. Do you want to come over?"

Selene glanced out the cab window. Almost home—almost to her car. "Could I? Oh, thank you, Alison. I'll be there by ten."

Nick's lungs still hurt. He was in good shape, but he wasn't Captain God-damn America, and chasing a bus up Centre Street pushed it. And when, three inbound stops later, he caught up with the bus, the one he'd been sure Selene must have been on—she wasn't.

He'd punched at the door when the bus drove off, which, he figured, made him look crazier than the average half-dressed guy pelting down Centre Street, and since they were near the VA Hospital's outpatient psych clinic, the level of random street crazy in the neighborhood was fairly high.

Taking just enough time for a deep breath, he'd run back to his own neighborhood and the restaurants and cafés of Centre Street. She had to be around here somewhere, couldn't have vanished into thin air. With an increasing sense of insanity, he dashed into every restaurant and bar and coffee shop, looked around frantically, moved on to the next.

She wasn't in any of them. No one remembered seeing her—not, he thought grimly, that he'd have given himself information like that at this point, because he must look like a classic psycho that a woman should be running away from.

Then he'd grabbed his car and driven to the Green Street T station. The station was empty, a train's lights disappearing toward Boston.

Probably that was the second or third train that had come through in the time since Selene had vanished. No hope there, especially since it wasn't a direct shot to her house on that line and she had several options of how she might transfer, assuming she was on the T at all.

But where the hell had she gone?

Had she taken the wrong bus because she was distracted or because she'd rather go all over Boston than risk having him catch up with her? Miraculously gotten a cab in the thirty seconds before he'd noticed she was gone?

Met up with something dire between his house and the

bus? His neighborhood was as safe as any in Boston—which meant it was unlikely but not impossible.

It had been almost two hours. He'd called and called, but she refused to pick up. He'd even called Alison and Garth on some lame excuse, too ashamed to admit what had happened, but hoping that if Selene had gotten in touch with them, Alison would say something. All that had done was confuse Alison.

Not that he'd blame Selene if she ran away and didn't ever come back. He'd broken half the unwritten rules of being a good dom and all the rules of being a good partner in one night. Any sane woman would run—and she more than most. He'd probably showed all the warning signs of an abuser.

But he wanted to apologize. To explain.

To say again he loved her, even if she didn't feel the same. And if he'd had a chance of that, if she just hadn't been ready to take the big leap from like and lust to love, he'd blown that out the window, hadn't he? Idiot.

He loved her and knew he'd fucked up big-time and would spend a lifetime making it up if she'd let him.

His phone buzzed.

Not Selene.

He almost ignored it when he saw Garth's number. If there were such a thing as a dom license, Garth would revoke his for some of the shit he'd pulled tonight.

But maybe Garth knew something.

He picked up gingerly.

And had to hold the phone back from his ear when Garth barked, "Get your ass over here. Selene just talked to Alison."

Chapter Twenty-Six

Selene considered it nothing short of miraculous that she managed to drive to Garth and Alison's without killing herself or anyone else. Between emotional upheaval and a strange sense of disconnection thanks to the abrupt way the scene—and her night with Nick—ended, she felt like she might as well be driving drunk. She couldn't focus on anything except that, if things weren't over between her and Nick, they probably ought to be, between her stupidity and his.

The longer she was away from him, the more she saw his side of the stupid. What kind of dumb did it take to say you loved someone you obviously didn't and then call her a cunt and whack her most sensitive bits with a cane to boot?

But then again, what kind of stupid did you have to be to fall in love with someone who'd made it clear from the beginning that he thought it could never work? Who, if he was in love with anyone, was still hung up on his ex?

She'd managed not to cry since running out of Nick's house. But when she walked into the kitchen, the kindness in Alison's eyes broke something inside her, some last bit of control to which she'd been clinging like a life preserver after the shipwreck the night had become.

As she started to cry, Alison crossed the few steps between them. Small as she was, she felt bigger than Selene when she folded her in her arms, a strong, loving, comforting presence.

"Come on upstairs," she said. "Garth's wrapping up a poker night. It'll be quieter in the bedroom."

Somehow, through her tears, she managed to make a joke

about finally being invited into Alison and Garth's bedroom.

She managed to take in airy blue and white accents and solid Mission furniture.

Then the room swayed.

No, she swayed, and Alison was right there again, guiding her to an old-fashioned oak rocking chair.

A rocking chair, she thought dimly. Who'd have thought they'd have something so homey in the bedroom of Kink Central? Then again, you could probably have good sex in the right rocker, and this one was both armless and suspiciously sturdy.

She winced as her tender bottom made contact with the hard seat.

"You okay?"

"Yes. No. I'm not sure." Feeling the damnable tears about to start again, she bit her lower lip. "I'm drained and I'm confused and...and I never got to finish dinner, so that's part of it. But I just feel weird."

"Dropped?" Alison asked. "Were you playing hard before..."

Selene nodded, cutting her off.

"Hang on. Let me get you a drink and a snack."

Some dim part of Selene's brain pondered the thought that only Alison and Garth would have a dorm fridge in the bedroom, presumably so they could refuel during particularly crazy scenes, but eccentric as she might have found it at other times, she was immensely grateful for the eccentricity. Alison pressed a cold bottle of sparkling water into one hand, a fruit-and-nut energy bar into the other.

Selene tried not to consider what kind of people needed to keep energy bars in the bedroom and unfortunately failed.

A broken heart, she thought, would be much easier if her libido had broken along with it. Unfortunately, the libido still seemed to be in overdrive, as if her body hadn't figured out yet that Nick wouldn't be coming back to end the scene properly.

Water and food helped give her a little perspective.

So did sitting in the calm, dimly lit room, not even trying to do anything but sit and collect herself.

Alison knelt next to the chair—not submissively but comfortingly, a quiet but strong presence. Didn't ask questions, didn't push, was just there.

For some reason, that made it easier to talk.

She started with the end. Might as well get the laughter out of the way. "I pretty much screwed everything up. I safe-worded, for one thing. He was caning me, and he caught my clit..."

"I damn well hope you'd safe-word that, sweetie. I certainly would. That hurts like a bitch. You need to catch your breath after something like that, and he needs to refocus."

"But I..." Something registered. "I thought slaves didn't have safe words?"

"Some don't. Some people drive without their seat belt on. Doesn't mean it's a good idea. I'm not going to stop Garth just because I'm not sure I like what he's doing, but if my hands are going numb or the tip of the singletail has wrapped around one of my rings—and both have happened—he wants to know."

"But Natalie..."

She fell silent, considering the source of the counterarguments. Let's see, who should she trust, the sane woman or Sister Mary Fruitbat? Easy one there.

"See, not so bad," Alison said. "It always feels weird if you're really into a scene and need to stop, like you've been jerked into another dimension. Nick wasn't a dick about it, was he? Because he knows better."

"No. He was pretty sweet. I think he felt bad for missing like that. But the rest of the night..."

And haltingly, she told the story, from her stupid jealousy of Natalie to Nick's annoyance to the wild, boundary-pushing (but, she admitted, hot as well as startling) scene.

Unfortunately, Alison was too smart for Selene's good. "Is that the whole story? It takes a lot to get Nick mad. Especially mad enough to be quite that dumb. What are you leaving out?"

"I don't know," Selene admitted. "He must really hate jealous women. He got to the point where he tried to convince me he loved me, just to get me to shut up. As if. He's told me a dozen times that love and kink don't mix for him. I don't know. Maybe I should go back to Lodi for a while, lick my wounds."

Alison shook her head. "You two—so smart and yet so dumb! You need something stronger than water." She darted to the fridge, returned with what proved to be a bottle of Pinot Grigio, poured Selene a glass and left the bottle sitting next to her on the floor, oblivious to the condensation dripping off it onto the hardwood floor—which, Selene thought vaguely, showed just how concerned she was. "I need to consult with a higher power. Be right back."

As Selene drank her wine a bit too fast, she wondered whether she was on to something with the idea of going back home. She could blow off Monday's classes and maybe Tuesday's too, and she was between contract gigs. Not ideal, but the idea of sitting on Molly's porch, looking out over Seneca Lake while the kids ran around the yard like little hellions, or helping her dad and brother out with the grape harvest, far away from love troubles, not to mention having to worry about crazy stuff like whether you were a "true slave" or not, sounded reassuringly normal and sane. It would give her time to sort things out.

The wine, hitting her hard after too much agitation and not enough food—not to mention the fact she was gulping it like iced tea and was already considering a refill—wasn't helping her thinking processes.

Maybe she wasn't ready to live in Nick's world. Maybe she never would be.

That didn't make her a bad person, she assured herself.

But it did make her a sad one.

Nick violated not just local laws but laws of physics getting to Garth and Alison's. He pulled into the last parking spot on the street with a squeal of tires that caused lights to flip on in an upstairs room of the dark home he parked in front of.

Ran again, ran as if he hadn't spent a good chunk of the evening in futile pursuit.

This time, at least, he knew his quarry was there.

And never mind that he was going to have to run a gauntlet of protective friends. Nothing he didn't deserve. He'd want them to help Selene keep away from bad doms and clueless asshats, and he'd acted like both tonight.

He crashed through the gate, pelted into the house, through the kitchen, peeled around the corner, skidding like a declawed cat on the hardwood floor of the hall and up the stairs. He knew they'd be in the master bedroom or maybe the upstairs office for privacy. Nothing was going to stop him.

Except Garth, that was.

Tearing around the corner at the top of the stairs, he crashed into Garth.

Suddenly he felt like a teenager caught trying to sneak in way past curfew.

Damn, he'd forgotten how effectively Garth could loom.

"Why did you tell Selene that you'd dumped Natalie because you were falling in love with her and that love would ruin a perfectly good dom-sub relationship?"

Nick tried to answer, but between sheer astonishment and being out of breath, he barely managed to get out, "Wha..." before he gave up and resorted to gaping like a fish out of water.

"Yeah, I thought it was pretty crazy too, considering how

many nights you spent over here nursing your broken heart."

Nick flashed to a couple of times Selene and Natalie had been curled up side by side on the couch, deep in conversation.

He'd thought it was sweet.

"Natalie..." Thanks to the shortness of breath, he sounded as growly as he felt.

Garth shook his head. The look on his face, too damn fatherly for someone who was definitely not his father, cut off Nick's urge to make melodramatic threats about what he'd do (but wouldn't, of course) to his lying ex-lover.

Garth didn't need to say a word.

If Nick had told Selene the whole story, plainly, instead of skimming over the embarrassing parts, the parts that hadn't done either him or Natalie any credit, she wouldn't have fallen for Natalie's lies. But it hadn't seemed important at first, because it was just supposed to be casual play. Once it started looking like it might be important, it had also gotten harder to tell her.

"I didn't actually lie," he said. "But I tried to save my pride and not sound pathetic when I told her and...well, basically I'm an asshole."

"Yup," Garth agreed, a bit too quickly—but hell, it wasn't like it wasn't the truth. "Selene's in our room."

Chapter Twenty-Seven

Nick tried to slip past Garth, but the other man turned, blocked his path in the narrow hallway. "Not so fast. How do you feel about her?"

"Why is that your business?"

Garth took a deep breath and actually seemed to think about the question for three seconds, which unfortunately wasn't enough for Nick to weasel past him.

"Because you're our friend, and we care about what kind of mess you may be getting into this time, but more because Alison likes Selene, and you know she doesn't make friends lightly."

No, she didn't. Alison was gracious to everyone, always the perfect hostess, but the number of people she seemed to get close to, other than Garth, was small enough that Nick had always felt honored to be included.

Nick thought about evading, thought about telling Garth it was none of his goddamn business.

But the truth was so loud inside him it had to come out. "I love her."

"Like you thought you loved Natalie?"

"I was young and stupid?" he said hopefully, even though it hadn't been long enough ago that he could pass as older, let alone wiser. Again he asked, because he didn't think he'd gotten the whole story, "What's it to you?"

"I was young and stupid once too, like you're being this time, not like you were with Natalie. So was Alison. And we almost missed each other on account of it."

"You two?" Hard to imagine.

"Us. And since Selene's apparently about to run back to New York because she's nuts about you but thinks you don't care, I suggest you get into the bedroom right now and start talking fast."

He moved aside just soon enough that he was only elbowed instead of bowled over by Nick in his eagerness.

"And watch out for my slave. I hear the National Weather Service has issued an overprotective redhead warning."

Even that wasn't enough to slow Nick down.

Although it did make him cup his hand protectively over his balls.

He knocked, not sure of the protocol of walking into someone else's bedroom when one, possibly two, righteously angry women were on the other side of the heavy oak door.

"Alison?" a small voice, so sad and broken he almost didn't recognize it as Selene's, asked.

He sighed with not entirely unreasonable relief that he wouldn't have to deal with the irate lover's irate friend as well as the irate lover herself.

Then he steeled his courage. "Nick."

"Why are you... How did you..." A pause during which he could picture her shrugging and sort of settling herself, deciding how she wanted to get through what was likely to be awkward, at best. "What do you want?" She sounded gruff but not convincingly so. He wasn't quite sure how to put a finger on the difference from those few words, but it sounded like the gruffness was her way of trying to hold it together, not necessarily the way she felt.

"What do you think?" He sounded just as abrasive as she had, he realized, and for basically the same reason— complicated, in his case, by years of dealing with Natalie, when his apologies made her feel like she'd failed, even if he had a good reason to say he was sorry.

Sad when you had to force tenderness and regret into your voice when tenderness and regret were what you really felt. He tried again. "I'm sorry, Selene. I'm really, really sorry. Tonight was just one series of mistakes."

"Yeah, I know." The gruffness was gone, replaced by a flatness that just about broke his heart. "I'm the one who should be sorry. I pushed."

Nick snorted. He had no idea what she was talking about, but he'd bet dollars to donuts that skewed Natalie-logic was involved somehow. "No, love. I pushed. I... Listen, can I come in?"

"You *can*. Door's not locked. Haven't decided if you *may*."

A trace of the Selene he knew and loved there, although the snark was delivered in a sad monotone.

"Please. I'm begging you. We need to talk, and we can't do it through a door."

He couldn't actually hear her sigh, certainly couldn't see her shrug, but he was sure she did both before she said, "I'm not sure how productive it'll be, but sure."

Nick reached for the doorknob. Pulled his hand back. Considered throwing up his hands and walking away if that was how she felt—with about the same degree of seriousness he might consider moving to Bali to be a beachcomber after a crap day of work.

Went to open the door again and found Selene had already done it.

Her eyes were red and puffy, her face blotchy, her mouth set in a hard, determined line. She ushered him in, closed the door, then turned on him, so like an angry cat he could almost see her back arching, her fur standing on end. "What's this all about, Nick? Masters don't beg their slaves to listen. Masters don't apologize. Aren't I just supposed to take it? I've fucked up,

235

and I don't think I can handle the punishment, so I guess I'd better walk away."

"What the..."

"That's how this is going to go, isn't it? I nagged at you, got you mad. Got you so mad you hurt me a lot. And you're saying you're sorry, but it's all going to come down to being my fault, that I asked for it. Classic abuser pattern, by the way, except that it really is my fault, and I really did ask for it—I mean literally asked for it—and I'm not sure I can handle what comes next."

He took a deep breath, trying not to fly off the handle at some of her assumptions, because flying off the handle again now would just confirm them in her eyes.

Maybe even in his.

He'd crossed the caveman line tonight in a bad way, not a fun, sexy alpha-male-playing-a-game way, and even though she'd been consenting, he *felt* like an abuser. "Explain to me how my losing my temper is your fault."

"I nagged you. I was going on and on about Natalie, and it pissed you off. For God's sake, you told me you loved me just to get me to shut the hell up."

Nick banged his head against the wall, not as gently as he'd intended. Then he turned around, put his hands on Selene's shoulders. She felt soft, warm, more fragile than he usually thought of her, and he wondered how he could have beaten her like he had, even though she'd shown every sign of enjoying it up until the stupid, clumsy end. "Is that what this is all about?"

"You don't love me, Nick. I know it. And if you do, that's not a good thing. You broke up with Natalie..."

Time to cut off that line of reasoning.

Make that way past time.

"She broke up with me, Selene. Left me high and dry. Told me I'd gotten too soft and mushy for her, that she needed a firmer hand." Despite the gravity of the situation, he smiled as he added, "Of course, being Natalie, she had to ask permission to leave, so you might say I dumped her, but I cared for her, so I couldn't expect her to stay if she was unhappy. That just proved I wasn't the right guy for her, because her right guy would make her stay even if it took locking her in the basement until she changed her mind. And never mind I don't have a basement."

"So you..." Selene's expression changed. A little doubt, a little incredulity, but at the same time a little more hope in her red-rimmed dark eyes. "You're saying that you and Natalie...but you said...right from the first you'd said that you didn't think love and BDSM would work together for you because of what happened with Natalie."

If the light-bulb-going-on-over-her-head expression had been any more obvious, she'd have grown long, floppy ears and turned into Bugs Bunny. "Duh! The problem was on her end, not yours, but you weren't ready to try again. Why didn't you say so?"

"With what you were looking for, that wouldn't have come off as a good recommendation. I had a really hot, fun woman who wanted to learn about BDSM and submission without romance or commitment involved. I'd have been an idiot to tell her I'd driven my last submissive away by falling in love too hard and I needed to keep things casual because otherwise I was afraid I'd lose perspective. Right? I mean, from my point of view?"

She looked like she was trying to fight off a chuckle but failed. "Yeah, I guess so." Then she took a deep breath and got a look of steely determination on her face. "About as much as I would have," she added, her voice softer, swift as if she had to let the words out fast or they'd never get out at all, "if I'd admitted to the guy who was all 'love and BDSM don't mix' that I was falling for him. But I might as well get it out in the open so we can figure out where to go from there."

She loved him! Or she was falling for him, anyway, which

was at least three steps in the right direction.

Then he focused back on the earlier fight. "Then why did you laugh it off when I tried to tell you I loved you?"

She put her hands on her hips and leaned forward, looking like a particularly cute Fury. "Because you sounded mad as hell when you said it! Usually when you say that and mean it, it's not in the same tone as 'get out of my face, you psycho bitch'. Wouldn't be the first time someone said something they didn't really mean to stop an argument."

"Who told you..." He realized his fists were clenching, his body poising to fight, as if he wanted nothing more than to strangle or deck whoever it was who had lied to Selene about something so important.

She must have caught it too, because she flushed a brilliant scarlet and looked away. "No one," she said, almost imperceptibly. "I did it to someone."

He'd have expected his fists to unclench, but he still felt like punching whoever had pushed her to that point. "Tell me," he said, surprised by how much of an order it sounded, even though that wasn't his intent.

"Will, this guy I was dating back in Rochester. He's a great guy. Molly was so into him, and my mom—they just loved him and thought he should be The One, with capital letters. He's good-looking, smart, really sweet. Eager to please, would do just about anything for me. Wanted kids, and soon. The kind of guy that a woman's supposed to want."

"Except you didn't."

"No. And I felt terrible."

Nick ventured a smile. "Let me guess. He was a gentle, tender lover. Always."

She nodded, a bit ruefully. "Most women would have been thrilled. I mean, he was cuddly and romantic and loved cunnilingus. What's not to like, right?"

"Except that's not who you are."

"No. But he wanted me, bad, and the sex being so-so didn't seem like a good reason not to want such a great guy, and I hate hurting people's feelings. He pushed and pushed for a commitment, but always in the sweetest way, and I couldn't think of a good way to say no. So I said yes. And the next thing I knew we were living together and planning a wedding, and I think by that time we both knew we'd be miserable together. For one thing, we'd both defer to the other so nothing ever got decided. He wasn't weak or dumb, but he really wanted me to be the strong, in-charge one, and that's just not me. At least not all the time. Maybe I should introduce him to Vicki," she added wickedly, naming one of their domme acquaintances. "I think I remember her saying something about her ideal guy being orally fixated and into being a stay-at-home dad someday, and I think Will would be great at that."

"So even before you were really aware you were a sub, you knew you didn't want to be the one in charge. Interesting."

She blinked as if she'd expected a different, perhaps more violent, reaction. "Not all the time. I'm...I'm not Natalie. I couldn't live that way. I'm not sure I could be like Alison, even. I like my independence. And I need to work with battered women. But I also know it's only part of me, that part of me also needs to yield, needs to surrender. Needs roughness and wildness and control—but mostly in the bedroom or leading back to the bedroom. If anything, I need the release so I can keep sane while doing something as stressful as helping battered women get their lives back. I don't know what that makes me."

She backed up to the rocking chair and sat down abruptly as if saying all that had taken a lot out of her. Then she blinked and seemed to wait for a reaction.

Nick crossed to her, crouched down in front of the chair, put his hands on the arms. Waited while he formulated the right way to answer.

"A woman I could love," he finally said.

"What?"

"You still don't believe me, do you? Maybe this will help." He leaned forward and kissed her.

Her eyes were wide when he let her come up for air again, pupils dilated with need, lips swollen from the force of the kiss. "That proved...something," she said dreamily. Then she blinked and added, "I thought you wanted a slave, eventually. Natalie said..." Blinked again. "But Natalie isn't exactly a reliable source. I know that. Why don't you tell me what you want?"

Nick shook his head. "Once, I did want a slave. Total control, total ownership. It makes a great fantasy."

"From the other side too."

"For a long time, I thought it was my ideal, the thing I should strive for. It's the ultimate expression of dominance and submission, and I'm the kind of person who likes the ultimate...whatever."

Selene laughed. "That makes two of us. I'm following you way too well here."

"For some people"—Nick gestured around the room in illustration—"it works. Garth and Alison have a great thing. But it's their thing. We could have a great thing too, but a different thing. One that works for us." He paused, then added, "If you still want to, that is. I was a real ass tonight."

"Yeah, you were. And so was I. I was a jealous cow, and you were angry, and we both jumped to conclusions."

"I hurt you." He took her hands. "Natalie would say a dom doesn't have to apologize, but sometimes we do—if only so we can live with ourselves. And this is one of those times. I'm sorry. I know better than to play when I'm angry, and I wasn't controlling myself as well as I should have. I pushed things way too far."

She bowed her head, tried to hide her face in her shoulder, muttered something he couldn't catch.

"What?" Very gently, he took her chin in his hand, turned her head. "What did you say?"

Her face was flaming red, a blush—or maybe a flush—extending down into her cleavage. "I loved some of it," she whispered.

He felt his own face flush at the bald admission.

"I didn't like the anger. I could feel the anger, wasn't sure how in control you were, and that scared me. And humiliation just pisses me off. But being tied up like that...and the paddling...and the cane. My God, the cane. It hurt like crazy, and while it was going on, it was almost too much. But at the same time, I could see where..." She took a deep breath as if gathering her courage. "I'd like to try it again sometime, but...slower, if that's the word I want. Give me time to get used to the feeling."

She bit her lip and shifted in the chair. She flinched a bit as she moved, but her face looked curiously content despite the flinching, as if her ass was sore but pleasantly so. "I can't believe I'm saying that. I don't even know if we should be together. If we should be doing this stuff."

"Of course we should." He said it with a confidence he wasn't sure he felt. "Why shouldn't two consenting adults who love each other..."

"I think maybe that's what's scaring me. As long as I could tell myself it was just casual and any thoughts of love were incredible sex warping my mind, I could cope. Wanting you to do hot, nasty things to me was just all good clean dirty fun. But it's more than that. I want you tell me what to do and...make me yours somehow. More than I expected, more than I ever thought I'd want. And I love you and you say you love me and how does that work? I know it can, but how? Now it all seems more complicated and darker somehow. I never knew I could want that much pain. Never knew I could need so much. Never knew I could like being treated that harshly. And never knew I could be so in love that thinking I'd lost you tonight hurt more than anything you could possibly do to me."

She began to sob, helplessly, hopelessly. Nick froze, not

sure what he should do, although all his instincts called out to take her in his arms.

But some instinct on her part drew her to him, made her throw her arms around him, snuggle close against his chest.

The rocking chair tipped too far as her weight shifted. She pitched forward.

They both ended up lying on the floor, her sprawled on top of him, laughing while she cried.

Nick's brain was going in six different directions, trying to figure out what to do next, how to handle all these new complications.

Nick's body and heart were more straightforward. A beautiful woman lay on top of him, soft in his arms, still smelling of rut and sobbing as though her heart was shattered? Arms go around sobbing woman. Lips nuzzle her ear in a comforting way, murmur soothing noises like those you might make to a dog during a thunderstorm or to a child woken from a nightmare—no sensible words, just crooning. Cock twitches, starts to harden. Doesn't get too insistent because of the tears, which seem to be serious tears, not the cathartic kind that can happen during great scenes, but starts to get ready just in case the warm, musky, soft woman decides that, being pressed against a hard male body, she might find something better to do than cry.

And heart reaches out in its own way, embraces her, vows to keep her safe, even though, his brain tries to remind his heart, he caused her problem in the first place.

Finally she quieted, both tears and laughter burned out.

"I love you," he said. "And I'm sorry. I'll never hurt you again." She flashed a ghost of a smile. "Not that way, anyway. Only good ways."

She sniffled, then wiped her eyes on the back of her hand like a little girl. "You can't promise someone that. Stuff happens. Things go wrong. People do dumb things. We both did tonight—all along, I guess, not being more upfront about some of the stuff in our pasts. And we will again. It happens in any relationship, but it seems there's a whole new level of dumb possible, as well as a whole new level of fun, when you start playing with dominance and submission. I saw it with Natalie, but it's easy to look at her mistakes..."

"And think you couldn't possibly be that boneheaded." He kissed her forehead. "And we couldn't. That doesn't mean we won't come up with our very own stupid stuff, but I promise I'll never lock you in a closet while I'm at work or tell you you're too fat and refuse to feed you. Especially not if you weigh a hundred pounds."

"Yeah, and hands off my shoes, buddy!" she mock growled. Then, suddenly sober, "But things like tonight—how do we keep them from happening?"

Nick opened his mouth to say, *I don't know*, but Alison's voice, outside the bedroom door, answered. "You talk. You talk a lot."

"How much did you hear?" Nick said at the same time Selene said, "You were *listening*?"

"Only to the last sentence. Okay, last two. *Hands off my shoes* caught my attention while I was passing and then..."

"Well, you might as well come in," Nick said reluctantly.

"It's your bedroom, and we did take it over."

She opened the door, peered in, saw them heaped on the floor. "Well, that looks promising."

"Uh...maybe?" Selene said. "A lot better than earlier, anyway." She sat up, running her hands down Nick's torso as she did, as if reluctant to let go. "So that's the solution to everything—talking a lot?" She sounded dubious.

"In any relationship, I think, but especially if there's BDSM involved, because that adds a whole new level of ways to confuse each other."

Selene laughed. "We were just talking about that."

"Just talk?" Nick said. "I knew that. I mean in theory. It even makes sense. But it never worked with Natalie, so I got out of the habit. She didn't want to let on anything might be wrong until it was far too wrong to fix it, and she'd go 'la-la-la' if I had anything to say that didn't fit the Master Mold." He realized he was saying it with caps on, the way Natalie always said certain words.

"Well, Natalie's..."

"Batshit?" Alison suggested.

"I was going to say 'not me'," Selene said tactfully. "Is 'batshit' the correct clinical term?"

"I'm not sure what the correct clinical term is. I'm a medical administrator, not a doctor. But speaking as her friend, the girl is running from something that's eating her up inside. She doesn't need a master right now. She needs a therapist. Preferably one who'll understand that once she gets more stable, she'll still need a master, or at least *want* one."

"It's like she's scared to think too much and wants someone else to do it for her. Whether he'll do a good job or not."

Alison nodded. "Exactly. And now that we've solved Natalie's problems for her, I'll leave you again to solve yours."

She withdrew.

"Talking, eh?" Selene said.

"Yeah. Communication. We talked about that the first couple of times. Then I guess we got swept up."

"A lot of things are hard to say to someone you don't know all that well, and we went awfully fast from strangers to...whatever we are."

"Lovers. We're lovers. A couple. A couple that has a few things to work out, sure, but what couple doesn't?"

"A couple. I like the sound of that." She snuggled against him. "I like that a lot. But if we're a couple"—she looked up, grinned, and even though her face was still blotchy and swollen and her hair was a crazy mess, Nick thought she'd never looked more beautiful—"will you still spank me and flog me and stuff?"

"Hell yes! If you still want me to."

"Hell yes! And set rules that are meant to be broken so I can get 'in trouble'." She made air quotes. "And make me give you lots and lots of blowjobs, and tie me up and fuck me, and all that other good stuff we've already tried. Other stuff too, but we'll figure that out together as we go along." Her smile was one of pure erotic glee—a bit at odds with the tearstains, but it went directly to Nick's groin. Blood pumped, hardening his cock, tightening his balls, sending waves of lust to short-circuit his brain.

"I have a few suggestions," he said throatily. "We could try some of them now..." Then he looked around, reminded himself where he was. Garth and Alison might pride themselves on accommodating their guests, but taking over their bedroom to kiss and nibble Selene's bruised and tender bottom, lick her to a series of screaming orgasms, and then fuck her senseless might be pushing it.

Especially since once he got started, Nick had no intention of letting Selene out of his arms until sometime late the next morning, when hunger would compel them from bed.

Long enough to eat something other than each other and then get back at it.

"By *now*, of course, I mean, *once we get home*. But I think we have time for a little taste." He ran his hands down her ripe body, just skimming her buns, but even that light touch made her twitch.

"They're so tender," she whispered, shivering. "It feels great. I love..." But when he raised her skirt, she shook her head. "Not so fast. Talking, right? I freaked out on you tonight. And I need to explain why, before we get carried away and forget and it just sits there waiting to pop out again.

"I can handle you calling my body part a cunt—but not me. Especially not in that angry voice. And then you tacked on worthless. That is not cool. I've told you about Molly. Her rat-bastard father used to yell that at her mom—sometimes at her too—even when other people were around. I didn't know what it meant back then, but it terrified me. I can't hear those words, especially not in an angry voice, without wanting to run and hide. Or better yet, hurt the person who's saying them."

Nick felt his heart—so recently put back together that the glue was still wet—crack again. "I'm so sorry. I had no idea. Play-humiliation is so tricky to pull off I usually don't try unless my partner asks for it and gives me ideas, but tonight..." He sighed. "Tonight I felt pretty humiliated myself, because I thought you were rejecting me, telling me I was only good as a rent-a-dom, not a partner. So I was trying to get some of my own back. Stupid. Can you forgive me?"

There was a second's hesitation, one that seemed to last longer than a second, than a minute, than a lifetime. Nick counted the beats of his racing heart—only a couple—but it still seemed forever before she answered, "Yes, I can. And you know why? Because if anyone else had used those words, I'd have bolted immediately despite the rope and probably kneecapped him on the way out. But I trust you, Nick. It wasn't easy, but I managed to roll with it, because deep down I must have known that if I did break, you could put me back together. Even though I was afraid you'd reject me for breaking when I did."

"Never be afraid to safe-word. I don't want you to be harmed, not ever. And if something does touch a nerve, I promise to be there and help you work through it. Always. Forever."

This time, when he touched her, kissed her, it was to comfort.

At least that was the intention.

But they both caught fire.

Bodies pressed together as if they'd been apart for years. One of Selene's small, strong hands sliding down his waistband, gripping and stroking his hard length. He raised her skirt, and this time, she didn't resist but spread her legs to give him better access. Her pussy was like molten lava, hot, thick juices flowing, and she bucked against him almost immediately, stifling a cry by biting into his shoulder.

Within record time, she'd found a condom in her purse, and he was in the rocking chair with his fly unzipped, a blazing erection sticking up, and Selene was straddling him. No extended foreplay, no games of pain and pleasure, just an overwhelming urge to mate, to merge.

Her warm, soft pussy opened, and she slid down onto him with one quick wiggle. Velvet and honey, he thought nonsensically. Then she whispered, "I bet they have a chair like this for a reason," and started it rocking. He gave up even nonsensical thought as a lost cause.

Back and forth, the movement of the chair assisted them, raising him to meet her tightening pussy, pulling them apart, then bringing them together, a slow, steady, delicious friction that—if they had been somewhere other than someone else's bedroom—they could have kept up forever, or at least a good chunk of forever. "Move me," she gasped. "Need more." He dug his fingers into her delicious, rounded hips and complied, slamming her down onto his cock over and over again, letting her clit grind against his pubic bone. He could feel her starting to contract again, to tighten around him, and his own body rose to answer, wanting to explode with her.

Or maybe sooner than that, if he wasn't careful. Between all the intense emotions of the evening, the risk of getting caught and the fact that they'd finally said it, that he was fucking not his sub but the woman he loved and who loved him, who, lucky him, was *also* his succulent sub, was too much.

"Touch yourself," he ordered, surprising himself with the dark whisky in his voice. "I'm going to..."

She grinned. Slipped one hand down to her clit. Circled and flicked as they ground together. Threw her head back and opened her mouth in a soundless howl as her pussy clenched and released, milking his orgasm from him.

He tried to choke back the urge to shout her name, to shout, *Love you*, as he exploded.

He failed.

As they came back to themselves, he looked at Selene, shook his head and said, "Alison and Garth are never going to let us live this down, are they?"

"Do you care?"

"Not in the least."

Chapter Twenty-Eight

They left Selene's car behind, promising to pick it up later. By the time they made it back to Jamaica Plain, Selene was dozing, wine, strong emotion and phenomenal sex combining with the late hour to make her cross-eyed with fatigue. Nick took one look at her, shook his head, tucked her into bed and crawled in next to her.

She scooted over, put her head on his chest and felt a deep sense of peace and belonging as he pulled her closer. They'd been sharing a bed regularly for several months, but this was the first time they'd deliberately fallen asleep so snuggled together. Selene hadn't thought about it until now, but it was as if they'd both been holding back from that level of intimacy even while they enjoyed erotic pleasures she couldn't have imagined sharing with anyone else. Now, after the evening's storm passed, they seemed to be ready.

In the morning, they were awakened by the sound of the front door opening.

Natalie, against all expectation, was home. "Sorry, guys," she called out cheerfully. "I'm just grabbing my laptop, then going back to Mom's."

"Hold on a minute," Nick said, his voice stern. "We'll be right out."

"No need. I'll be out of here in a sec..."

"No," Selene said, already grabbing the bathrobe she'd taken to keeping there since Natalie moved in. "We'd like to talk with you."

They'd had a brief, almost wordless exchange while they

reached for clothes, him asking if she wanted him to do the talking, her saying it was her job, at least to get it started. She still couldn't figure out how they'd said that without really talking. Lots of gestures and expressions, and a deep current of understanding that, she realized, had always been there but was now flowing unimpeded.

She had to be the one to ask the questions, at least at first. Natalie would tell Nick what she thought he wanted to hear, try to appease him. Selene understood that. Already, she knew how easy it was to leave out the difficult stuff when you were eager to please someone.

Not that she was looking forward to the conversation. Confronting a troubled woman and asking her if she'd deliberately tried to screw up their relationship or did it from sheer idiocy wasn't her idea of a good time, especially not before coffee.

When she actually saw beautiful, graceful, crazy Natalie waltzing around the condo like she belonged there, tact didn't seem so important anymore.

Not with Nick standing behind her, radiating strength and support.

"Natalie," she said, "were you screwing with my head or are you just an idiot?"

"What? Selene, I have no idea..."

In her consternation, Natalie dropped the Dunkin' Donuts cup she was clutching. Coffee splattered everywhere, and the room filled with the rich smell of vanilla-flavored java. "Oh God, I'm sorry, Nick! It's all over your rug now. Let me get that..."

Natalie tried to dart past them to the kitchen in search of paper towels and distraction.

Selene blocked her path. "But the carpet... Shouldn't I..."

"Leave it," Nick growled.

Natalie looked so fragile and bewildered that Selene felt a pang of guilt at pressing the issue. But only for a second. "You broke up with Nick, Natalie. Everyone knew that except me. And you broke up with him because he was falling in love with you, and you couldn't handle that."

Natalie glanced around wildly, trying to look for an out. Thought she saw one in Nick. "Sir," she said in her most ingratiating voice, "I don't know what she's talking about. Tell her you released me."

"Because you begged me to." Nick's voice was cold, and not in the detached-but-sexy mad-scientist sort of way it sometimes got in the bedroom, but in a way that said, if you were paying attention, that he was done.

Natalie, apparently, wasn't paying attention. With three steps, she crossed the living room, put her hand on Nick's arm and looked up at him, eyes as wide and pleading as a puppy at the pound. Even Selene, who wanted at this point to hit the woman repeatedly with a clue-by-eight because a clue-by-four wouldn't be big enough to make an impression, had to admit that if she were more into women and even a little bit toppy, that little-girl-lost expression might have melted her heart.

She wasn't, though, so it didn't. "I think you need to talk to me, Nat. Not to him."

"I...uh... Oh, hell. Selene. You've done so much to help me. Why would I have wanted to hurt...?" She sat down abruptly on the nearest piece of furniture, which happened to be Nick's favorite green comfy chair. She'd never sat in it, as far as Selene knew, in the time she'd been living there, and she looked down at it as if it might burn her.

Nick put a gentle but firm hand on her shoulder when she tried to jump up again.

"That's a good question," Selene said. "Because apparently you did. Either that or you're really dumb, and even though you play that game sometimes, I don't buy it."

The long, pained silence was finally broken with Natalie jumping up and darting for the door.

"Natalie," Nick said, a warning growl. The instinct to obey him must have been strong in her still, because she caught herself short, hand on the doorknob, and waited, her skinny body trembling like a frightened fawn. Remembering the broken woman she'd first met, Selene pitied her. Maybe Natalie didn't deserve her pity, but it would make her smaller somehow not to feel it when someone was so fragile both physically and emotionally.

"I like you, Selene," she finally said. "That's important to say, I think. When you first started asking me questions, I really did just want to help. You don't seem like a slave to me, more someone who likes to get her freak on in the bedroom and be equal the rest of the time, but I don't know what's in your heart, and you wanted to learn. When I first knew him, it was something Nick wanted, to be a master, a really good one, to have a slave and love and cherish her. What he wanted didn't work for me, but it might work for you, so at first I wanted to help because I still care for Nick."

She glanced from Selene to Nick, her eyes wide and wild. She'd wrapped her arms around herself as if that would hold her together, but she was still shaking like she might fall apart. "But it's been killing me seeing you guys so happy! The longer I've been here, the harder it's gotten. I'm not sure anymore what or who I need, but I'm pretty sure it's not romance, and you need to give your girl that, Nick. But it hurt. Seeing you two... It hurt in the worst way. And I realized neither of you were seeing how right you were for each other, and that just made it worse because you had the start of something great, and you didn't even fucking appreciate it."

"Oh, we did," Nick said, a rueful smile on his handsome face. "We just didn't have the sense to tell each other how much we appreciated it until it was almost too late."

"So I started playing games. Not lying, exactly, but my truths, not yours—what works for me, but not what would probably work best for you guys. I fed you a few ideas that I knew would push Nick's buttons, maybe provoke a fight. I thought maybe it would be a good thing in the long run, that either Selene would find her slave-self, or she wouldn't, and you'd both know and could decide what to do from there."

The strange thing was that Selene could see how Natalie, confused and miserable, trying to put her life back together and not sure how, could convince herself that this behavior made sense, that it was even serving Nick's interests and helping Selene figure out what she wanted.

"And then I started talking to Craig, and he..."

"Wait just a damn minute," Nick exclaimed. "Craig's in on this too?"

"Don't blame him," Natalie said, her voice firmer than usual. "I guess he put some ideas in my head, talking about how he never saw how you two ended up together, how Selene wasn't right for you, not enough of a slave at heart, not like me. I got worried about Nick. Then I got worried about me. Where would I go if you two kept going the way you were? What would I do? I'd gotten what I thought I needed and it was hell, so I've been questioning. Maybe I was wrong, maybe I left too soon, maybe I should have stayed with you and tried to learn to be loved. And that maybe if things didn't work with you and Selene, I'd have another chance."

"What made you think I was going to let her go?"

"You let me go."

"Because it was what you wanted and needed. We weren't working, and I wasn't going to keep you against your will. You've never wanted all I had to offer. You wanted the whips, the leather, the control, not the man wielding them. Selene does."

"Your loss, really," Selene said, her voice sweet with malice. She found she could forgive Natalie's games with her head a lot more readily than the damage she'd done Nick. Selene had been naïve enough to let Natalie manipulate matters—more fool her.

Nick had loved and trusted Natalie once, though, and she'd hurt him. That, Selene couldn't forgive.

"But Craig said that you'd be much better with someone else. That you really needed a playmate... someone more like him, really, who wasn't in a position to commit and didn't want to. I managed to convince myself that maybe it would be the best thing for everyone," Natalie smiled weakly, one of those smiles that was more like a defense mechanism. It was clear from her eyes that she knew how badly wrong she'd been. "I don't know what I was thinking except Craig said I was the only woman who'd made him think of leaving his wife and that's kind of a brain-melting thing to hear, you know..."

A flash of understanding hit Selene, and with it, a flash of solidarity with Natalie. "That arrogant bastard! Natalie, that rat was playing you twice over. He wanted a chance at both of us. Not that he had one with me, but I think he was hoping if Nick and I broke up, he might. And if that didn't work, or even if it did, since he's not exactly the monogamous type, he'd have a crack at you."

Another flash of insight. "Natalie, I know you're lost right now, trying to figure out what to do next. But I know you have better judgment than to go from one bad situation to another, from Derrick to being someone's guilty little secret." Okay, Natalie was messed-up enough at this point that she didn't have better judgment than that, but Selene was putting all her counseling classes to use. "You can do better than helping Craig Whittaker cheat on his wife. He'll do it one way or the other, but let's leave you out of the equation, shall we?"

Natalie looked back at her, stunned. "But he's a master. He can..."

"Don't you have to earn that title by being worth serving and respecting? He's a cheater who was trying to figure out a way to two-time the person he was hoping to two-time his wife with. You don't need someone like that. You're too good for that, even if you don't believe it. Nick believes better things of you, and so do I. I'm angry enough I want to choke you right now, but I still know you deserve better than that."

Impulsively, she crossed over, gave Natalie a hug. The smaller woman was stiff in her arms, then yielded, bonelessly and fully, to the embrace.

Natalie began to cry.

"Derrick never tried to find me," she finally said.

"Thank God," was Nick's dry response.

"I know. I've been here instead of at Mom's because I figured you guys could handle it if he did turn up. But at the same time...he'd said I was his forever, that I couldn't leave, that he'd always find me and bring me home. I'm glad he didn't try, because it would have gotten ugly. But part of me still feels abandoned, and I know it doesn't make sense because he really was crazy, and I'm so lonely and Nick didn't need me either and... I'm sorry. I need...I need... I can't believe I ever thought doing anything that might mess you up was a good idea. You guys have been so good to me, and it just doesn't make sense that I did this."

"Nat," Selene said, as gently as she could, "you need therapy."

Selene felt her stiffen before she pulled away. "Don't want someone to cure me of being a slave."

"Not that. There's nothing wrong with that, once you get a few things straightened out, but you're doing stuff that doesn't make sense even to you. Maybe it's something to do with losing your dad so young, maybe something chemical, maybe it's just the after-effects of Derrick, but something's wrong, and you need help to fix it."

"When I find a master again...the right one this time..." She froze, her mouth opening and closing silently. She was wearing a boat-neck shirt, and Selene could see the tight lines of her shoulders, like steel cables strained past their capacity.

"I'm sure the right master is out there for you, but to give him what he deserves, you need to be healthy. I don't know that much about being a good slave from the inside out. You're right that it's not who I am. But it seems to me a good slave should be like, oh, a good butler or executive assistant or something. Able to take on whatever needs to be done at a moment's notice. Even if he's making the decisions, you need to be able to carry them out. You need to be strong for him when he needs you to be, and not just handling a whipping or something but being a rock for him when he needs one. What if your master was in a bad accident or got cancer or something? You'd need to be able to be strong for him, to take care of him, to make decisions in his place, maybe. When free people flub up, it only screws up our own lives. You're a reflection of your master, so you have to be the best *you* that you can be. And that means dealing with whatever demons are haunting you. A master who cares for you will help, but you have to start the work yourself."

She was making it up as she went along, but Natalie's clouded face brightened a bit. "So I might do better finding the right one if I weren't so scared all the time? Scared to act, scared to make decisions, scared to love or be loved, but scared to be alone..."

Selene, hoping she was telling the truth, nodded. "At the very least, you'll be more likely to recognize a good guy when he comes along."

"Do you know someone," Natalie said, "who wouldn't try to change the parts of me I like? It's so hard. I know there's something not quite right inside me, even before Derrick got me so I didn't know which way was up, but I've been scared to get help because I'm afraid they'll tell me I'm *all* wrong, that I need to stop being who I am. Stop being kinky."

Selene slipped her arm around Natalie's narrow shoulders. "Alison handed out a list of kink-friendly therapists when she talked to my grad school class. She said she knows some of them."

"I should get back to my mom's," Natalie said in a small

voice, "and get out of your hair, but I'll take that list if you can find it, and I'll talk to Alison later. And talk to my mom about moving into her place for a while."

After she left, Nick pulled Selene close and gave her a resounding kiss. "I'll be damned," he said. "I think she listened to you. She never listened to me that well."

"Maybe some people would say that making herself a better slave isn't the healthiest reason to see a shrink," Selene said. "But hey, if I thought it would get her to therapy, I'd tell her she'd find a pot of gold in the office after her tenth session." She paused. "And I think I've just learned something important for my work. Someone can be an abuse survivor and deserve help and compassion, but that doesn't necessarily mean she'll be easy to deal with. Sometimes people who've gone through hell can be awful, to themselves and everyone else. And sometimes the most compassionate thing to do for someone is call her on her bullshit."

"Natalie always was a little damaged. What she went through this year just made it worse. But I never had the guts to call her on it because I loved her and I couldn't handle the hurt in her eyes." Nick hugged Selene again. "I may be the dom and act all tough in the bedroom, but in a lot of important ways, you're tougher than I am."

Chapter Twenty-Nine

Selene took a deep breath, took Nick's hands and looked into his eyes. "I want to try the cane again."

"Are you sure?"

"Yes..." A split second's hesitation. "I hate being afraid of something you like. I hate being afraid, period."

"You don't need to push yourself. Of course, if you really are ready, whee! I like canes. But I like you more."

She grinned a little weakly, trying to hide the way she was lurching between arousal and terror. "It's not unselfish, Nick. I need the closure. That was an awful night and I feel like we need to redo it again and do it right this time. And besides," she added, a little more confidently than she felt, "I bet it'll be fun when we're not fighting."

It was afternoon when they got started this time, broad daylight. Selene asked for that specifically, to have the autumn sun streaming in through the blinds as Nick beat her, to make this a normal, bright thing, not a thing of darkness. Nick had drily suggested using Jimmy Buffett as scene music, and she'd smacked him. This allowed them to get into a playful wrestling match in the living room.

It ended with them on the living room floor, Nick's cock in her mouth and Nick's head between her legs, as he licked her clit and she sucked him. He moved in her mouth, shallow strokes because of the angle, and she thought he tasted like heaven, and each flick of his tongue sent shimmers of pleasure through her entire body. He felt so hard, so powerful, and yet his tongue was gentle and soft. At the same time, that gentle tongue and that cock in her mouth controlled her utterly, as much as bonds or orders did.

When the shimmering turned into a nova and she exploded, Nick said, "Love you," in a voice that started out as a harsh whisper and ended up as a strangled cry. He flooded her mouth, hot and salty and utterly delicious.

Still, by the time they moved from the living room floor to the bedroom, Selene had moved past sated and back to aroused, and Nick's cock was stirring and stretching again. Nick threw open the curtains. For a second, Selene wondered if this was such a good idea. What if someone saw in?

Then she decided she didn't care. She wanted the light to witness this scene, because they weren't going to let things get as dark as they had that night.

When Nick said, "Lean over on the bed and stick your butt out," she figured it was time for the caning. She closed her eyes, took a deep breath, then let it out slowly, bracing and centering herself. Excited as she was, she was also nervous. The good mood, the arousal, the playfulness earlier, not to mention the playful sex in the living room, would make sure this was a good experience emotionally. But canes still hurt. A lot.

Her gut roiled anxiously, anticipating that sharp, hot sensation, wondering whether she'd be able to enjoy it or even take it at all this time or if it would turn out to be something that didn't work for her. She hoped that wasn't the case. She knew she could stop the scene if she needed to, and Nick would find something they could both revel in, but dammit, she wanted it to work. Wanted to like it, even if she hated it at the same time. Wanted to find the fiery pleasure she'd sensed amid the turmoil of the failed scene.

She felt Nick move in behind her and took another deep, steadying breath. His hands cupped her ass, and she leaned into the caress, figuring he was going to stroke her skin as he often liked to do before spanking or flogging her. Instead, Nick parted her ass cheeks. She felt a cool trickle of lube. One of

Nick's fingers worked into her ass, then two. As always, there was a second of burn, a hint of resistance before the pleasure kicked in and she let herself open to the exploring fingers. She groaned. They hadn't done full-on anal sex, and she hadn't pushed for it. There were so many other things to explore, and butt-fucking was something she'd tried before. Even super-vanilla Will had been game for that.

Maybe it was time to change that. The plugs they'd used were lovely, and right now Nick's fingers felt so good. Maybe, assuming her butt wasn't too sore to ponder the pounding, she'd ask for anal as a finale. Worst he'd say was *not now.*

As if he read her mind, Nick said, "I'm going to plug you now, and when we're done with the beating, when you're lovely and open and floaty and tender, I'm going to fuck this beautiful ass. How does that sound?"

"Oh God, yes," she exclaimed, perfect punctuation as he slid his fingers out and a well-lubed plug in.

She expected the beating to start then, now that she was quivering with need, full of a butt plug, about to fly apart from excitement.

Nick instead had her stand. And then he lovingly wrapped Selene in deep red rope, not to restrain her at this point but to arouse her further. Rope coiled around her rib cage and between her breasts, forming a harness that thrust them out and made her more aware of the weight and sensitivity. Rope slithered between her legs, one strand tugging gently on either lip, spreading out from a strategic knot right over her clit. Wherever the ropes touched her, she felt the echo of Nick's hands stroking as he tied her. "We're going to need to wash the ropes," she said, half giggling and half sighing. "I'm getting them all wet."

"That's why I didn't use hemp this time. This stuff washes well." Nick ran his fingers between her legs, tracing the path of the ropes over her labia and up between her cheeks. She shuddered and bucked, as much at the husky love in his voice as the touch. "I love how wet you get. I love the way you respond to rope." He put his now slick hands on her shoulders and captured her mouth. She wrapped her arms around his waist, parted her lips and fell into the kiss.

Sweet and possessive. Fierce and tender. He tasted of her juices, and some subtle spice, but mostly he tasted like Nick, delicious and beloved. She moved her hands over his skin, loving the play of heat and muscle. The last caning, the one that had gone wrong, he'd stayed dressed. She much preferred him like this—naked, just like her, a kind of equality within the power game. Besides, this way she could cup his hard ass, feel the slight fur of his thighs against her skin, gaze at his muscular body, and enjoy his cock jutting against her, so much better bare than through clothes.

She was reaching for that cock when Nick caught her wrist. "Oh no. Not until I say so. In fact, maybe we better tie those hands so you don't distract me."

He had her lie across the bed, hands extended in front of her. A couple of quick loops fastened her wrists together, and from there, he extended the rope to a tie-down point hidden on the far side of the bedframe. Selene squirmed experimentally. She could move quite a lot, but she couldn't get away, and every wiggle would tease at her already hypersensitive clit and full ass.

She couldn't decide if that was an argument against wiggling or for it.

"Beautiful. You look so beautiful tied like that." Nick ran his hand down her back, an innocent gesture that made her shiver with pleasure and need. He moved away and started rummaging among the toys.

Selene made a determined effort not to look. They'd already deviated in several wonderful ways from the original night—besides neither of them acting like utter assholes, which was the most important difference—but he'd probably go for the paddle. He got a kick out of the NAUGHTY imprints on her butt.

When he positioned himself behind her, she braced herself for the sharp slap of the paddle.

What she felt was one of their lightest floggers, stingy yet soft and sensual, a caress with a bit of bite. Lovely. She pushed back as much as her bonds allowed for more. The movement shifted the ropes between her legs and she gasped in pleased surprise.

"No coming without permission," Nick said, although his tone suggested the consequences of failure wouldn't be too dire.

Still, that settled the wiggle versus not wiggle question. Not wiggle, as much as Selene could manage.

Nick flicked the flogger again. This time just the tips caught her, stingier but still sensuous and sweet. Then again and again and again. Soon she was sighing, "More please," and counting the strikes, though he hadn't told her to, to distract herself a little from the firestorm building in her pussy, the smaller one in her ass.

She lost count, inevitably. She lost herself. She lost everything but the sensations: the stinging blows on her butt and thighs, her stretched, sensitive ass, teased pussy lips and blissfully tormented clit, the embrace of the rope, Nick's hands warm on her skin when he paused to stroke her. He was hitting her hard now but still it felt like a caress. The right word would make her come, but oddly, there was no real urgency. For now, riding the waves of sensation was enough. She was babbling *yes, yes, yes* under her breath, but if Nick had thought to ask her, she couldn't possibly have explained why, just that she needed to affirm something.

When he finally set the flogger down and reached for the cane, she was flying so high that the first strike felt like a love tap. Or maybe it was a love tap, a warm-up, leading her into the caning gradually? It felt good, whichever it was, sharp and hot but good, like the rush of eating spicy food. She let out a breath she hadn't known she'd been holding with a little *aah*. Nick laughed softly as he caned her again.

This time was definitely harder and caught her right in that sweet spot where her ass curved to her thighs, that spot that hurt a little more than the ass proper yet radiated pleasure so wonderfully to her clit and pussy—and, with a butt plug in, to her ass too. She couldn't help flinching and crying out at the initial pain, but she couldn't help clenching either, couldn't help the flames of need that seared her. She wiggled back into place, letting the ropes tug and tease at her drenched cunt.

"How does that feel?" Nick asked.

When his words sank into her foggy brain, all she could think was that she wanted more of that fire. So that was how she answered, with a groan of, "More."

Nick complied, this one cutting like a hot knife, but at the same time, delicious. Selene jumped and shrieked by reflex, but the pleasure overcame the pain. The next didn't hurt, exactly. She was aware of the cutting strike, of the fire in its wake, but the fire was so sweet it burned away pain. After that, she floated away, the pain transmuted to bliss, feeling each hot strike as a pulse of pleasure, almost a caress. The need was building. She was going to erupt like a volcano.

But she couldn't. There were words she needed to say and hear before she could let go. Words were hard, though. She couldn't remember many. But she did remember, "Please, sir, please," and she repeated it like a prayer.

"One more, Selene. Just one more. This one will be harder."

She remembered a few more words then. "Yes sir, but please...please..."

"Love you." He struck again, and it was harder, hard enough to shock through the euphoria and actually hurt. As the cane smacked down, though, he said, "Come, Selene. Come now."

The inferno broke free, consuming what was left of Selene's consciousness in an explosive orgasm. The orgasm encompassed not just her long-teased clit and pussy and ass, not just her delightfully tender butt, but the soles of her feet, the hair on her head and everything in between. She'd never been sure if there was such a thing as a soul, but she was pretty sure she felt her soul coming, bursting into flame in its own way. She came keening and howling, shaking like she was caught in an earthquake, pounding and tearing at the bed with her bound hands. It took a long time for her to start to come down.

And just when she thought she had, just when she thought she could start breathing normally, Nick removed the butt plug.

Her body clenched and released in anticipation. She pushed back. When Nick's cock began its slow, inexorable journey into her ass, that triggered another firestorm, smaller than the last but still powerful.

"I feel you," Nick groaned. "So tight. Your ass clamps down when you come." He came to rest, his hips against her ass, his cock fully inside. "I'm almost scared to move. Once I start, I'm not sure I can hold back."

"Move." There—another word she could manage to speak. "Please?"

"I may not be gentle."

She squeezed deliberately this time and pushed back against him. "Please. Move. Please."

He did.

He'd been right. He wasn't gentle. He went hard and fast, slamming against her sore cheeks, fucking her ass like he normally would her cunt. Fire and darkness and a bright, lovely edge of pain when he pressed his fingers into the cane marks as he gripped her. It might have been too much at some other time, a time when he hadn't taken her as far before they reached this point, but it was just right now.

All the time he fucked her, he was muttering words of love that sounded like obscenities, obscenities that sounded like words of love, a vulgar litany that rose to a crescendo as he came.

He didn't even manage to untie her hands, just helped her to crawl onto the bed and curled up around her. "Love you," he whispered into her hair.

"Love you," she whispered back, and then, "thank you."

Much later, after a nap, and a shower, and a snack, Selene said, "I don't think you hit me as hard as you did that first time. I had bruises for days after that fiasco."

"Look." Nick led her over to the mirror.

She had to crane her neck to see her own ass. But sure enough, her ass was striped with distinct red double lines with bruises forming around them. "I...I..." She couldn't speak, just turned and buried her face in Nick's chest.

"You're welcome," he said.

Chapter Thirty

Nick rolled over in bed the next morning—okay, it was more like afternoon—looked at Selene and said, his voice still harsh with dreams, "I love watching you wake up. You look so gorgeous."

Selene laughed. "Yeah, right. With just-been-fucked hair on top of bed-head, my eyes bleary and probably swollen, pillow wrinkles on my cheeks... You must love me."

Of course Nick looked disheveled himself, his hair all over the place. But that just made him look like deliciously wild, like a naked pirate, all long limbs and hard muscles, his blue eyes keen and intent on her. And he smelled well fucked, just like she did—but it was easier to enjoy it on him.

"I do love you," he said simply. "But honestly, you look beautiful all rumpled and sleepy and soft. Especially rumpled and sleepy and soft with my marks on your sweet butt."

"You can't see those," she said in a teasing singsong.

He took that as a challenge, just like she'd hoped he would, and the next thing she knew he was wrestling with her and the sheet, attempting to flip her over and pull the sheet down.

He won, of course. Since he was bigger, he would have even if she hadn't wanted him to, but she did want him to.

Wanted to feel him overpower her, overwhelm her again, in a lighthearted way this time, in contrast to the previous night's fire. Wanted to feel his strength, his energy, his mock fierceness that could become real, intensely sexual fierceness at the drop of a hat, or in this case, a sheet.

After the inevitable result—tracing the lines left by last night's caning, giving her a few delicious smacks to redden her again, warm her up, make her sex swell and dampen and her need for him, which had been dulled a bit by sleepiness, rise again, a quick, furious, good-morning doggy-style fucking that brought her over the edge and tumbling into the oblivion of space—after all that and the cuddling and the laughter, he looked at her again and said, "And I love to see you like that too, all flushed and tender and sweaty from sex."

"Now that I'll believe. I love you seeing you that way too."

"Doms do not get not flushed and tender!" he proclaimed in his most pretentious voice.

She couldn't resist.

She hit him with her pillow.

He retaliated, and before they knew it, they were chasing each other through the condo, buffeting each other with down.

This time, she wasn't going to let him win and smacked at him with the pillows for all she was worth.

And in the middle of the laughter, Nick said, "Yeah, I definitely love waking up with you. Move in."

The pillow that was about to come down on Nick's head without mercy fell to the floor. "Nick, did you just ask me to move in?"

"You're not on the lease at your place, right?"

She shook her head. "Moved in to fill a vacancy. I need to give Lashonda time to find someone new." She hadn't gotten close to her roommate, but she didn't want to leave the other woman in the lurch, stuck with more rent than she could afford. Lashonda was fresh out of undergrad, without the savings reserves Selene had from selling her house in Rochester.

"Funny you should say that," he said. "I've got a new coworker. Nice kid, moved out here from Cincinnati to take the job. She's living on a college friend's couch now, but she's kind of desperate for a room of her own. I think she and Lashonda would get along okay. How about it? Eventually we'd need to find someplace bigger, where we could have pets and throw parties and stuff, but this could do while we're looking."

The reality of the question hit her, and she threw her arms around Nick and squealed like a happy little girl. "Of course! I'd love to. I love you. I..."

She stopped abruptly. "Am not very coherent at the moment?" Nick suggested helpfully.

"Yeah, that too." She stayed silent, thinking. Of course she wanted to move in. That wasn't a question. She loved Nick, loved being with him, wanted to see if they could make it work on the next level.

But something was niggling at her.

"If I move in...when I move in... will there be rules?"

"Yes," Nick said unhesitatingly. Then, a little more hesitatingly, "If it works for you too. Not slave rules, nothing too strict. Just little things to remind you that you're mine."

Her heart fluttered. "Yours?"

"Mine. Not my slave, just mine. Mine always, because I'm not going to let you go. Mine."

He grabbed a handful of hair at her nape as he said *mine* the final time, and Selene felt herself melting. She thought the recent lovemaking had left her sated, boneless, but all it took was those words, that gesture, to make her pussy swollen and slick, her nipples achingly taut.

Nick's blue eyes bored into hers, and the world narrowed to him and her and that was just as it should be.

"Yours always," she said softly.

And that was all the talking they did for a long, long time. At least with words.

About the Author

Teresa Noelle Roberts started writing stories in kindergarten and she hasn't stopped yet. A prolific author of short erotica, she's also a published poet and fantasy writer—but BDSM-spiced contemporaries and hot paranormals are her favorites. She's hard at work writing the kinky tales of hot dominant guys and smart women who submit to them—but not anyone else!—and making more sexy Duals and Donovans magic for your reading pleasure.

Teresa is a crunchy granola girl who enjoys belly dance, yoga, medieval re-creation, playing in the ocean, cooking, and growing more vegetables than she and her husband can possibly eat. She shares her home in southern Massachusetts with her husband, a Leo who works in law enforcement, and two overstuffed cats, who deserve their own shout-out as inspirations for her works. She and her husband often plan vacations around food, history, and/or proximity to water.

To learn more about Teresa Noelle Roberts, please visit www.teresanoelleroberts.com.

Follow her on Twitter (@TeresNoeRoberts) or on Facebook: www.facebook.com/teresanoelleroberts.

What happens in Vegas lasts forever...if you're lucky.

Fox's Folly
© *2012 Teresa Noelle Roberts*
A *Duals and Donovans* story

Las Vegas is the wrong place for an inexperienced witch like Paul Donovan. But he has no choice; his family owes a debt of honor to a half-fae casino owner, whose guests have been dying under mysterious circumstances. The normy police haven't connected the dots between the deaths, and the owner has called in his marker.

When Paul literally runs into fox dual Taggart Ross, the instant, powerful attraction between them bristles with red flags. Not only should there be no sparks between him and this "hillbilly with a tail," the fact is a dual couldn't have committed murder-by-magic. But until he's got proof, caution rules.

Tag's own suspicions are on high alert. Magic killed his favorite uncle, and Paul, who senses Tag's dual nature way too easily, should be a prime suspect. Except Tag's libido responds to the witch in a way that shouldn't happen.

Whatever this thing is between them, the raw sexual energy feeds a power that becomes their best hope of drawing out the killer before he, she, or *it* strikes again. Until love gets involved, and things get real complicated, real fast...

Warning: Sly foxes, smoky Southern drawls, sex magic, dangerous demons, tacky Las Vegas glitz, and did we mention the hot guy-on-guy sex?

Available now in ebook from Samhain Publishing.

It's all about the story...

Romance

HORROR

www.samhainpublishing.com